A Cedar Friend

A Cedar Friend

A Tale of Visions of Jesus and the Heavenly Woman

ROBERT RHEA

RESOURCE *Publications* • Eugene, Oregon

A CEDAR FRIEND
A Tale of Visions of Jesus and the Heavenly Woman

Resource Publications
An Imprint of Wipf and Stock Publishers
199 W. 8th Ave., Suite 3
Eugene, OR 97401

www.wipfandstock.com

PAPERBACK ISBN: 978-1-5326-5185-4
HARDCOVER ISBN: 978-1-5326-5186-1
EBOOK ISBN: 978-1-5326-5187-8

Manufactured in the U.S.A.   09/19/18

To my mother, Sara, and all of those whose belief in and devotion and dedication to our Lord Jesus of Galilee, the Anointed One of Israel, gave her and them the joy, happiness, and contentment of life, even in the face of strife, adversity, and hardship.

"The wind blows where it wills and you hear the sound of it, but you do not know whence it comes or whither it goes; so it is with everyone who is born of the Spirit." Nicodemus said to him, "How can this be?" Jesus answered him, "You are a teacher of Israel, and yet you do not know this? Truly, truly I say to you, we speak of what we know and bear witness to what we have seen; but you do not receive our testimony. If I have told you earthly things and you do not believe, how can you believe if I tell you heavenly things?"

—John 3:8–12 RSV

Contents

Preface

As a youth I was very much baffled by the differences and discrepancies between the biblical world and the modern era into which I had been born. It was not only that the peoples of ancient times had not developed the machines, technologies and other advanced industrial and scientific advancements of the modern world, the pages of the Hebrew and Greek Scriptures were filled with a spirituality that seemed most incongruous with the religious belief and simple prayer life of those Christians I knew and with whom I grew up. Each Sunday we attended Sunday school and a worship service where stories of the most unearthly and phenomenal events were read and discussed that had no comparison to the mundane unfolding of our lives from day to day. We were led to believe that God had sent his spiritual presence along with dreams and visions to the ancient Hebrews but not to many other peoples on the earth and certainly not to us some two thousand to three thousand years later. If the writer of Samuel reported that during those days visions of the Lord were rare (1 Samuel 3:1), then during our time they had somehow and for some reason been totally suspended.

On April 12, 1961, a Russian missile carried the cosmonaut Yuri Gagarin into orbital flight around the earth. For the first time in recorded human history a human had left the earth's gravitational field and flew through some of the space of the solar system. During the spring of 1957 I had became a confessional Christian when I was baptized and received as a member of the Presbyterian Church US. Though my father was a descendant of Scottish Presbyterians and a descendant of the father of a well-known Scottish pastor, he had stopped attending church before I was born. I assume that it was his decision and not my mother's not to have me circumcised or baptized as an infant. She was a devout believer and always took me to church. At that time we attended the Methodist church, since my grandfather had married outside the Presbyterian Church and for that and doctrinal reasons had been ostracized by most of his Presbyterian friends. But at the age of eleven I decided to return to the Presbyterian Church so that I could be baptized and confirmed at the age of twelve.

Had I made the right decision? I believed then that I had, but for the next six years I grew more and more skeptical of the prophet and Messiah, Jesus of Nazareth, and religion per se. The Cold War and the space race dominated our lives during those days, and the more I read about science and technology, the more I began to doubt the validity of Christianity and religious belief. Though at that age I had not read theology and philosophy, the marvels of science and then at that time what most considered to be the real possibility of space travel had definitely altered our understanding of the past—above all, our human perception of earthly reality with religion as the underlying basis.

Then just weeks before Dr. Martin Luther King led the March on Washington and delivered his "I Have a Dream" speech, and some four months before President Kennedy was assassinated, I saw a series of visions and left this earth not bodily but spiritually as countless people had supposedly done through the centuries before the modern era. I knew as a result that the religious worldview of primitive and ancient peoples had not been altered or suspended and that there was definitely another world.

During the year 1975, archaeologists in the eastern Sinai at Kuntillet 'Ajrud unearthed two large *pithoi* that bore three inscriptions that petitioned the blessing of Yahweh and his wife Asherah. This discovery astounded scholars throughout the world. Although some people have used other inscriptions on the *pithoi* to argue against their Hebrew origin, many archaeologists and biblical scholars now make the claim that Asherah was also the Hebrew Goddess who became the wife of Yahweh. This should have had a tremendous impact on our concept of the monotheistic Hebrew Godhead. But other scholars, clergy, ecclesiastical hierarchy, and some archaeologists such as Ephraim Stern—who, for example, limits the worship of Asherah to the Assyrian period—have sought to minimize this discovery and its significance for the Judeo-Christian world.

When, during the summer of 1963, I saw visions of a heavenly woman and later those of Hebrew people, I had no idea who she might be and why she would have revealed herself to me. Some thirteen years later when I saw a series of visions of Jesus of Galilee, my first reaction was to consider the visions of the heavenly woman to be false and misleading. For a good while I had thought there might be another religion centered just on her. But with time and the archaeological discovery it has become rather apparent that both of them complement one another.

Robert Rhea
Bristol, Tennessee
June 2018

I

Beyond Beginning

THERE ARE THOSE WHO say that this story begins at night, that seemingly eternal night before even the glimmer of dawn. Others say that it appeared to have begun during the great age of gloom and darkness that followed the flowering fruits of the first great Christian empire on earth. Some, though, say that at the beginning there was just nothingness, and night as they see it is nothing but nothingness. But night is the opposite of day, and the morning is the awing spring of day, when the air blows fresh from an often dew-covered, cool earth across my face and down my neck, when the sun is still a bit asleep and just waking up and there is a tangy tingling in the air that tugs at my heart and nudges ever so slightly at my feet as they set forth on the adventure of the day.

There are, though, a few who say that this story began not at all so long ago in a remote and uncivilized corner of the greatest nation on earth, and not just that but that the greatest Christian empire the world has ever seen that grew up simply out of a vast pagan wilderness that lay unknown to the civilized world for thousands of centuries. These few go on to say that this story seemed to have begun in the deserted, forgotten, verdant, almost junglelike hill country where once the savage Cherokees flourished and lived in the great harmony that issues forth from the earth and all that springs to life as the sun rises over the earth's night and brings the daily sweetness of light. But for the most part, such an observation is wholly dependent upon the dictates of a modern-day worldview and the accepted criteria of that state of being civilized and the accepted manner of attaining the Christian life, which in the vast world of the West is not always the same. Yet further-more, a few others would cry rather loudly that such a view of civilized and pagan emerges from nothing but an extreme bias not only on the part of the secular civilized but also those who espouse the Christian life. After all, how does one go about deciding what criteria should be used to determine what areas and peoples of the earth are civilized or not, or remote and deserted? The latter few wonder if some of most of the populated, civilized, intellectual, and cultural centers of this world are not some of the greatest deserts this earth has seen in quite some time.

But all of that aside for the moment. If this story is to have the validity it professes to have, if it is to become what it should be, then it must be understood that it doesn't actually begin here on earth. It never really began. There where the light shines eternally; there where the sun of suns radiates its eternal, golden glow; there where the sea of eternal light flows on and on forever, there is no beginning, there is no end, there is only unfretted being, joy, and happiness. There where the light reigns supremely there is no trace whatsoever of darkness, for it was never there. This vast realm of splendor has never caught the first glimpse of the darkness; it never entered nor did it ever come to the border of the vastness of the light. Here the earthly questions—how, where, when, and why have no meaning; here they do not exist.

But the earth did not begin here, even though it came from here. So it was that one day sometime, somewhere, somehow, this earth did begin, and with that event the tiny questions of how, where, when, and why began to reverberate though time, space, and matter, bouncing about clumsily, threatening hatred, greed, war, famine, and the great uncomfortable disagreement. So it was that one day somewhere amid the great time that floats around the earth somewhere, this story appeared to have begun. But appearance is not reality, and since then women and men have never ceased to puzzle over this unfathomable mystery and the great story that only appeared to have begun.

Exactly when it began cannot be precisely determined. It is more than likely that it began long before Abraham and Sara sat in the door of their tent at Mamre in the scorching late summer heat and were suddenly startled to see three divine beings come wandering their way. Many believe that it began sometime before the Goddess made herself known—but on this point there is much debate, for others are certain that God appeared to many peoples long before the Goddess or that they both appeared simultaneously during one great theophany. As for Adam and Eve there is a slight misunderstanding here, for it is rather certain that there was no Paradise on earth. Earth is not heaven but a definite reflection of it. As for the Aborigines and the great Dreamtime and the days of Gilgamesh and Utnapishtim and Noah and the great Flood and the time before that when the gods and goddesses came to earth and lived for a while until they tired of daily work, many believe that this story began even before these events. Then there are more than a few who are convinced that it did not begin until Paul saw his visions and was able to explain what Jesus came to tell all the peoples of the earth. But many were not satisfied with Paul's exuberant expectation of the end of the world, and they say that it was not until the great Augustine with a little help from Mani and a great deal of Plato was able to explain what Paul meant that the story was set aright. Still somehow the somewhat mystical Augustine left out more than a good bit of the story, especially Paul's treacherous debunking of the sacred Jewish Law, the essence of which was around long before Moses; and so for that reason some believe that it did not begin until Luther at last understood Paul and began to flatter the pope with his observation that he—the pope, of course—was a solitary island of virtue in the midst of a vast sea of wicked cardinals and bishops. Others are rather convinced that the real story of this story did not begin until Immanuel Kant synthesized among others the works of Descartes and Locke and proved that there is no God-talk. But more than a few deserted philosophy in favor of the machine and hold the view that it could not have begun until Lindbergh flew from New York to Paris. Of course, many of the English are rather certain that it was the beheading of Charles I and Cromwell's rise to power as Lord Protectorate that turned the right switch and added the final taste of truth. But not long after that happened, the Catholic King James II beheaded the ninth Earl of Argyll after a brief religious war and imprisoned his relatives on the Isle of Mann. No prison could hold the Campbells for long, however, and they soon escaped and fled to Northern Ireland, County Donegal, where they took the most unusual name of a Greek goddess, the mother of Zeus, seemingly to provide some kind of camouflage. From there after a few generations on the peat bogs they fled to Philadelphia with one notable exception. One named Joseph made his way across the sea to Glasgow where he studied theology and became a Presbyterian minister, before he embarked on the long, dangerous, but exciting Atlantic voyage to the City of Brotherly and Sisterly Love.

Joseph arrived just about half a dozen years before the great birth of that great new experimental nation, and his son John might well have observed the signing of the revolutionary declaration that declared that no one is dependent upon anyone or anything; therefore, everyone has the right to become independently wealthy at the expense of thousands or millions or even more. Then the Liberty Bell cracked, an unexpected tragedy for all, and Joseph packed up his family and some of their belongings and set out from that newly founded center of Western civilization to wander about with the revolutionary troops among the unknown but sun-filled wilds to the south, where not only the savage Cherokee but other fierce pagans had lived for thousands of years. At that juncture where they crossed what would later become the border of the tidy southern tidewater of colonial Virginia and with extreme caution walked slowly into the almost junglelike, extreme wilds of the central hills and mountains of western North Carolina that lay east of the Mississippi, Joseph suddenly ceased his wanderings for no real tangible reason. Here he bought up a large tract of land—which really meant that he claimed some of the land where the Cherokees hunted—built a home, began to farm, preached but to whom is not clear, and founded a church. What the original church looked liked is not known, and it cannot have had many members, unless somehow he persuaded the local Indians to join him and there is no record of that and seems rather unlikely.

What it must have been like to live there in that breathtaking, awing countryside during the early 1780s one can only try to imagine. It is known that the Europeans later called the Northeast "the howling wilderness." Those who went south called the land they came to simply Paradise. No doubt life was not easy, but the fertile earth blossomed for them as it had for the Cherokees, and the land that he claimed was passed on to eight or nine generations of his offspring. There is today something but not much left of those most ethereal and alluring sounds and most enticing sights and marvels he and his friends saw and heard as Mother Earth welcomed them into her bosom. It seems rather certain that they felt very comfortable and content there surrounded by the vast canopy the countless trees spread over their forest home, the food that sprouted up from the earth, and the innumerable creatures that lived around them.

It was not too long after their arrival, just over a hundred and eighty years, that he lay sound asleep one balmy July night on his living room hideaway bed. His family lived then in the east wing of a modest duplex apartment on the south side of the town that grew up some twelve miles from Joseph's old homestead and church, just across from the south wing of a local high school. Parental strategy had paid off with more than a little success. On that June's graduation night he walked across the stage more than once for several awards and was decorated with the laurels of the salutatorian of his class. Then, when a prestigious Presbyterian college awarded him almost a full scholarship, his parents were immensely gratified and the house was filled with a hidden and subdued euphoric rejoicing. After all, only one parent went to the graduation and by no means would one want to allow one's emotions to run about untamed. Nonetheless, those real future visions of wealth that engender the true feelings of happiness danced in those parental heads that summer, since not too long away was that day when a rich, young executive of some sort would provide for those to whom he was indebted for most all of his success. On that day the rest of America would take note and marvel at the fact that even in its poverty belt, even in the Bible belt, the great American Dream blossoms. Yet little did anyone know that the golden sun of next morn would not dawn bright and rosy on Queen Street until the dream of dreams had swept away his hideaway bed.

II

Racepeople and Cherokees

THE HILLS OF EASTERN Tennessee cannot be described as majestic mountains. At first glance there is little about them that is startling and awe-inspiring. They are not those kind of high-up mountains as the famed Rockies, Alps, and Himalayas are. One would never hear a member of the Sierra Club say that it was a lifelong dream to climb White Top Mountain, and few mountain adventurers and hikers from distant lands come to walk and climb along these ancient peaks. No, there is little of that high-flying spaciness swirling about them, for the hills of eastern Tennessee roll and flow along something like a river does, something like the gentle hills of Essex and Devon do, though they are by no means really like the waltzing and swaying hills of the southern English countryside.

Looking across a typical Appalachian valley to the ridges that rise up on either side, one perceives something like the imprint and outline of prehistoric dinosaurs wrought into the contours of the hills. At times he had been filled with the eager expectation that the hills might arise at any minute, gather support from the earthen legs that are piled up against the backbone of their ridges, and walk merrily away to a swinging dinosaur party. But the great irony here is that these old, rounded-off peaks have not been noticeably moved for hundreds of thousands of years, at least not too much in one of the earth's four directions. But the Cherokees have seven directions and centuries of weather have worn away the Appalachians' former, majestic peaks in the fifth of their directions, depositing them in the great abyss that once wound around and through them, filling up the previous depths with the earth that once towered high into the sky in their sixth direction.

But little about the Appalachians moves in the seventh Cherokee direction, along a level line or the inner way, at least not from a mountain's height. When all is said and done, no one can deny that the Appalachians are mountains. A life spent among them is a life spent looking up at them. They make the sun climb higher into the sky for the sunrise, and allow it to end its day at least a third of an hour earlier than it does on the level plains that begin just east of the Mississippi. They flow like a river and glow like the sun and shine like the moon, and they let many young souls slide along their backs. He could recall countless golden autumn days when he bounded out of the front door of the house, and in a matter of minutes was soaring and gliding along a soft carpet of orange, yellow, and golden leaves that washed along the old path that edged along the top of the ridge of a nearby knob, as the locals called the hills. From the clearings of the small hilltops that rose up along the backbone of a knob's ridge, he often peered out into the vast expanse of trees that covered the earth in all of its four directions before it simply disappeared into infinity. This was his first home, though he would not have said that then—the home that lay beyond the fence that surrounded the family house, beyond the limits of town, the home that floated through but beyond the earth to the vast realm where everything is.

But he didn't know it then, or if he did then only intuitively. He didn't know for sure that everything was, but he felt it. There was something deep within him that stirred around and around even when he thought about it. There was something about the marvelous world around him that told him it was, but he could not describe it. But the grass and the plants and the trees and the birds and the squirrels and the chipmunks and all the thousands of other animals of the earth lived as though something was there with them but beyond them. They were a home beyond a home, and one could feel it, just like the Cherokees had felt it thousands of years before. But he didn't know about them then. Certainly he had heard the name of their people. He knew that Indians had lived here before him, but they were then just Indians.

The earth and the people world that sprouted up on its divine face had undergone a vast metamorphosis during those hundred and eighty years since his ancestor Joseph came wandering about those hills. Farmers wanted cleared land, and more and more farmers came who wanted cleared land, and so almost overnight the great verdant canopy of trees that grew up from the divine Mother Earth and towered upwards toward the Father

Sky and sun, beyond which lay the divine Creator, was simply decimated. The new people who came didn't really like the earth the way the Cherokees had left it and had no regard for the way they lived on it. It was nothing but a vast wilderness and had to be rebuilt. Oh, they agreed that God had created it; the Cherokees were right to worship a Creator. But the God of the new people had given them the right to rule over it, not just live on it. Their God was divine, but the earth was not, and surely she was no Mother Goddess. It had to be built, it had to be constructed, it was not finished, if for no other reason than it had to yield forth the vast reserves it held and give the new people wealth, and with wealth came great enjoyment, fun, and unbounded pleasure.

These days not far from where Joseph built his home and church is a most bisarre- looking round concrete and metal structure that towers high into the sky. If by chance somehow any Cherokees from the days of Joseph or settlers of the new people from the early time were able to see it and walk past it, it is rather hard to fathom what they might think about it. The only aspect about it that would be familiar to them was that it was constructed in a complete harmonious circle, like many temples of ancient times, like the direction of the divine dance the Cherokees danced to celebrate the life given by the Creator. The circle is a divine image that transcends earthly life and time and signifies the eternity of God; it calls forth a time without beginning or end, a time that is no time but only unending life.

But this hideous structure shows no sign whatsoever that it has been constructed to embody such a view. Early new people and Cherokees alike would be shocked and dismayed to see nothing left of the animals and forests that once flourished here. The land lies bare around this tower circle, and the man who last bought it issued a great proclamation to all the people who live around it that God had given him the right to use great earth-moving machines to move some of the knobs that lay on the west and south side of the tower circle. There are some trees that have been left growing on the sides and ridges of nearby knobs, but the scorched grasslands around them grow larger and larger each year. Crisscrossing the land surrounding the tower circle are countless wide black strips that extend miles and miles in all directions. The people who come here and who pass by the tower circle do not walk, nor do they ride on animals or wagons. They sit in square metal boxes mounted on black wheels that are powered by a macabre-looking motor made of heavy metal taken from Mother Earth that is made to turn round and round by a black fluid extracted from her. It is from this black fluid that the black strips are made, and over these black strips thousands of the metal boxes roll each day as the new people zoom around and around what is left of the verdant countryside.

A few times during the year thousands of people come to the great tower circle, riding in and bringing with them thousands of the glaring metal boxes. Where once wondrous trees decked and laden with fruits and nuts stood rising skyward, the glaring boxes are parked on huge, wide black strips in one row after another until thousands and thousands of them sit basking in the golden sun or under dark and foreboding clouds of rain that often arise when the people come to the great tower circle. One after another they leave their metal boxes, walk into the tower circle, and take a seat on one of the thousands of metal seats mounted on concrete rows that wind about the tower from its bottom upward, hundreds of feet into the sky. Then they look down onto a tiny, round concrete circle that has been laid out in the very center of the bottom of the tower circle. Were some of the early settlers and the Cherokees who lived and hunted there hundreds of years ago able to come to the tower circle and sit on the metal seats, one wonders what they might think about it. If they were asked what might take place next, some of them would say that the new people have come here to dance, either to celebrate a harvest or to worship the Creator. They would surely be appalled to see some of the new people driving the metal boxes enter the tower and drive around and around the circle for some three hours without stopping, while thousands and thousands of other new people sit on their metal seats simply eating or drinking and talking loudly, some not even bothering to look at the metal boxes swirling around the concrete circle. There is little doubt that they would feel strange sitting there surrounded by metal and concrete and thousands of people who never look up at the canopy of sky that separates earth from heaven and who never dance. They would be even more puzzled to see the metal boxes leave the circle after three hours followed by the new people who then get up, walk back to their metal boxes, and drive away on the black asphalt strips.

When he was that age, though, the tower circle had not been built, though of course people rode in metal boxes because he and his family were some of the new people and his father and mother were very proud of their metal box. There was also almost no sign of the Cherokees. It was said that the new people had discovered gold on some of their land, so over a hundred years before this the Cherokees were rounded up and sent to the great level plains on the other side of the Mississippi. He had no real idea what it must have been like to see the Cherokees living alone on this sparkling, jeweled earth. He had no idea that only some one hundred and fifty years ago or less the Cherokee used to gather at certain times of the year in vast numbers and sit on four sides of a huge arena in the center of which was a large circle of earth that had been dug out a considerable distance down from the earth's surface. At the very center of this earthen circle was placed a great fire that was lit hours before a most mysterious ceremony began and whose flames soared up and fluttered high into the sky. All seven tribes of the Cherokee were present, dressed in their marvelous ceremonial dress of many colors. After the chief lit the sacred pipe with a coal from the Sacred Fire, it was passed first to the medicine men of each tribe and then to each member of each tribe, who took seven puffs for the seven directions of earth and sky. The Cherokee chief then met with the medicine men, the priests of the tribes, and the tribal leaders, and with their approval he announced that it was time for the Sacred Fire Dance or Stomp Dance to begin.

This was the moment the dancers had prepared for hours and days before. They had first sacrificed meat to the Sacred Fire and then listened to sermons that reminded them about the love of the great Creator for all of humankind. A tribal stickball game followed next. After that they drank a special drink that was somewhat intoxicating, and then they went to the river to bathe in the crystal-clear waters that ran cool over their skin and cleansed them with myriads of bubbling, crystal droplets to prepare them for the divine presence. Then the women put on their ceremonial dress and the women who were to be shakers tied the turtle shells filled with pebbles around their ankles and legs, and the men adorned themselves with their leather trousers and colorful vests and feathered headdresses. Each tribe had its own primary color—red, blue, brown, yellow, purple, bronze, and so forth. Selected song leaders of each tribe were called to begin the dance followed by the lead woman shaker, then came other groups of singers dancing before the other shakers who were followed by the rest of the thousands who came to the dance. One by one they danced around the great fire with their left hands reaching toward the fire and their right hands extended toward the heavens. And as they danced the boundary between heaven and earth began ever so slowly to disappear. The music of their tongues rose in rolling waves around them as their feet moved in eternal rhythms over the vibrant Mother Earth who had given them life and sustained them each day. They began to feel her presence move upward around them and on toward the Father Sky above where each day the Sun, the sign of the Creator, rose over them, the plants, and the animals and gave the life that welled up upon the earth and within themselves. They danced on and on until they began to feel the presence of the Creator who had come to earth many years ago and chose four men—red, yellow, blue, and black—the four people of earth who believed in him the most. To them he had given the sacred fire to help them with life on earth and to symbolize the Great White Spirit who bound all of them to the Creator and led them on the journey to the other realm.

Round and round they went, feet moving, voices ringing with the celestial sounds of the sacred songs. For hours the fire burned and the deep night descended upon them, but as they danced on and on the earth melted beneath their feet and the sky above lit up with a wondrous light and they began to dance among the stars, flying on the wings of eagles from one star to the next, soaring toward the never-ending light that burst forth into celestial song, which reverberated all around them and carried them on and on with unending joy. The great Creator had put them here, had made them to reflect his love, and they had heard his voice and had turned their lives toward him. With all the sweet earth around them, the earth that gave them life, with the help of the Mother of them all, they danced on and on to worship the wondrous Creator moving from the earth toward him from whom they had come and to whom they so earnestly desired to return forever.

III

Nocturnal Spiritual Flight and the Madonna

ON THAT BREEZY, BALMY summer night in mid-July, meandering waves of warm air drifted through the windows of the living room and hovered over the hideaway bed where he lay sound asleep. Wave after wave floated over the bed, tugging at the thin cotton sheet that only partially covered him and caressed his legs, chest, and arms as myriads of cicadas hummed and chirped in the otherwise serene calm of night.

It was that magical summer just after his first graduation. Although the one girl with whom he was wildly infatuated for no real earthly reason had slipped through the cracks forever, and though he had not married another who told him that he had the choice to marry her or let her go to another, and though a third girl would not be attending "his" prestigious college because it was all male, this was the summer when he was most on top of the world. Success rang out from the streets, the grass, the trees, and the sky, and the secular word "electric" was the word he used to talk about the euphoric atmosphere that literally engulfed him and pulled him like a magnet three times the speed of light through each day. 'Course the old-timers would have used the ancient word "glorious" to describe all of this, but for a year or so now he had fewer and fewer thoughts about the past and the old world. Though not totally convinced, he was becoming more and more certain that the old world no longer really existed, and if not, then it would soon become extinct. The modern world had almost completely descended upon him, and from the waves of success buzzing around him, he could only hear "scholarship, achievement, prestige, southern Ivy League," and soon the world would bow before him and he could do anything he wanted and go anywhere he wanted. If someone then had offered him almost anything else in the world, he would have asked for nothing more than what had just come his way.

Yet he had not completely given up the old quest for understanding that he felt came from the earth around him, the "real" world, and thousands of new questions floated around his head. He knew that he was stepping off the "flat" world of the knobs he knew a little bit and was bound for a distant foreign land that he only knew through books and hearsay, a world with which he had not the slightest experience. He had spent years dreaming of this day, dreaming the other dream, which was not the real dream, or was it? The longing for it was just as strong as the moving desire to stay on the way of the old quest, and he was bursting with the sizzling longing to embrace the "other" world to which he had been admitted and for which he was bound at long last.

It still seemed, though, that he was giving up the puzzling something that came and went and floated about him just when he least expected it. The valleys, the streams, the hills, and all the creatures who lived there were its home, its "real" home, and he knew that but he didn't know it. There lingered there that most enigmatic, mysterious something with which he had never really come face-to-face. It was as though some great indescribable, amorphous cloud hung about the earth, dragging its dark, frayed corners from one day to the next and over the lawn, and streets, and meadows, and out to the knobs and over to the great high mountain that looked out over the town and the numerous ridges of knobs that crawled and creaked along from day to day.

He had come to suspect that that particular summer might be special not only because of his success but because there was this something that hung in the air and swirled around his head, and flowed in Beaver Creek not far from the house, and walked with him in the morning when he rambled past the mansions of the wealthy along Cedar Creek on his way to work at the swimming pool. It was as though he were waiting and watching for something he had never encountered before, but something he somehow knew surely existed. He thought that it was that wondrous and splendid something that lay both deep within the earth yet soared high and above and beyond the clouds as it disappeared into the vast blue of the heavens. Though he sensed that it had existed for centuries, he had for some time now pondered over the likelihood that it might uniquely manifest itself in his lifetime. For fiery rockets were sending satellites to roam high above around the earth; huge air machines flew to all corners of the world; thousands of scientists sought to unlock the so-called secrets of the origins of the earth, life, and the cosmos; and a man of African origin named after his father who was named after Martin Luther led hundreds of thousands of former Africans along with some Cherokees and other native Americans on a long march to repair the Liberty Bell. Swirling about his head was the thought that an incredible age was emerging that would soon blossom as the exquisite flowers bud, blossom, and then burst into full bloom in the springtime, so very slowly and quietly at first before all at once they open their petals fully to the sun. He was brimming over with such a naive expectancy that it was a wonder that the expectant air within him did not inflate his body to a size some thirty times its normal proportions and send him riding on the gentle summer breezes that washed around those lush, verdant hills.

Sometime in the black darkness of night well past midnight he awoke. As far as he could remember he had never been awake at that hour before, and for certain he had never heard a stillness so solemn and silent as that which surrounded him at that moment. He felt a wondrous tingling glide throughout his body as he turned his head toward the window to greet the streetlight that shone through the room onto his hideaway bed. At that moment he knew that he was not alone, and for a few minutes he was filled with a feeling of foreboding and fear. He looked around the room. Nothing, no one was to be seen. He was alone and only silence rang out throughout the house; no one else was awake. Still he could feel it, a definite, invisible, intangible something that flowed through the air and penetrated his body. It was in the light, too, that drifted from the streetlight above. He knew that light well; its rays were unavoidable whenever he climbed into bed each night. He was very familiar with the ordinary light it cast into the night and knew that it was not the ordinary light that now beamed through the window.

Strangely, though, after just several minutes he became accustomed to this presence that permeated the room, filled the air, and moved around him. Then all at once presence and light seemed to merge into one, and it became a definite entity that transmitted waves of translucent feeling deep into his body and eyes. It radiated with an unfathomable magnificence that made him feel all pink inside as marvelous waves of motion moved throughout his body, and the tingling began all over once more. For a moment he thought that he was floating on a cloud, hovering over an unearthly land, and at that moment he saw a definite, vivid image. There in his mind's eye was the distinct and clear picture of a girl he had known since his first school years. For no apparent reason and not at all related to his previous thoughts, it simply coalesced out of thin air. It was certainly ethereal but nonetheless as real as a picture from a book. She was sitting against what at first appeared to be the south wall of Dr. Harkland's house, cuddling a real baby in her arms. But then a closer view revealed that the wall was not that of Dr. Harkland's house at all but rather the south wall of Dr. Taylor's house, which was a block or so farther south just across the street. As he continued to look and gaze with utter amazement at this most unexpected vision, he saw the actual outline of a tall cross superimposed over the wall that towered over her and at the foot of which sat Lea Oxbridge, her arms wrapped in a loving embrace around the baby boy.

He sat there literally amazed. Nothing like this had ever entered his mind. He had had an occasional dream now and then, and he had read many of the Bible stories that reported dreams and visions, but at this point he was much less likely to consider them actual events, possibly nothing else but pure mythology. At first he was somewhat reluctant to concede the reality of all this, and for a few fleeting minutes he could not rationally rule out the possibility that it was mere fantasy. It all seemed so very strange. Then soon came the sobering thought that he could not deny that he had seen the vision, and at that moment the presence that he had felt before became more palpable and more corporeal. *Was it real?* he wondered. *Was this a real child she was holding in her arms? Had Lea had a baby boy?* The thought was rather absurd, since he knew that she was never pregnant. He had gone to school with her from the first grade to the twelfth and they went to the senior prom together. But she had simply become his friend; the relationship was totally platonic, and he went to see her because she was the only girl he knew who would literally sit for hours listening to him babble on and on about the great questions he had those days. She was one of the most proper of all the girls he knew— attractive, not luring and vampy— and though during the past few years she and one of her best friends had become a bit rambunctious and daring, playing tricks on others and picking up some of the slang that was making the rounds those days, she kept company with none but the best and most behaved students of the school. There was this other side to her that was not at all daring and close to the accepted status quo. This specter had often raised its head during their conversations, when she either became silent or retreated to the safe side of an argument, taking refuge in the complacency that was so comfortable those days and that was so easy to imbibe from the middle class. Has Lea had a baby, and is this just a baby or is he the new Christ child?

As he abandoned these wandering thoughts, the presence that had engulfed him seemed to take over. For some while he wondered if there might be an angel in the light that entered the room from the streetlight just outside the window. But try as he may, he could not see the definite shape of an ethereal being of any kind. Still there was a certain feeling that the presence was an entity of some sort and with whom he seemed to be communicating. The so-called real, rational world seemed to drift off into the past the longer he sat there; within a matter of minutes it had become almost completely inconsequential. The boundary between this so-called real world and the other had simply vanished, and there in the midst of the presence surrounding him he knew that he had no choice but to get up and go Dr. Taylor's house. He had to see for himself if she was actually there. But now he retrospectively and thoughtfully asked himself if he would ever really do that. He had never ever before been awake at that hour, somewhere around 3 a.m., and he knew that his parents would never willingly allow him to leave the house at that hour.

Only a few seconds passed after those thoughts when he got quietly out of bed, pulled on a shirt and a pair of pants, and then speedily tiptoed barefooted out the east door of the house, the exact direction to Dr. Taylor's house. Why he did not put on shoes or carry them in his hand until he reached Queen Street, he had no idea; but then, after all, most people know that "real" Tennesseans do not wear shoes. Then, too, he had not really decided to leave the house, nor had he had any second thoughts about what he was doing or where he was going. On the spur of the moment, he got up and left, and within a matter of minutes, he found himself padding gleefully along the warm, worn, gray asphalt that the new people had poured over Queen Street.

Never once did he consider returning; he knew instantly once he left the house that he had set out on an adventure that would from many points of view probably never end. He felt like a bird that had just been set free from years of caged captivity, and it was so amazing to feel his wings cut through the air and propel him along the street with the greatest of ease. The balmy night air was so marvelously soft as it licked at his arms and face, and he felt his feet aglow beneath him as they glided and soared over the smooth pavement stretching before him. He wondered why on earth he had never been out in such an exhilarating night as this. Not a single car was to be sighted on the streets, and no one but he alone moved against the natural contours of the lawns, houses, and trees. There was no moon, only a beautiful canopy filled with millions of twinkling stars, myriads of stars that hung like glowing bright torches overhead in a vast, pristine, clear sky that at first sent a most enthralling and unearthly silence down his way, washed the earth from under his feet, then lifted him up and sent him sailing through the Great Milky Way toward the outer reaches of the universe. The stars seemed so near to him that it occurred to him that he might reach out and grab one to take with him as he went soaring by. Only a few minutes fluttered by as he passed Edgerose Avenue and made his way to the entrance of Deerborn Estates. He was alone in an immense night—or was he really, and was this really only night?

As the earthly night and the light of the stars began to soak deeply into his skin for a few fleeting moments he sensed that he was truly alone, that the town, the cities, the villages, the entire world was asleep and had left him alone to wander over the face of the earth in the great quest for the end of the universe as prehistoric people and ancient prophets and prophetesses might have done from the beginnings of the life of humankind on earth on to the civilized eras that followed. The great Gilgamesh was compelled to wander on without his friend Enkidu, whose death brought him such remorse he set out alone to find the hidden sage Utnapishtim who was the only one known to have been anointed with life eternal. Odysseus was abandoned by his fellow friends as he wandered toward Ithaca, and the daring Hebrew prophets Jeremiah, Ezekiel, Isaiah, Amos, Joel, and others were left alone and set at all odds against the thriving and fastidious Hebrews who populated Israel during the triumphant reigns of the kings. So he walked on, he flew on, bidding adieu to his home and the earth, saying farewell to earth's space and matter and its seemingly time-filled time in search of infinity, on the quest for the golden fleece, embarking on the audacious search for the timeless time, the other realm, his real self. Once more he became aware of a deep, pervading silence that sat upon all the land and reigned over the four corners of the earth. Yet it did not prevail; it did not reign supremely but gave way to an immense happiness and joy that reverberated from the heavens and the stars, and a great joy bubbled up within him, and he felt as light as a feather and forgot that he was alone. The silence had vanished, and the heavens and the stars began to vibrate with a most ethereal, enthralling, wondrous celestial music as thousands of angels sang marvelous songs of joyful wonderment that rang out over all the earth and penetrated deep into his breast and soul. He felt as though he would be able to walk on forever.

At last he reached the street that ran perpendicular to the avenue on which Dr. Harkland lived. From that vantage point he found himself standing in a tiny, shallow valley looking up at three houses on his left: one belonging to Dr. Harkland, one to Dr. Taylor, and a third to a financier named Hancock. He paused there for a short while, collecting his thoughts as it was a rather arduous task to relate to both worlds. Dr. Taylor's house was the first house on the left, and the south wall—made of rough but light-colored beige, dark tan, and speckled red old brick—would soon come into full view. Lea should be sitting there if the vision was to have an actual concrete reality. But would she actually be there? After pondering the matter another few minutes more, with that question ringing and bouncing around his head, he decided that Lea would be there when the bottom of the south wall came into view. The vision had been so very vivid, and he was more than certain that it was real. He felt his feet move under him as he crossed to the left side of the street, now within seconds of a full view of the south wall. With his eyes fixed, glued to the spot where she would be, he quickened his steps as he hurried on toward the house. Standing there at last on the spot that afforded a clear view of the wall, a shudder rippled through his entire body, and he stood rigid and aghast, recoiling from the sight at which he gazed in painful disbelief. An empty, drab wall filled his eyes, his head, his limbs; there was no one there! With ladened icy disappointment dripping from his eyes, his shoulders, and his arms, for the first time he began to ponder the possibility that this was all nothing but his own subconscious fantasy, a wishful figment of only his own imagination that had so abruptly awakened him and disrupted his lavish and pleasant nocturnal, summer slumber.

But no! There was another possibility. He had at first thought that she was sitting against wall of Dr. Harkland's house, or at least that was the location the vision seemed to have initially sent his way, and that house lay only a few minutes away. His feet padded speedily on past the Hancock house, which sat squarely and opulently on the corner of the intersecting streets, with a back side that faced the south wall of the Harkland house. Once he was there, less than a block from what might have been the first scene of the vision, he could see the top half of another brick wall that might have been the wall at the foot of which Lea sat; but thick, verdant shrubbery hid the bottom half from his view. There at that moment he had the distinct feeling that no one was there; but mustering up all the courage he had left, he stepped ever so quietly and slowly forward to the shrubbery and peered through. He saw nothing but the dark contours of a grassy lawn and an empty brick wall!

There was no new Christ child! Lea Oxbridge had not had a new baby boy, and he told himself that had he at all considered all of this from the perspective of the real world, he would have known that Lea Oxbridge of all the girls he knew was the least likely to have had a new baby boy. The real world was just like it had always been. Yet still the presence that had come to him just about an hour ago lingered there in the vastness of the night, and he could still feel the ringing of the spheres of heaven that had engulfed him as he had sallied forth through the immense quietness of a lazy, southern July night. His subconscious! *It must have been my subconscious*, he thought to himself, and he wondered how he could have been so naïve to have acted on such that from the vantage point of the real world was nothing but an unfounded, most fanciful, imaginary impulse. Even then at that early assessment of the matter he could think of no one who would even begin to believe the vision he had seen, no matter how elaborately he might have dressed it and adorned it with the flowering and budding imagery of convincing literary and rhetorical garb.

Try as he may, he could not deny that some of the splendor and glorious intoxication of his celestial walk had faded as these unsettling and disappointing thoughts drifted and swirled through his head. Yet no matter how much sober, rational, throbbing reservation was generated by such cold reflections, the celestial waves and glimmerings of his nightly escapade still hovered and floated around him, and he had the distinct feeling that they would certainly remain with him as the night gave way to the brilliance of a sunny, golden dawn. He turned swiftly about and quickly made his way westward across the streets that were the actual and social borders that divided Deerborn Estates from the environs of Queen Street. Had he continued on eastward not more than some five blocks he would have arrived on the front lawn of Lea Oxbridge's house, where either he could have had a final searching look or, if he had been so bold, could have knocked at her door. But such an idea never occurred to him. It was obvious that she had not received the celestial message. The vision might have nothing really to do with her. He was surely certain that the vision was real; someone had sent it to him. His house came quickly into view, and he scurried softly through the fence gate, opened the house door ever so quietly, and slid with a sigh of relief safely into the hideaway bed. For the first time since leaving the house that night he was aware that his feet were very warm beneath the skin. They had not only gathered up heat from the hot July pavement, but it seemed that they had begun to generate a curious, firelike glow that warmed the bottom of his feet and rose somewhat up around his lower legs.

At first, after all that, he had absolutely no desire to doze off for the rest of the night. He couldn't imagine what he should do next. One of the other baffling things about it all was the fact that no one had heard him leave or return from his heavenly voyage. This was astonishing considering his domineering father's reputation as a somewhat light sleeper. He suddenly recalled a conversation he had overheard his father have with a sister of his about the time he had been sighted sleepwalking by his mother early one morning, and he wondered if this could have something to do with all that. Impulsively he got to his feet, stalked quietly to his father's bedroom door, and knocked gently, hoping that he just might know something about the strange events he had just witnessed. But the door remained closed, and more than several minutes passed drearily before he heard the usual, belated, bellowing reply emerge from the confines of the room: "What is it? What do you want?" he loudly groaned in complaint . He opened the door only slightly and reduced the hours of the night's enigmatic and wondrous experience to a nimble and efficient statement, the only solution he could conceive of at that time. "Daddy," he said, "I think I'm going to be a preacher!" "What?" he cried out with a tone of certain disbelief and apparent disgust, which was swiftly followed by nothing but a command from the great ruler: "Go to bed!" Recoiling from the expected rebuff, he wheeled about and fled to his hideaway bed. Already he had learned to keep his distance from his father, and though after this he made more attempts to discuss matters with him, he knew then that nothing would come from it.

He first awoke early the next morning to the ringing metal sounds of his father getting his breakfast. A heavy weariness hung over him and drifted throughout the house. Never before had he missed three or four hours of a night's rest, and he was unaccustomed to the deep, weary haze that he felt settling over his eyes and clogging up his ears. But even then so early that morning after the routine ritual of awakening to a new day, he knew that this was no ordinary day. He felt the presence that had descended upon him during the night still lingering around the living room, even around the house. The sounds that came from the kitchen seemed to him at first to be his father's, though usually he was still asleep when his father got to the kitchen for breakfast, which usually his mother made for him. But the sounds that rattled through the house seemed to be those his father made, as it was his practice to put a heavy hand to things, the pans and plates, knives and forks, which resonated with what could be understood as the sounds of power and decisiveness. Yet not long after these initial sounds sailed past his ears, he sensed something there beyond all the usual, expected daily clattering of breakfast. For whatever reason it felt as though the human presence there in the kitchen was no ordinary human presence at all but that of some otherworldly being that had arrived with the coming of the previous night. Whatever it was, it generated an aura that penetrated the house around him, imparting the definite sensation that it had come from a place far beyond the stars. He was strangely elated yet at the same time utterly frightened by the thought that this presence could actually be his real Father, some kind of manifestation of God himself who had come and invisibly superimposed himself over the human frame and personal stature of the man who was his father. He trembled but marveled at the thought that as he lay there he perceived the spiritual hand of a transcendent being that had reached through the depths and vastness of eternity to grasp and take hold of a bit of matter and time into its palm as it piled fluffy, yellow eggs onto a plate and spread butter and jam onto the surface of crisp, brown toast. A delectable bite of eternity was eaten that morning by a man who didn't give "two hoots and a nanny goat" for anything but the earth on which he put his feet every day and the scores of things he could put into his hands. He who was his father was not his father but for a few precious moments that morning had become his Father. Not soon after that, only silence drifted out of the kitchen. He heard the side door of the house close, the roar of the metal box as it was started and driven away, and he dozed off once more.

An hour or so later he awoke to a bright, golden sun streaming through the east windows of the living room. Though he wanted to get up, he felt almost none of the usual energy that propelled him to his feet each morning. The bed was a warm magnet that still held him there, and thousands of soft rays of sunlight erected an impregnable wall that provided no access from the bed to even the room where it stood. But despite this barrier of light he eventually rolled out of bed, sat up, and looked at his feet. He knew they must be terribly dirty, and they were indeed so thoroughly soiled and blackened, it looked as though he had spent an entire day outdoors barefooted. He had to wash them before his mother saw them and made sure she did not see him as he scurried to the bathroom, zooming past the kitchen where she stood getting his breakfast and beginning the noonday meal.

His mother like his father had no idea what had happened the night before. He was glad about that, for he knew that his mother would have no idea how to react. He fixed a couple sandwiches for lunch, added a banana or apple to that, and went to the dinette for the breakfast she had put on the table for him. It was the usual morning chatter that passed between them: she was happy that he was working again this summer. Then all at once as he sat eating his cereal, he trailed off into a trance. He did not remember when he entered the trance nor what he thought while it lasted. It seemed only as if the presence came to him as he sat there eating, and he simply floated off. It was as though he had entered a state of meditation, as a spiritual aura came and sat with him and around him and he just forgot that he was sitting there eating breakfast. The next thing he knew, his mother was shouting to him, "Are you alright? What is the matter with you?" He quickly came to himself and assured her that he was alright. He finished breakfast, gathered up his lunch and things, and walked to work, padding along over Queen Street, through Deerborn Estates, past Lea Oxbridge's house, and along Cedar Creek.

He arrived a bit early at Cedar Swim Club as a heavy dew was slowly disappearing from the grass, flowers, and shrubs that grew on the lawns and walkways around the new pool. A refreshing breeze nipped at his legs and face as he polished off one after another of the routine morning chores from the filter room to the concrete decks of the pool. Most all of the staff were all smiles as usual, and the lifeguards piled thick streams of suntan lotion onto their skin, as it looked as though it would be another hot, dry, sunny day. Some mothers and children came sauntering and waddling up the stairs to the clubhouse from the lawn below well before time for the swimming classes were to begin, and he grabbed the daily register and money box for the usual guests and trudged through the large lower lawn, through the parking lot to the admissions gate that lay on the far south side of the club. There he put up his super-wide umbrella, let it drop into its stand, placed the register and money box on the makeshift desk fastened to the wire fence just to one side of the entrance gate, unfolded his chair, and sat down. As each carload of members approached and stopped at the gate, he rose to greet its occupants with a friendly smile and handed them the register.

He was one of some three or four gatekeepers and groundskeepers. When he wasn't sitting at the entrance gate, he mowed the lawn and various picnic areas, did some of the gardening, and helped with the daily cleanup. He was also a member of the first-ever Cedar Swim Club swim team; his best stroke was the backstroke, and he was on the first-ever diving team. The club then was four years old, and he had worked there all of those years.

Some weeks he spent five entire days at the entrance gate, and there were often long lulls between cars. This left him with a good bit of time for reading, mostly novels, and one that he remembered best from those hot summer days was Don Quixote. The entrance way and parking lot were not paved for a number of years after the pool was built, and after the first couple of weeks of June, rains were rather infrequent. As the cars rambled in and out over the often dusty, rock-covered ground, clouds of dust rose and swirled all around him and merged ever now and then with a flapping wind that blew past the gate and skipped over the cars that sat roasting under the grilling rays of the sun just like their owners who lay basking around the pool a couple of hundred yards away. As he eagerly followed the exploits and sufferings of Don Quixote and his sidekick Sancho Panza and the consequences of the illusions of grandeur that befell Cervantes's hero, the flying, dry, thick clouds that blew around him with each wave of arriving and departing cars lent a touch of realism to the unfolding story and helped transport him to the wind-blown, sun-drenched plains of medieval Spain through which these two, and now three, courageous adventurers rode.

Each time he approached the entrance gate during those days that he was reading Don Quixote, he felt as though he were leaving the stuffy confines of modernity behind him for the almost primeval, vast reaches of Castille and Aragon, a fascinating, near-ancient land shrouded in mystery. Years later as he reflected on these exploits, he wondered if Don Quixote had not sought out the armies of the enemy, damsels in distress, the wicked, the poor, the oppressed, dragons, giants, and of course windmills much the same way some of the earliest of prehistoric nomads, perhaps spurred on by a natural and almost subconscious curiosity for the different facets of the earth, its plants, animals, and the aura of the numinous that they often perceived surrounding them, had wandered from place to place in search of food, and later pasture and fertile ground. He knew that these people had found meaning and romantic adventure in the natural world they were a part of without even attempting to begin to unveil all of the intricacies of its natural structure. As he peered back in time to the glorious days of chivalry a la Mancha from the south end of that dusty, scorched, deserted parking lot, he had easily imagined that he had caught sight of that indelible pair riding slowly but with much bravado and a determined demeanor over a majestic landscape in search of their next windmill.

On that particular day, though, those two absurd silhouettes did not appear on the horizon of the entranceway to the club and he was not so preoccupied with the past as he was with the present. Car after car stopped at the gate to register, most brimming over with children. The pool had been built without large dressing rooms because of a lack of funds, and this situation had still not been remedied. The bathrooms were large enough to accommodate a few people at a time, but most the members and their guests got around this inconvenience by dressing out casually in shorts and so on with their swimsuits underneath, or they just put on their swimsuits and headed to the pool. One pool director was known for his notorious comment to some of the members who seldom but sometimes came fully dressed just to talk and visit rather than swim: "Sorry I didn't recognize you. You're not wearing your bathing suit today."

Almost every car was driven by one of the mothers of the children, and as car after car passed with them came views of bare, lovely shoulders and enticing upper breasts and of course usually warm, smiling faces. Most of times before this he had been able to remain rather indifferent to all these scenes and the dozens of women who came day after day to soak up the sun and meet their friends. That day, though, was no ordinary day. The charge that had ignited within him that morning had not faded, and the earth around him had been set aglow as he had never seen it before. Everything around him was intensely and compellingly beautiful: grass, shrubs, trees, birds, and sky shone with an unearthly aura of loveliness he had never seen and felt before. They were the same but not the same, as they appeared to have been transformed by an underlying presence and glow of energy he had never been aware of before. He had never imagined that such beauty existed, and sitting there he began to ponder the thought that a wondrous, harmonious, life-giving energy penetrated every particle of the earth, and its plants and its creatures reflected here on earth an even more beauteous, blossoming, splendorous hidden world. It seemed clear that he and his body were a part of this other world. A splendid, tingling vitality surged throughout his body, and he marveled at the waves of captivating feeling that linked this earthly sphere in physical time, space, and matter with a marvelous, rarified, heavenly realm that lay within but yet beyond it. As the waves of bare, feminine shoulders topped off with lovely womanly faces meandered and flowed past him and blended with all the other waves of unearthly radiation, there were moments that he sat and stood beside the entrance gate that day seemingly suspended in time and absorbed in a lovely bewilderment as he watched an unending display of life-giving rays of light dance around him.

He was amazed that no one else he talked to that day had made even the slightest comment about all this extraordinariness, and from them came not the faintest word about any kind of intriguing transformation of reality. Some of the swimming team came to do their regular daily workout and laps. A few used the stopwatches for timed swims and raced from one end of the pool to the other. Everyone was planning their new strategy for the next swim meet. The concession stand was open and hotdogs, hamburgers, and drinks went swimming out the window all day long and landed all around the terraces. He talked to friend after friend and the lifeguards, and everyone was filled with the happy summer that had come to sail around them and carry them on their carefree summer escapade. Boys and girls flirted with each other, steady couples came and went, and the grown-ups had their usual fun in the sun, mingling about and avoiding or not avoiding the juicy gossip of the day. He was both disturbed and comforted by all this. It would have been great if Lea Oxbridge had come to the pool that morning and said, "I have to talk to you. I had the strangest thing happen to me last night and I have no idea what it's all about." Whether she came that day, he didn't remember, but she had not yet said anything like that. And not one other soul said anything about anything being different. It was all so routine, so everyday, so just like any other day, with only one exception: The swimming pool was leaking.

IV

Alone but Not with Lea Oxbridge

A FEW DAYS CAME and went most routinely. For this he was at first very thankful. It seemed as though he could and would be able to put all this into some kind of sober perspective, and there were moments and days when he began to view it all as some kind of mystical fantasy that really did not intersect with the real, secular world. After all, no one he knew had ever talked about such experiences, and no one knew of the vision and the star-walk that had somehow made their way to him. To be sure he thought of them every day; he pondered them over and over, and he was awed by them as though they were some kind of precious treasure that had been unearthed and given to him by an unknown person. He had often wondered years before this if there were such things and how it was that the ancient people knew about them but moderns seemed to have no clue about them at all. He wondered how the Hebrew scribe or prophet had been able to write, "And God said to Abraham, 'Rise up and go, and leave this land and your kindred, and go to a land which I shall show you, and I will bless you and make you a great nation.'" Or how had the biblical writer had known to write of Samuel, "During the night the Lord came and spoke to him, and he did not know that it was the Lord, so he got up and went to Eli." Or how did he make a record of God's words to Isaiah: "During the days of Uzziah . . . the word of the Lord came to Isaiah, and he was in the temple, and he saw a vision of the Lord who was seated high and uplifted above the altar." How had all this happened? He did not have to ask his friends and the grown-ups he knew. He knew that they somehow knew that all of these things had not really happened. But God had not spoken to him, Jesus had not appeared to him, and he had not seen the Mother Mary, or had he? He found it all more than a bit bewildering.

He had talked to Lea Oxbridge once since that starry night, and she had had nothing unusual to say or tell him. Before that he had hoped that she too might have had later some other experience she could not explain, even if nothing had happened to her that same night. But nothing at all out of the ordinary came up as they talked, and she was the same old Lea who moved and talked rather slowly and who really liked what for her was routine. Over the years she had become something of a buffer for him, absorbing and soaking up a lot of his energy and his sometimes unusual, extraordinary, unsettling thoughts and ideas. He had told her before that the apparently sedate modern world was possibly not what it appeared to be and not what it should be. But she had never bought into that argument, and as they stood there that day in the parking lot at the swim club, he dared not mention a word to her about the vision.

The first things he could remember from his earliest childhood were for the most part routine and mundane. He could still see himself riding his tricycle around the house from the kitchen to the dining room and to the living room; around and around he would go, sometimes almost as fast as he could go, and then his mother would tell him to stop zooming around so fast. Those were days when the sun shone brilliantly even during the winter months, and the rains were abundant, and from the garden came bushels and bushels of potatoes, corn, beans, onions, squash, and cabbage. Then once his father planted the vacant lot next door with popcorn. That was a year or so after he and his friends found at least a dozen or more long sticks, five to eight feet long, and after the rains had almost formed a small pond in the middle of the lot, they divided up and took sides and fought a fierce war against each other in the middle of the pond, which then soon became a large, sunken mudhole. They used to play smear football there when grass was finally planted and on the high school lawn across the street, and he could keep up with the neighbor players even though he was smaller. There was a quietness about the earth and the land around them then; the creeks and rivers and valleys and knobs sent their presence and good feelings even to town back then, even to their backyard and front yard, and to their doorstep. Yet he never saw a ghost of a Cherokee and he never found an arrowhead like many of his friends, and he wondered why, because he could always find four-leaf clovers, just like the Irish shamrock.

Then one day when he was three years old, something happened he could never really explain. The tall, attractive daughter of the Lovejoys who lived in the new, big house on the corner east of them came to visit his mother. They were in the kitchen talking and laughing, and he had wandered off to the living room where he found the front door open. As he came closer to the door, he thought he felt someone there. He could see nothing, he heard nothing, but he apprehended a definite feeling of some other presence. Someone was there who did not appear to him and who said nothing to him but he felt this uncanny presence, and when he did, he tried to tell his mother and the Lovejoy daughter about it, but they did not hear him. He called to them and they did not come. So he stood there alone and all he could do was cry, and then they came around the corner of the dining room to see what was wrong with him. He remembered that and he pondered his new visions, and he could say to himself that God had not appeared to him. He had seen visions of women and a baby boy. Was he the baby Jesus?

He kept hoping that Lea Oxbridge had seen something—or if she hadn't, then she might at least have had some kind of strange dream or something might have happened to her that she hadn't been able to explain. After all they had gone to the senior prom together, and they had been dating for about the last half of their last year of high school. He had to admit that he was comfortable with her. He could talk to her on his intellectual level as he had not been able to talk to any other of the girls he knew, and whether she understood it or not, she at least tolerated it. Over the past year or more he had spent hours at her house just sitting, sometimes casually half-sprawled on the floor, talking on and on about diverse topics, but usually about religion, science, and the ancient world and how it was seemingly so different from their world. Along with these topics he felt compelled to mention the poor people of the town, maybe a bit of the civil rights movement and politics, and then all of the rest. But what did she really believe and what did she want out of life? He didn't know and had no real clue, other than she seemingly wanted a quiet life that was productive and allowed her to do something she wanted to do and which benefited some people around her. He had nothing against that. It was just that it did not seem to go far enough for him; it did not allow her to go exploring around the human psyche, around the country, and around the world with him. It seemed that she was lagging rather far behind him, either because she didn't want to keep up with him or because she just could not—not because she didn't understand on the one hand what he was talking about but because it really had no intrinsic meaning for her. But maybe she hoped that he would soon outgrow all this and there was something about him she liked, so she hung on and sometimes they did have fun together or seemed to.

So not too many days passed before he called her; he had to find out if anything even vaguely related to the visions had happened to her. He forgot whether he went over to her house or whether they met again at the parking lot at the Cedar Swim Club. He had already talked to her in the swim club parking lot for a short while. But this time he had a plan of sorts, particularly if all went as it did the last time, and this time they talked on for a good while, longer than they had for weeks. She was all excited about going off to college and he was too. She was having a great summer with all her friends, and they talked on about them, leaving out very little of the latest. Yet somewhat to his disbelief nothing even remotely out of the ordinary surfaced; she was almost the same Lea he had known from the first grade, the same Lea he knew from Sunday school and the youth group, the same Lea he had taken to the senior prom. There he was, remembering the starry night walk, and her at Dr. Taylor's house sitting at the south wall cuddling a baby boy, and the golden stars flaming through the night sky! She had seen nothing of it and probably would have laughed aloud had he told her about it, before becoming frightened at the mention of such absurdities. So at last he had no choice. Maybe she had decided not to tell him about what had happened to her, and so he said, "Lea, I had a vague dream about you and your father last week. You had both decided to go on a long trip. Are you? Are you going on some kind of trip?" "A trip," she replied. "What kind of trip? The only thing I know is that he is taking me to university the first week of September." That was it, that was the final word; it was clear that the Lea of the real world and the Lea of the vision were two distinct people, if of course the second was a real person.

The midsummer days waffled by, toasted by the scorching summer heat that from time to time hit one hundred degrees or a little more. The lifeguards kept a thermometer on their chairs, mounted on metal stands that rose some seven feet or more from the pool deck, and whenever the temperature hit a hundred or more, word flew quickly around the pool. Thick suntan lotions were a must, though back then sunblock did not exist and people did not know much at all about skin cancer. When the temperature hit ninety-five degrees or more, the guards would take a quick swim before they climbed up to their chair and after they were relieved for the next shift. He made sure he had a wide umbrella at the gate, but he did not wear a hat when he mowed the lawn and did the gardening. The pool manager was something like the Egyptian overseers of Moses's day might have been and went out of his way to keep his reputation for being tough and demanding. He went to great lengths to show and prove how innovative and progressive he was. The gardening had to be done efficiently with no waste of time, and he often checked the time cards and matched them with the work done. But his powers did not end there because this modern-day taskmaster was also the swim team's head coach, and from time to time he gave the team swimming lectures, which they rather reluctantly had to admit were mostly helpful. He knew a lot about swimming but less about diving, and the boards he bought for the pool were the new, stiff, fiberglass types, much too stiff for good diving.

Somewhat to his own amazement he kept going. He worked and he swam and he dived. He got along with those at work and on the swim team, though his performance at some of the swim meets after the vision was not what it had been before. The routine of it all was comforting, he had to admit, and there were more than a few moments when he began to wonder if he shouldn't just let bygones be bygones and move on from there. It occurred to him that the vision could be nothing more than his vivid imagination called to the fore by the robust libido of the sexually budding young man he was at that time. If he continued pondering all this along these lines, he could well conjure up the argument that his somewhat puritanical ways and views of sexuality had had a repressive hold over his body and his psyche, all of this leading to a late puberty which then burst forth with such vigor that it had thrown the normal flow of things way out of whack. It seemed like not such a bad way to go with all this. After all, no one else he knew had ever said anything about any such things, and he had not been able to tell even the closest people to him about them. So he tried it for a while; he did not make the attempt to deny that they had happened. He just let them float on by him as though they were part of a fantasy movie he had seen at the theater, just like Jules Verne and his *Twenty Thousand Leagues under the Sea* or Orson Welles and *The War of the Worlds* or even Edgar Allen Poe and his "A Descent into the Maelström," or even Washington Irving and his *Rip Van Wrinkle*. From here it was not far to the thought that the Lea Oxbridge of the vision was a symbol of some kind, that she was a figure who pointed to a future learning, for example, or actual academic study, and that with time the cloud surrounding her might or would give way to a true, ethereal light of wisdom.

Yet somehow all of this did not work. Try as he might, he could not deny the reality of it all, especially the presence that had come to him. It was clear to him that some kind of correspondence between himself and the other world had taken place. Despite all his attempts to deny it, deep within him he had to admit that he had been spoken to. It was this presence that he was certain of, and he was led to relate it directly to the Hebrew Bible, to those passages that told of the revelation of God to the patriarchs, the matriarchs, the judges, and the prophets. "And God appeared to him and the Spirit of the Lord came mightily upon him and the Presence of the Lord came upon him." He could not deny this, but then he had not seen a vision of God, and Jesus had not spoken to him—or had he?

He had really no idea what he should do next, when one afternoon at the pool he decided he ought to try to talk to his pastor about all this. It was one of those hot, sultry summer afternoons, and it seemed as though half of the town had decided to come for a swim. The pool decks were covered with dozens of children incessantly coming and going to and from the pool like he imagined the swarms of locusts might have looked in Palestine or Babylon when they came from Africa and ate grass and crops and flowers and shrubs for days on end. He went to the phone, called, and to his great surprise his pastor told him that he had time that very afternoon, that he could even come to the pool to meet and talk with him there! He made sure that he told him that he didn't have to park in the parking lot, but that he could drive up the private drive on the right that led to the clubhouse. After he hung up, he was brimming over with excitement. If anyone could shed some light on these absurdities, then it ought to be the person who was considered to be closest to God. He still felt that God and Jesus had a hand in all this, as they were the two religious figures he knew most about and to whom he had devoted himself on the religious side of things for close to a decade now. Despite all his questions and his criticism and doubts he still believed that Jesus was the true Hebrew Messiah, and for years before this he had almost decided to become a pastor.

His pastor was a man of medium height, a few inches taller than he, and well past middle age. He was one like many who had been to the last great war to end all wars. Yet even when that was all over, he had not gone to seminary but entered the business world before deciding to become a man of God. A good Presbyterian of Scottish descent like himself, he had a wide wrinkled face that lit up when he smiled, and he most always smiled when he talked as he was kind and very personable, liked immensely by the congregation. The great theme of his ministry was "Missing the Mark," his attempt at modernizing Jesus's message of repentance and religious understanding, and it was a good thing that his name was not Mark.

He waited on the pastor at the clubhouse, questions and visions swirling around his head at such a speed he felt a little faint when he saw the car drive up the private drive. His expectations had soared into the stratosphere minutes after the call, and it was almost as if he expected Jesus himself were coming to his rescue. He had made the resolve to tell him all that had happened, and if he could explain these matters, then he would offer to enter seminary after college. The car door opened, and the pastor emerged, shook his hand, left his coat on the car seat, and pointed to a shady spot under one of the tall poplar trees that grew along the drive. His familiar smile emerged and drifted over his face, leaving no noticeable trace of the thick glasses he wore, and eradicated and washed away what seemed to be half of the wrinkles that lined his face. For a few minutes there was a buzzing excitement about this meeting, as though some great secret was about to be unveiled even as the sun boiled overhead in the sky and tiny droplets of sweat bubbled up on their arms and faces. Then it was when all the pleasantries were exchanged and he began to try to explain and talk about that starry night that he confronted an impenetrable world or worlds, those of the modern pastor, a devotee of the church and its sacred tradition. Of all that welled up inside him and swirled around his head, he could offer only diffuse and vague sketches. Did he say that he had seen a vision and that he thought that he should enter the ministry? No. It was more like he had been thinking for years now about the ministry, and now that he was going to college, he wanted to ask about it. He wanted to ask the pastor if he had ever had a vision of Jesus, but he was not able to do that. So they sat there smoldering on the green grass, not like Jesus with his disciples on the mountain overlooking the Sea of Galilee as he miraculously divided some five loaves of bread and a few fish into hundreds and then thousands, but more like a cat cornered by a huge dog, just before the cat darts around him and sails gleefully to freedom.

The longer they talked, the more it seemed as though his resolve was a bit ridiculous and that the pastor was only bemused by the reflections of a youth trying to put religion onto the right shelf of the modern world where it belonged. Somehow what could have taken a few minutes or more dragged on for close to an hour, before the pastor leaned over, patted him rather listlessly on the shoulder, and with what seemed to him an incredulous, condescending tone of voice told him that he should enter the ministry only as a last resort. There was a hint of sincerity in the quick analogy he gave of his own life's story and how he was just not able to avoid the ministry, but he gave no specific reasons for this. It was vaguely something like what might have transpired between Samuel and Eli, and Eli's advice to go and listen to the Lord. How the pastor had gotten his call from the Lord was not at all clear, but one could surely say that he hadn't the faintest idea what a vision was. As for going off alone to listen to the Lord, which seemed what had been recommended, how was he to do that when he had just seen a vision of a woman in the middle of the night holding a baby boy and myriads of flaming stars soaring through the night sky?

Evening came quickly that day. He wished that time would stop and he could remain suspended in some kind of eternal time warp. He wanted to go home and eat and watch TV, and then he didn't. It would mean that he would have to get up the next day and come to work and try to understand what he really did not understand. He didn't consciously know then that one of the things that was really bugging him was how to explain all of this from the viewpoints of his friends and the grown-ups he knew. If Lea and his pastor would think it all absurd, what would his father, mother, the pool manager, the mother of one of his best friends he liked—actually Dr. Taylor's wife from Vermont, who he thought knew almost everything—and even Lea's mother say? Then it was that the thought came to him that was to color the next several days: perhaps, just perhaps the vision had been sent to him because something like the end of time was just around the corner? He had had these thoughts years before the vision, but for the most part had brushed them aside, though he still had the premonition that this was some kind of special time on earth. After the Lovejoys moved out of the big house on the corner, another family with three sons moved in. They were staunch Baptists, and the oldest was allowed to begin preaching when he was only about sixteen years old. He remembered he woke up one morning wondering if his new neighbor could be Jesus come to earth again. He never went to hear him preach though; he got his earful just talking to him from week to week. But what if the vision was some kind of sign sent to him that he was to tell and impart to those he knew best who did not believe? How then was he to explain the absence of God and Jesus in the visions, or was Jesus really not there? Who was the baby boy? Had he, too, been able to walk about the stars?

V

The Golden Woman

SOMETIME JUST BEFORE OR after he took that starry-eyed walk around the world and past some of the stars, the pool sprang a leak. It was not a really bad leak, but it was not a tiny leak either. Every day the water line dropped some two to three inches below its regular level, and tens even hundreds of gallons of water disappeared mysteriously from the pool, leaving no trace around it whatsoever. The lawn did not become wet and swampy, a small creek did not flow anywhere from the pool, and all the decks remained high and dry. Some, even the founder of the club and manager of the pool, doubted that a real leak existed and were working on the assumption that there must be a flaw somewhere in the filter system. Working on this hypothesis the manager then either made or rented a swimming pool stethoscope, which was a regular doctor's stethoscope with large, hollow metal feet attached to the patient's end of the rubber tubes. These metal feet were then placed on the sides of the pool and on the concrete deck surrounding it as one moved about the pool listening to the water flow in and out of the pool from the filter system. But of course this could not be done during the day because of all the noisy children and people swimming, diving, climbing in and out, and walking and talking all about. So special, secret night missions were planned and carried out over a period of some two to three weeks.

On several of those nights the manager himself had asked him to go along with the secret leak team to help listen to the water flow and filter system. Maybe the manager thought his ears might be better than those of the others who had gone before; he didn't know. But he had gone anyway, meeting them well after the thick darkness of nightfall on the terraces and decks of the pool when the sky was ablaze with the twinkling lights of the thousands of visible stars of the Milky Way beaming their sparkling beams down upon them as they walked around and around the pool counter-clockwise and then clockwise, placing the metal feet methodically here on the side of the pool and there on the concrete deck. If the moon were up, the sky was awash with light and they could see for the most part without their flashlights or the light that had been put up on the roof of the concession stand. So they listened to the pool for hours at a time with the night and its starry light surrounding them. They heard the hum of the filter motor in the background, and the rushing of the water along the pipes under the concrete decks or at least something like it, and the flowing of the water in and out of the pool or at least something like it, but never anything that sounded like a leak, whatever a leak was supposed to sound like. The days passed and the leak did not go away. Each day the pool had to be filled with fresh water, and swimmers began to complain that the water was too cold.

The other approach naturally was to dig at various places under the decks and around the pool; but before that course of action was decided upon, one last stopgap procedure was tried: colored dyes were poured into the water system at various places in the attempt to determine where the flow of water was being disrupted. But when no one was able to pinpoint anything like a leak, the manager put him and a few others to the task of digging. Even when things looked grim and pessimism was seeping into all their bones, he had decided to put them under the ground where maybe a groundhog would have done a better job. Any other manager would have called in the services of a professional crew, but their hardnosed leader would not hear of such. He was determined to save money and demonstrate his innovative, pioneering competence to the swim club members. It was decided that the digging was to begin beneath the decks and terraces on the south and east sides of the pool as a maze of pipes was located there.

He was to begin digging under the south terrace, and another ground-skeeper was sent to the east terrace. The pool had been built on a gentle sloping hill that rose in a north-south direction from the floor of a small valley. Adjacent to the south terrace was a grassy lawn that gradually gave way to a moderately steep incline leading to a large center lawn below the pool and on to the parking area. The manager told him to clear the grass as sod squares between the upper lawn and the south terrace and to tunnel under the terrace. So he did and soon began to dig under the terrace. This he could do standing for a while, but once some three to five feet of earth were cleared away from under the terrace, he could no longer stay on his feet and reach farther under the decks with the long shovel and hoe. So after a day or so he found himself lying on his belly digging with a small gardening tool much the way he imagined that a mole or a groundhog dig their holes and burrow with their long teeth and front claws.

As he moved farther and farther under the deck and worked his way to the side of the pool and along its southeast side, the heat and humidity in the tunnel rose to pretty high levels. Every half hour or so he found he had to crawl out of the new pool tunnel to fill his lungs with fresh air and take a drink of cool water. For days he and a couple of others kept digging at a steady pace and were making good headway along the pool. But they found nothing, not even the slightest sign, that might indicate the location or presence of a leak. A week slowly and wearily passed, and as the end of the second week approached, there was still no sign of any damp ground. Odd, he thought, that only days after his nocturnal flight to the stars and his soaring ride through the universe that he should have landed there beneath the earth something like Osiris, who was slain and sent to the underworld. At least Osiris had the sun's light underground at night, but he had nothing but earth and darkness surrounding him day after day. It felt somewhat as though he had embarked on another spiritual adventure of some kind, which sprang from the mundane reality of those days, such that somehow the uncanny vision of the Christ child and the great mystery of the swimming pool leak were not at all unrelated. If the leak were not soon found, the pool might have to be closed and a major renovation of the filter system undertaken to prevent gallons and gallons of water from disappearing into an unknown abyss day after day.

As the first days of this new adventure passed, the digging became routine. Days went by, and digging there underground like a groundhog he began to collect his thoughts about the vision and the starry night walk, but he kept his thoughts to himself. It seemed good at that time to leave things as they were. Friends at the pool were the same as they had always been, and he did his workouts with others who were on the swimming team, diving from the low board and sometimes the high, steaming and pumping through the pool with most of his usual energy. He had talked to Lea Oxbridge a few more times, but they were disappointing and discouraging talks. She seemed to him to have retreated more and more to her father's side, and her new opinions on a number of matters they had discussed of late resembled his more than ever. He had seen her a few times at church and at the pool, and each time he could see only her expectant wish for everything right the way "it ought to be." He could see her father trim and fresh, wearing his bowtie, brimming over with enthusiasm as he bounded out of their house each morning on the way to his dental practice, where he could take what was wrong with that part of the world he dealt with every day and make it right again. He remembered her saying that her father loved his work, and whatever she did with her life, it would be something she loved to do. He had nothing against that, but only he thought, what if there is something basically wrong with the world the way it is? What about that? But for her as far as he could tell, she would have never had such a thought. It remained painfully clear that she knew nothing about the vision and there was no need to try to mention it. She had not been at Dr. Taylor's house that night. Then she called one night and invited him to a party at her house; it was to be a big party, a splendorous summer party. Dozens had been called to come and celebrate and ruminate about their eighteenth summer and finally becoming at least part of what they had dreamed of becoming.

If the days of that summer were extremely hot and humid, back then the nights were still pleasant, washed by the cooling breezes that swept gently out of the damp valleys below the hills. The night of the party was one of those nights. It was one of those lazy southern summer nights when cool drafts of air puffed and chased the sultry heat of day away, when southern people felt more than any other time of the year that all was right with the world because they had made it be and become what it should be. And all this rightness came cascading around them and piled up those fluffy waves of good southern feeling which just simply made everybody happy. He was to wonder many years later if this was the way things were way below them in Rio and Buenos Aires. Of course, back then he had few thoughts about South America; for years though he had thought and pondered much about his own country and had not been able to understand the America he saw swirling around him. That night was crystal clear and calm; myriads of stars dotted the night sky, and only an occasional, feathery, random cloud sailed overhead. He walked over to Lea Oxbridge's house, walking along Queen Street, the same street he had walked along when he walked to Dr. Taylor's that starry night. When he came to Deerborn Estates, he looked up and saw Dr. Taylor's house and the empty brick wall, and then he looked past the Hancock house toward Dr. Harkland's house. He didn't stop, though; he walked past them and kept going on the street that would take him to

Cedar Creek. But before he got there, he hung a quick right and after a few blocks landed at the Oxbridge abode.

He rang the doorbell and waited as waves of loud chatter and laughter penetrated and rushed through the windows and kept him company until the door swung open and Lea popped gleefully into view. "Oh, hi," she said. "We been wondering where you were." He felt flattered to hear those words, but if they were true, then almost nothing else that happened that night lent them even a hint or trace of veracity. The others were on the patio eating, and he followed her over there. He knew almost everybody, as most of her guests were their fellow classmates from the advanced classes at the high school. They had been gathered and shepherded together into all of the advanced classes supposedly so that they could learn better and faster. There were a few other of the usual people there from school and other friends mostly from church and from the other side of town, really the other state. The town was divided by the state border that ran through the center of it. He moved from one person to the other, talking about what each had been doing for the summer and about all their plans for college and something about summer sports and movies. It was fun to see them all, and he ate and lulled about with all the rest and followed along after that to watch television, still a great novelty those days as there were some there who had been watching TV for only some nine years or less. He lowered himself into a deep, soft, comfortable seat and became quickly absorbed into the program, whatever it might have been. There were those, though, who did not watch and kept wandering about from room to room, moving with a friend and from friend to friend.

After only a few minutes he felt that he again was not alone. Of course he was not alone; there were friends sitting to his right and left. But that presence was still there, now far more palpable than a few hours ago, and he felt a bit suspended in time. Most of the others were quickly lured away and captivated by the program, and he also sort of went along with it all, but all at once he saw his Christian name flash across the screen. At first that was not unusual, as his was a common name. But it reappeared several times and then he heard a voice, a woman's soft voice, and he thought at first that it was Lea Oxbridge's mother calling him. She was a tall, beautiful, voluptuous woman with long, flowing dark brown hair, sparkling fleshy cheeks, and captivating eyes. He had often thought that she was not really at all like her daughter and her husband or even her son. She was an island unto herself, and often when he saw her from a distance, she took his breath away. He turned around abruptly, expecting to see her standing behind the seat. But not a soul was standing there, or maybe one could have said that only a soul stood there, which he did not see at first. No one else had heard her voice, or that is, no one asked who was calling him. He turned around to the TV and saw his name paraded again across the screen. Then that quiet, uncanny voice called his name once more, and there was nothing he could do except get up and leave the room.

But he didn't just leave the room. He knew all at once that moment that he had to leave the house, and so he bounded quietly though the front door. No one saw him leave. He plodded slowly with excitement though somewhat bewildered through the thick soft carpet of lush grass that been mowed only a few days ago toward one of the tall, full magnolia trees that stood on the south and east side of the lawn a good distance from the house. As one foot floated after the other, swishing through and over that deep grass toward the tree, he saw a flash of light in his mind's eye, not below him and not above him and nowhere on the lawn to be seen but only there in his mind's eye. The lower limbs of the tree were bedecked with a thick canopy of leaves, and behind and under these he stood wondering what this unfathomable call and the light could be. Then he saw her and he could scarcely believe it. He saw the full figure of an extremely, wondrously beautiful and handsome woman who smiled at him with the radiance of the stars and who was bathed in a marvelous celestial light, something of which had come his way when he first saw the flash of light. He had no idea where she was, only that she was there, up there, above him both in his mind's eye and then, too, somewhere gently floating and pulsing through the night sky. A thrilling, exhilarating, uplifting wave of joy flowed through his body and his soul, and the earth around him came alive and turned real just as it had for him these past several weeks when the presence let itself be consciously manifest. Through the earth, the grass, the shrubs, and the trees he could feel a pervasive naturalness and a primordial essence that now rose up around him and ascended above him to greet the brilliant, golden light that emanated from the body and face of the celestial woman who smiled at him with the warmth and love of the heavenly spheres and lifted her caressing hands and eyes toward him as she tossed wave after wave of loving feeling to him through the pristine night sky. He could only stand there looking up at her, and then to his great amazement he began to wonder how he might reach her and how he could find out where she really was.

He was truly awed by her presence, but then, during those first moments he saw her, a bit baffled all the same. She said no other audible word to him, and he could not really see her. He could see the vague yet real contours of her exceedingly sensual body but not her actual body, and he saw or at least he thought he saw her wondrous absorbing lips, cheeks, eyes, forehead, and hair. But all these features were bathed in the marvelous, sensual, almost erotic golden light and aura that appeared to him with a fantastic glow at least a dozen times brighter than the brightness of the evening star, the planet Venus when it sets on the horizon of the night sky. But this somewhat baffled hesitation must have been his last sober thought that night, and as he stood there a few minutes more, he became totally absorbed by her presence. His body tingled and glowed all over as the earth around him—its grass, flowers, shrubs, and trees—seemed to vibrate with a living, animate, pulsing presence that danced and rang around him. And then it was that he could only see her, see the rays of golden light cascading down all around him and he felt as though his body might actually rise up any minute and fly to her. No longer did any of this seem absurd to him; and then he saw where she was, and he was overjoyed to see that she was not too far from earth. To his great amazement he saw her hovering high in the night sky above the pool at the Cedar Swim Club. His felt his feet glowing again as they had done the night of the first starry night walk and the day after when he went to work at the pool. Longing to feel the cool earth beneath his feet and the caressing night breeze against his breast, he tore off his shoes, pulled off his shirt, and set out at brisk pace toward the pool, which was just over two miles from Lea's house, filled with the glorious anticipation of a more complete and intimate glimpse into the realm of the heavenly spheres.

The street in front of Lea Oxbridge's house ran perpendicular to the street beside which Cedar Creek flowed. He bounced gingerly with brimming expectation along the east side of it until he came to the intersection of the two streets and then turned south. It was a rather often-traveled street connecting one southeast section of town to its center, but on that particular night he was surprised to find it almost deserted. Only a few cars passed him through the entire walk, which was much to his benefit since most of the west side of the street was bordered by a rather high, tree-covered bank and its east side by a moderately deep ravine, through which Cedar Creek flowed so deeply hidden by the ravine that one did not see it until it seemed to emerge from underground and came into view just before the entrance to the swim club. There were no sidewalks, so he strode nimbly over the dark, warm asphalt, moving over to the rough, gravel-coated shoulder of the street whenever a car passed. During those first minutes of this daring night escapade he could still see the goddess beaming at him with all her glory, yet still a great distance from him and very high in the dark vault of the night sky. She hovered there where he thought she was above the pool, but as his feet fled on at a heightened pace, she seemed to be moving toward the east, beckoning to him, and somehow he had the impression she was pointing to the east. Over halfway to the pool he became preoc-cupied with the walk, making sure to give way to the occasional car that zoomed by, though it seemed to him that only a few seconds had passed before he turned into the entrance way to the pool gate and padded over the small bridge that crossed Cedar Creek some ten yards from the park-ing lot of the swim club. During the day, ducks came to glide sometimes noisily over those gurgling, bubbling waters, but none were out that night. A rather high weed-covered mound to the east blocked out the lights from the bowling alley and restaurant that lay to the east of the pool; and the parking lot fence and gate stood silently, shrouded in a deep darkness that encompassed them and the lower lawn of the pool. The scene felt so very unfamiliar to him, and a fleeting sense of foreboding came over him as he took his last determined, excited strides before reaching the gate. He was so used to the radiant sunlight that poured over him each morning he arrived there. Now, though, as he stood there wrapped in the thick blanket of the night, the only light he could see was far in the distance, the moderately bright light set atop the concession stand and small clubhouse, which sent its light beams streaming out over the motionless, silent waters of the pool and on northward into the thick gloom of the small forest above it.

He reached the gate, stopped, and peered with the utmost reverence and expectant exuberance through the wire mesh that now held him cap-tive and blocked his access to the pool. To his great dismay and disbelief he could not find her anywhere in the night sky above the pool, and even more disheartening, the vision of her had faded out of view. He could remember the last images of her as she seemed to be floating slowly to the east, appar-ently waving to him, and yet he had not had the impression that she was leaving him. From that vantage point at the gate, though, he could not get a full view of the sky above the pool. Still enthralled by her celestial pres-ence and awed by the visionary sensation of flying through the sky to her golden glory, he was convinced that she had only momentarily disappeared and would reappear to him once he had walked onto the south terrace of the pool. Spurred on by these—for him at that moment—the greatest of all expectations, he miraculously climbed over the eight-foot wire mesh fence, crowned on top by three stands of barbed wire. How he was able to do this remained even to him years afterward quite a mystery. There might have been a small piece of wood lying near the fence that he used to stand on to get up the first few feet or so, and of course the wire mesh was porous and he could easily push his toes through the one- to two-inch squares of wire for a painful footing. But for the most part he must have relied on his hands and shoulders and pulled himself up to the point where the barbed wire began; his swimming had enabled him to develop strong back and arm muscles. Then, too, he crossed just opposite the gatekeeper's stand, which was some five feet high and had been fastened sturdily to the wire mesh on one side of the large double gate that had a smooth round pole on either side of it and provided for a slight gap between the barbed wire. He remembered planting his feet firmly on this stand once he had cleared the sharp spikes of the barbed wire. He jumped to the ground, crossed the parking lot, and was quickly immersed in the pervasive darkness that draped and drooped over the lower lawn and picnic area.

To his left rose the vague silhouettes of the large willow trees that grew along the banks of Cedar Creek; their large half-circular, drooping limbs swayed over the creek and lawn and marked the end of the thick darkness that lay close to the earth and the lighter shades of the night sky above. A grove of large poplar trees to his right blocked a direct view of the east side of the clubhouse. Overhead a few finger-shaped clouds caught the reflections of the suburban lights that drifted over the pool from several surrounding neighborhoods. He forgot about the stairs next to the clubhouse and made his way through the middle of the lawn, directly toward the pool. That was not far at all but it seemed an eternity before he began to climb the soft incline that led to the large south terrace. The light atop the clubhouse washed out more of the night's darkness than he had expected. But despite this he could still see the dark sky above, and on this he focused intently as he made his way on to the east terrace of the pool where the spell of the night still held sway. There he stopped, peered into the heights above him, and waited. Minutes passed slowly and drearily by, and he looked eagerly all around him, hoping that at any minute she would stand there above him robed in all her celestial glory. It was here that he had seen her hovering, here that she had come into view; it was this very location that she had given him. Yet there was no sign of her at all. Not the faintest hint of un-earthly light, not the least trace of a golden ray, no glimmer of anything but only darkness that sat there above him. He strained to pull himself upward and turned about to search the sky and all its four directions. Not one of the myriads of stars above moved or grew larger, and no new or unusual light burst forth in the midst of them. He thought of the empty brick wall on the south side of Dr. Taylor's house; had it become the empty night sky above the Cedar Swim Club pool? For the second time within a matter of weeks what seemed real had not become real. He still had to decide what was real, but now he was certain that he had been given the ultimate choice.

It was somewhat like when one's magic golden bubble bursts: all that was euphoric and effervescent evaporates quite unexpectedly into thin air without warning and the transformation that seemed so complete gives way to the old or a more sober mode of everyday living. What seemed so baffling to him about this was the total unexpectedness of it all to begin with. He had had no idea that he would see such a vision. He knew the Hebrew prophets had had awing visions of the Hebrew God; he knew that Jesus supposedly had visions of this God. But who had had visions of a heavenly woman floating through the night sky? He did not know then that people had had visions of Jesus or the Mother Mary. Yet these rational thoughts arose and vanished in a few brief seconds, and he did not even ponder them long enough to consider whether they were valid or not. He now knew surely, though, that there were at least two worlds, and then he remembered his shirt and his shoes under the tree in the front lawn of the Oxbridge house and the party. He had to get back there before it was over.

He turned and ran to the gate at the entrance way, climbed atop the tall desk adjacent the gate, and then eyed the stands of barbed wire jutting at a slight angle over the top of the fence. He didn't know how he had managed to climb over them, nor did he know how to get over them again. He only knew he had done it once and he would do it again, even though this time there would be an eight-foot drop to the ground on the other side. Exerting almost every muscle in his body he dug his toes into the wire mesh, reached for a good hold of the wire mesh with his hands, and pulled himself up so that he could take hold of the smooth dome of the iron pole of the gate that divided the strands of barbed wire. Then somehow he pulled himself over and free of the barbed wire that threatened to lash out at his flesh at any stray movement, once again dug his toes into the wire mesh on the other side of the fence, and descended a few feet before jumping off the fence so that he only dropped some four feet before he landed safely on the other side. He really didn't know how he did it; he only knew that it was a wonder he did not cut himself anywhere nor did he have a bruise of any kind. The creek gurgled and bid him farewell as he scurried over the bridge. From there he alternated running and walking on the side of the asphalt street that took him northward to the Oxbridge house. Only a car or two whizzed past him, and he was a bit amazed that no one stopped him to ask why he was running half naked through the middle of the night on a street with no sidewalk. Gasping for breath he reached the tree, swiftly pulled on his shirt and shoes, and walked toward the house. To his great surprise no one was on the other side of the door when he opened it; he was halfway to the den or TV room before he saw a party guest, who simply smiled at him and asked if he was having a good time. A couple of people were leaving the den when he got there, so he stopped to talk to them, and then realized he was hungry. He guessed that some of the food might still be on the patio, so he wandered past a handful of other partygoers and bumped into Lea, who told him that there was plenty left for him or anyone else who wanted it. No one had missed him. Not a soul knew that he had left the house, at least no one who had come to the party. Somehow he felt strangely relieved by all this as he ate, talked, and then bid all adieu.

VI

The Leak, Galileans, and Hebrews

THE NIGHT GATHERED THICKLY around him as he plodded along past the large houses (they called them "mansions") of Deerborn Estates; past Tremont Street, which for the most part marked the divide between the little old houses and the big new ones; then gliding and floating along Queen Street. But he was not really there, or was at least part of him now somewhere else? He felt supremely deserted and abandoned on the one hand, as though the golden woman of heaven had left him sitting alone in the middle of the Sahara with no sign at all of an oasis. She had been so absolutely spectacular. Who was she? Where had she come from? He had no idea, and the strangest thing of all was that once she called him, once he saw her, it was as though he had known that she would be there and that he had known that she had been there all his life. The sensation of perhaps being able to fly to her was a bit different; it could have arisen out of his humanness, his desire to partake more closely of that which seemed to be also human but was actually not human at all. Then the utmost question of all came to him as he made his way exuberantly home. What did all this mean? How could he have seen a vision of a golden woman and not God or Jesus? What on earth was happening, and why had no one else at the party been able to see the flaming, golden woman of heaven?

As the sun rose bright and shiny on Queen Street the next morning, it found him more than a bit weary and baffled and yet at the same time filled with the most profound exuberance and expectation. When he first awoke, for a few fleeting seconds everything seemed like it had always been. But as he pulled himself out of bed and draped his clothes around him, he could think only of her. She had not left him; she was with him although he could not see her and could tell no one about her. The marvelous aspect of it all was that he did not really have to tell anyone about her, and at no time did he feel compelled to explain that flaming vision either to himself or to those around him. She was just there, and yet on the flip side of it all she was not there. With and without her he had breakfast and may have gone into another trance momentarily, and his mother saw him sitting there motionless and asked him if anything was wrong. At that he came to himself and told her it was nothing, grabbing up his lunch bag as he got up from the table hoping that he would not be late for work. It was a good twenty-five-minute walk to Cedar Swim Club. He glided through Deerborn Estates to the street with no sidewalks and walked cautiously, moving to the extreme side of the street to make way for the passing cars. He crossed the bridge over the gurgling creek, sailed through the entrance to the parking lot, and within a matter of seconds stood on the south terrace where he had been just hours before peering high into the night sky, stretching almost every muscle in his body like swimmers do when they head toward the end of the pool on the last leg of a race for the finish. But his muscles had not pulled her out of heaven and he had no idea where she had gone, but instinctively he knew she was there.

Weeks had passed with absolutely no sign of the leak. The other two groundskeepers let it be known that they thought the wrong areas had been chosen for excavation and complained vehemently about the possible futility of all their efforts. As he crawled underground to his tunnel, he began to feel as though he had already spent at least part of eternity underground below the terrace. For a couple of hours or more it went as usual. The tunnel was dark and musty, but he took a flashlight with him and some sunlight came through the opening and a few small holes overhead where the side of the pool met the overhead terrace. With the garden tool he dug and scratched along the water pipes for half an hour or so at a time before he crawled out to rest and tank up on fresh air. It looked as though this would be another day just like all the rest and that the mystery of the missing water would remain with them for some time to come. Then during the late morning while he was extending the tunnel yet another three feet or so toward the east end of the pool just to make certain that there was no reason to keep digging there, he heard a faint rushing noise. At first he thought it was the regular sound of filtered water being pumped into the side of the pool, but a few seconds later he heard a definite, sustained hissing sound that gradually grew louder and louder. The excitement mounted as he began digging at a rapid pace in the direction of the bellowing sound when without warning a small wall of water washed the remaining dirt from the pipe in front of him and came racing toward him. He had found the leak! Almost ecstatic he crawled out of the tunnel, stood up, and walked about the terrace. There just a few hours before in the thick darkness of a balmy summer night he had peered deep into the unfathomable heights of heaven searching in vain for the golden flames emanating from a heavenly woman he had never known of before that night. When she first appeared to him, though, she had been here on this very spot, and the morning after she vanished before his eyes, the evasive, mysterious leak had at last been found.

He was somewhat amazed that he felt so literally overwhelmed with joy and at first if for no other reason than that for days they had begun to doubt the leak would ever be found. It could not be compared with the happiness that had engulfed him at graduation. Like it or not, this was another, entirely different reality, and of course no one in the real world would even begin to compare the simple finding of a leak and the culmination of the first level of academic learning. But no one else, not a single soul, knew of the visions and his night walk and the presence that hovered there still around him. Crawling under the deck day after day had become almost supreme drudgery, and at times it looked as though he were doomed to spend the entire summer, if not longer, underground. Yet at the same time his tunnel existence had somehow merged with his celestial walk and the visions. He had been singled out and given an almost impossible task, and the presence had been there with him through the ordeal that at long last had come to a successful and joyous end. The starry-eyed night-walker who not so many days ago had been blown away by the utmost fantasy of a journey to the heavens had ventured now into the depths of the earth to find an elusive, mysterious leak that had threatened the heretofore undaunted reputation of the pool manager and the rest of the sunny, fun-filled summer swimming season.

But then again that was all still on the surface or just below the surface of those things that flew by him those days with all the rest of his friends and those who worked and swam at the Cedar Swim Club that fateful summer. The real mission he had been given revolved around his understanding of the night visions and the seemingly elusive leak itself, seen from the point of view of his new reality. For from the time he was given the task of finding the leak, he somehow understood that it was not the manager who gave that to him or oversaw his work. Whoever it was who had sent him the visions had also sent him underground to search for the leak. And it was as though the leak came about and had to be confronted because the night visions had been sent his way. But surely the great paradox of it all was that it was a statement the presence itself had made not only to and for him but to the carefree, sun-baked swimmers who came to exercise only their bodies or wander and waddle lazily about the water and lie with utter abandonment on the sundecks. Yet it seemed that he alone was aware of this. For all the rest of them it was just a leak somewhere around the swimming pool. No one else he talked to seemed to have any awareness of the presence that had come to visit him. But why? Why had not at least Lea Oxbridge had some vague premonition that the earth and the plants and trees and air and sky were not the same as they had been before, even though when those around him looked at them they appeared to be the same? The night visions had singled him out and imparted some mysterious message to him that he really did not understand at all, but which he only felt and only experienced and only marveled at. He had even sometimes wondered if they could really be real. Then, with the finding of the leak, the so-called fantasy of the visions and earthly reality merged into one fabulous reality. Seen from the symbolic viewpoint the presence had become embedded in this true-to-life reality, and his finding of the leak was a real verification of the vision of Lea Oxbridge, a verification brought to him by the golden woman of heaven. He had not found Lea that night sitting at the bottom of the south wall of Dr. Taylor's house. But the empty, abandoned, and deserted brick wall outlined with the cross over it no longer gave him any conclusive answer. It was now superbly clear to him that the presence that came with the appearance of the golden woman of heaven that night just past had also brought him the vision of Lea along with the others that propelled him to the stars, yet furthermore this same presence had led him to the mysterious leak. It had all become for him a wondrous symbolic event that affirmed the transcendence of an invisible, heavenly world most of his friends professed to know about and believed in, as most all Christians he knew did. But why did his fellow workers and his friends not feel all this? Why was no one else seemingly aware of what he felt and saw those days?

Brimming with excitement he ran to find his two coworkers and a lifeguard or two. They were at first a bit reluctant to believe the leak had been found. But with the water rushing out of the tunnel now, it was a bit hard to deny that at least one leak had been found and no one had yet come up with the thought that there might be two. He celebrated with the other two workers and a lifeguard, and then went to the concession stand to get a bite to eat and something to drink. On the way he stopped to talk to an older woman he knew well. She had four sons, all a few years younger than he, and a tall, handsome, robust husband who was extremely kind and friendly and must have been the apple of the eye of many women before he met her. She herself, though not as tall as he, was a wondrous budding flower whose suntanned skin and womanly curves beamed as beauteously as her lovely face and dark, captivating eyes, and she was always a joy to talk to, even when they only exchanged a few words and flew on past one another. She had been told that he had found the leak and extended her congratulations, saying that he had done well. They talked on a few minutes, during which she leaned over to fetch something on the bath towel she sat on, unknowingly presenting him with almost a full view of her shining, ripe breasts. A smell of sweet honey seemed to fill the air, followed by a feeling of transcendence that beautiful scene seemed to afford. Something stirred deeply within him, and he knew that he wasn't looking merely at the breasts of a woman but rather at an intangible, celestial harmony that rose from her bosom and carried him beyond the winds of time.

From the concession stand he made his way to the employees' lounge next door to eat. Some lifeguards were just finishing lunch when he got there, so he had the lounge to himself. It was a welcome reprieve from all of the morning's excitement that gave him a chance to collect his thoughts. For a few brief minutes as he sat there with a bit of quiet and solitude hovering about him, he was a bit startled by the fleeting thought and hope that these sensational episodes and all their related thoughts and feelings might subside at least for a while so that his feet might plod and meander over the earth with a carefree and casual air about them as they had usually done so many years before now. *Could it all be reversed?* he asked himself. *Could it all be just my imagination?* he wondered still again for a few brief minutes. The face of Lea Oxbridge drifted by once more and with it a wave of brief sadness as he remembered that she had nothing to do with all this. He knew that though he sat there in that quietness looking through the screen door that afforded him a panoramic view of the swimming pool, he was actually peering instead into a fantastic, mysterious, and rather unfathomable land that had been and was still welling up inside him.

Who was the golden woman of heaven? She was now the most confusing and bewildering aspect of all this, and yet somehow it seemed as though she belonged there, as though as he had felt when he first saw her that she had been there all along, wherever of course "there" was. He then accepted the Christian creed and the doctrine that Mary the Mother of Jesus had been a virgin when she gave birth to Jesus, but for a good Protestant such as he, that was the end of the road for her. She was not for him the intercessor to Christ, and she played no other role than that of being the human mother of Jesus. Like good Jews, good Christian Protestants were patriarchal, and there was not the least mention of a feminine aspect of the Godhead. Christian Trinitarians surely described the Hebrew God as Three in One, but there was no trace whatsoever of a Goddess. He had always thought of and prayed to God and Jesus, and it had never occurred to him to consider a feminine deity along with them. But why had she come and why at this particular time? If she were a messenger sent by God, then would she not have said just a few words to him other than his name? For some reason it didn't occur to him that he did not even know her name.

At that juncture his thoughts began to fly around in circles, and the recurring cycle that had preoccupied him for days now returned. Was this all just pure fantasy? He could even ponder once more the belief that most of his peers and the grown-ups he knew held, some not so consciously, that the ancient stories of the Bible were simply a mythology, the result of the fantasy of the ancient peoples who had not yet developed a scientific and rational philosophical understanding of the earth and human life on it. Surely at that time he did not know all that much about the intellectual aspects of the modern world, but his high school science and history plus literature gave him immediate contact with the modern world of two hundred and fifty years or more. He knew that Jesus and Mary and the disciples did not watch TV, at least not the kind he saw daily. But was the presence that had come to him and the enthralling sensation of being suspended between this world and the next pure fantasy? How could he now tell his friends that there was no such thing?

Around and around those thoughts swirled as the patter of feet and the chatter of boys and girls and men and women echoed from the south terrace of the pool through the screen door of the small lounge, and the sweltering heat of midday began to seep through the shade of the umbrellas and the poplar trees that stretched out their limbs and leaves over the small clubhouse. The thought that it was all mere fantasy was tempting. If this was the real essence of it all, he could for the most part just forget about it and let time take its course. It was phenomenal and perplexing that at no time had he been told anything definite to say or to tell the others anyway.

And what about the golden woman of heaven? Who would even begin to believe him if he did actually tell someone about her? But he could not forget the baby boy, and then at that moment it became an unmistaken fact for him that this son of someone was the Christ child and Lea perhaps not just a symbol of but the actual Madonna. He had for years already in his early life debated the divinity of Jesus back and forth, and he had decided that Jesus was the true Messiah of Israel, the Anointed One, the one true God. Could it be that the golden woman was his messenger of some sort? Had she come to announce to him the coming of Jesus the Christ? If so, then he had been given a definite task, and Jesus or God or both were holding him accountable.

This would mean that he had to act and that he had to make a statement to the others about this. But why him? Why had the presence not come to the others around him? Why was it not clear to them that this world and the other world are uniquely interrelated and that one could actually move between them, from one to the other? If only one of them, if only Lea, had somehow become aware of this—or if only a few people at work had been able to apprehend the presence when it was there—then they would know something about what had taken place. And what about Jesus himself? Why had he not appeared to him or to others he knew? Was not the task that he now felt had been given to him the task that Jesus himself should have? Should he not then come to him and to the others and make it clear what was happening? At that moment he clearly understood that, no matter how long he might sit there that day, all those feelings and thoughts—though extraordinary and seemingly imaginative—were truly genuine and would remain with him. Resolutely he got up and went back to work.

A good bit of the soil that had been dug up from underneath the terrace could not be put back, as there was no way to compact it all so that it would fill the original underground space. They were told to load it up and take it to a landfill several miles from the club not far from an old sawmill. Then, too, since new tetherball poles had been added on the upper lawn adjacent the filter room, a good bit of sod had to be removed from around them, and the players circle needed to be filled with sawdust. So they were told to make a stop at the sawmill to take on a load of sawdust. Together they began to shovel the leftover dirt onto the truck bed, and as he lifted shovel after shovel of the soil into the air, he was surprised to sense that he was drawing on unlimited store of energy that extended to every muscle in his body. Shovel after shovel of soil literally flew into the truck bed, and it was obvious that though he should be tired, he was working now much faster than he had worked that morning. He then had the strange thought that he might be able to stand there forever piling the truck bed higher and higher with soil.

Not long after this he became aware of a definite burning sensation in his feet and hands. He stopped shoveling and looked at his hands. They were literally white hot, and though he had not taken off his shoes, his feet felt almost the same way. He felt his feet glowing with almost the same intensity as they had the morning after his starry night walk, and this time it seemed that the warmth had reached his hands. He had not put on any gloves, and surely the friction between his hands and the shovel handle would have generated a good amount of heat. He kept shoveling for another ten minutes or so, when beneath the skin on his hands he thought he sensed another inner glow. At that point he stopped once more to look at his hands. He was astounded to see that the upper layer of pink skin on the palms of his hands had been loosened in the shape of a hot, white circle that now hung dangling from the center of his hands, held only by a slight sliver of thin skin. Skin from his palms that should have remained a blister had become warm and had somehow become white circular patches of skin that now dangled loosely from the palms of his hands. They immediately reminded him of the Eucharist wafer the priest imparts to each communicant Christian at the Eucharistic celebration of a Roman Catholic Mass! But he had never attended a Mass of any kind in his life, and he was astonished that he felt the urge to eat this skin, thinking that it might somehow have been transformed into the truly holy Host. His hands and his feet continued to glow for hours after that, and in spite of the remaining now-open circular blisters that covered the centers of the palms of his hands, his hands did not hurt at all, not even slightly. He restrained the initial urge to eat those circular patches of skin, simply pulled them off, and continued shoveling by moving the shovel handle to another portion of his hand. Yet as the bed of the truck was filled with soil, he wondered very much about these patches of skin and strangely sensed that they were truly symbolic signs of real spiritual food, that they could well be signs of the very spiritual presence that filled him from within and surrounded him with circle after circle and wave after wave of invisible food.

The truck bed was soon filled, and shortly after they piled into the front seat, they were rambling along the road that led first to the landfill and then to the sawmill, which lay to the south and east of the populated borders of town in a remote countryside. A radiant sun beamed and poured down upon them as they reached a stretch of road that was not at all familiar to him. As they bumped and bounded on southward, they came to a landscape that was markedly different from the usual verdant hills that surrounded most of the town. There were far fewer trees, even some barren reaches of almost flat pastureland sparsely covered with grass, and only an occasional rolling hill. They reached the landfill, offloaded the soil, and meandered on along the eerie road.

Not long after that he saw the sawmill looming there before them, lunging high into the sun-drenched sky. He had never seen such an old, rusty metal structure before. Not only the yard but the surrounding landscape was brown, barren, almost desolate. As they stepped out of the truck and made their way toward this seemingly century-old tower jutting high into the blue canopy above them, he had the distinct sensation that instantly and without warning they had been swept up and transported to another land around the world or to another planet. The reddish-brown, rust-coated metal support tower and wheels of the sawmill exuded the aura of an earlier century, reminding him of those antique engines and flywheels built at the beginning of England's and Scotland's industrial boom of the mid to late nineteenth century. Obviously the drab old mill had been used for almost a century or more. They had parked at first a good distance away and now made their way cautiously toward a few, weary-looking men who stood near the mill watching several other men at work. They wore grimy, sweat-soaked overalls, sleeveless shirts, and some a tattered straw hat set at an angle from one ear to the top of their head. They all moved at such a slow and lethargic pace it seemed to him as though they had entered some kind of time warp that set them some fifty years at least back. He heard one of the groundskeepers mumble something about sawdust, and then the ordinary sounds of that encounter faded out.

He turned to look over the countryside and then back again, and at that moment he was startled to sense that the presence of an earlier ancient era had descended around him. The men, the conveyer belts, and the sawmill all disappeared momentarily before his eyes, and in their stead stood a maze of small buildings set to one side of a small agrarian village surrounded by a lush, verdant countryside. A vivid view of ancient Palestine flashed magically before his eyes. Centuries of time floated quickly by in the aura of timelessness that whisked him away from the twentieth century, and when he turned to look at the village and surrounding landscape again, it seemed as though he stood near a small stone mill where village workers were grinding freshly harvested grain into flour somewhere in Galilee of Jesus's day. But the aura of timelessness was not content to leave him there. No sooner had he arrived than, as he looked out over the distance to the south and east, he saw a band of Galileans dressed in the costumes of that day, trudging along, some riding donkeys and a camel or two, making their way along the rough road that led to the stone mill. As they came closer, though, he noticed their rather subdued demeanor. They spoke in a very low tone of voice, and on the breeze that blew the sounds of their voices his way he felt a marked sense of expectancy and excitement that hovered about them as they approached the stone mill. They stopped not far from it and gazed at the scene: men throwing fresh grain on the primary stone, and others gathering the ground grain from the other side as a donkey paraded merrily around the circle of the stone to keep it turning.

To his amazement he felt as though they were peering into an even more remote time than their own, and he saw that they were awed by a vision of yet another, more ancient group of wanderers who had at first left Uruk and later Haran to the east to seek out a western plot of ground on which they began to build a small but impressive altar. It was a supernatural, visionary tunnel of time that afforded him a kaleidoscopic, primeval panorama of history dissolving the twentieth and even the first century into those pristine, quintessential days when heaven and earth were almost united and when Terah, Abraham, and Sarah wandered along the rivers of the Tigris and Euphrates through Syria into Canaan, a heavenly flash of the Israelite past that gave him the awareness of one, long, monolithic continuum of time through which the presence of the one true Hebrew God had penetrated the souls of humankind. A definite feeling of the earth during those earliest days drifted past him and then soared to its timeless origin in the stars, that marvelous eternity that turned the eyes of not only the Hebrews but the Edomites, the Ammonites, the Moabites, but others of the Fertile Crescent and the rest of the earth upward to the great love of heaven.

As he heard someone tell them to move the truck over to a mound of sawdust, he came to himself somewhat and walked in that direction. A shovel was thrust into his hands, and he went through the motions of helping fill the truck bed; but he could still see himself standing there breathlessly spellbound, for there was nothing he could ponder or do that would dispel those flying visions and their peaceful continuity, which had seem-ingly arisen out of the earth around him and bound some of the earliest of earth's times with the twentieth century—even though its new science and technology had all but obliterated the essential feeling of those previ-ous eons from the face of the earth. Time stood still as he peered into the eternity of love.

Then it was that the titles of the four canonical Gospels began to re-verberate around and around his head, and he began to repeat them over and over: "Matthew, Mark, Luke, and John." On and on it went, and the repetition of the names became something like a soothing mantra that calmed him, and the shovels hummed as a kind of background chorus that sent the sawdust flying high over the sides of the truck. To his amazement he began to consider these the names of the first four disciples of Jesus, and he forgot that they were not their names with the exception perhaps of John according to one Gospel tradition, and he completely forgot about Peter and Andrew whom many consider the first disciples of the Lord. But then he realized that the names of the two groundskeepers with him were ancient biblical names. One was even named Peter, the rock, who according to one tradition proclaimed that Jesus was the true Messiah of Israel, the very disciple whom Jesus called to become the ultimate foundation for his church on earth. The other was named Paul, the great apostle who actually founded the church and took the gospel to the Gentiles. At that moment he could no longer restrain himself; he had to say something about all the visions that had come his way. Yet what he said amazed even him, and it seemed then that he had no choice but to say it. He turned to Pete and told him that he was the disciple Peter; he looked with a penetrating gaze at Paul and told him that he was the Apostle Paul. Then came the pronouncement he himself could scarcely believe: he told them that he was Jesus the Christ!

After only half an hour or so, a heaping pile of sawdust rose over the rim of the truck bed, and they climbed in and set out for the swim club. The truck first lurched and bumped along over the uneven country road but not for long, and they were soon zooming over a newer, smooth swath of asphalt tar that made even the old truck hum underneath them. They were almost there when someone let out a cry that rang through their ears, "Out of gas! We're almost out of gas! Did we forget to check it before we left?" Instantly a quite unexpected and startling thought whizzed past him: *Sometime, perhaps even in the not so distant future, there might be a shortage of gasoline that would threaten the economy of the country!* He had never thought of it before, but there it was, wandering about with all the other thoughts and sights of the past few days, and it seemed to say that the time when oil would be scarce and most of the world's oil reserve would be depleted was inevitable. Then an eschatological aura arose to surround and color this thought and the words rang out: "The day will come when even nations would be out of gas." He started to say something to the others about all this, but then realized the paradox of it all. At that time of inevitability, gasoline would no longer be for many the primary source of concern; then people would know that they had used too much gasoline for far too long and that they had neglected the real and essential fuel of the soul. What they had thought might be fuel for the soul was only the beginning of it all; then they would know that there was a gasoline that could never be depleted. So he simply said, "Keep on going. Keep on driving. We'll get there before we're out of gas."

VII

Where Is Jesus?

WHAT PETE'S AND PAUL'S reaction to all this was, he really couldn't tell. They did not seem to be too much concerned, and the return trip to the swim club with the exception of the shortage of gasoline was uneventful. They backed the truck up to the tetherball pit and began to unload the sawdust. For some reason now he thought he ought to have two other followers to bring the total to four, and one of his good friends was named John. Where they were to go and what was to happen next he really did not know, but he thought that they ought to gather together to see what would happen. He rushed to the phone to call John and tell him to bring his car.

The swim club was full to overflowing with all those who had come to seek a reprieve from the heat that had descended after noonday and now rose all around the lawn and the pool, baking the concrete terraces and the people who lay there to sunbathe. It was toward the end of July, and the bodies of most all the regulars had for weeks now been roasted to a glowing golden tan to brown color. Only occasionally did one catch sight of a newcomer who, if not all white, sometimes had tan legs and arms contrasted with a glaring white upper legs and torso. He called John's house, and his mother answered the phone to give him the somewhat sad news that John was not there. She wanted to know what message to give her son, and he hesitated at first, but then went on to try to describe ever so briefly the scene as he saw it at that time. He told her that, as far as he could tell, something extraordinary was happening and that he was not sure what it was but that it had definitely something to do with Jesus. He went on to say that if at all possible John should get his car and come to meet them at the church. It was not at all clear to him how she would react to all this, but anyway he felt that he had to say something about this at that time.

Whose idea it was to go to the church was not clear, and exactly what he had told Peter and Paul he did not remember. The heat that had oppressed them for weeks now, the digging for the leak along with the routine work, and the visions—especially the coincidence of the vision of the golden woman of heaven, the finding of the leak, and the visions of ancient Palestine—began to take their toll on him. He was certainly tired and from this point on he became just a bit confused. It could well have been his idea to go to the church, because he thought that they ought to seek out a quiet place where they could talk and ponder these matters together as they waited to see what might happen next. As far as he could tell, that was their primary task at the moment, because so much had happened during the span of less than a day that he could not imagine exactly how to proceed from this point on entirely on his own. It seemed to him that God had to intervene in the lives of those around him for this to continue.

He left the clubhouse and walked back to the tetherball pit with the names of the four Gospels still ringing in his ears: "Matthew, Mark, Luke and John." On and on the mantra went, but he didn't say anything about it to Pete and Paul. He told them to hurry up, that they had to get to the church as soon as possible, and that there was a good possibility that John would meet them there. With Pete at the steering wheel they slowly edged their way along the lower lawn to the parking lot and then quickly zipped through the exit gate over the Cedar Creek bridge as a duck or two flew up from the gurgling waters. Then they turned onto the street with no sidewalks named for the church that an ancestor of his had founded almost two centuries ago. It seemed to him that no sooner had they left the swim club than they arrived almost magically at the church and parked in one of the vacant spaces in front of the mid-nineteenth-century structure built on the model propagated by the rise and dominance of the American Protestant movement of that earlier century. The sanctuary was not level but descended at a substantial angle toward the pulpit, which was centered at the front of the apse before the altar and rose abruptly to a great height above the sanctuary floor. It was from this vantage point that the divine word was proclaimed to the sinners who came each Sunday to allow that word to reach their souls, the essence of the Protestant sacrament of the spoken word, which for some four centuries now had been developed to supersede the Eucharistic feast of the Roman and Orthodox Churches and a few others that had survived from antiquity onward.

The church was open, as it was the custom then to keep its doors open during the day for anyone who wished to go there. They bounded up the stairs, scurried through the sanctuary, and gathered in the center of it just below the pulpit, a place that he had long considered sacred. There were no children's sermons back then, and he and his mother usually sat toward the back a good distance from the pulpit. Not at all accustomed to the sacred altar of the typical Catholic church, he had come to associate the pulpit and the area around the pulpit as the most sacred part of the sanctuary, for it was from there that the divine word of the Lord was proclaimed to the sinners of the Protestant Church. So he did not go too close to the sacred pulpit, but kept his distance. Pete and Paul must have been more than a bit dumbfounded by all this, but if so, they said almost nothing about what they were thinking. He hoped that they might at last have some kind of experience of their own, but it soon became clear that they really had no clue what this was all about. It looked as though he would have to try to relate to them most of all of the things he had seen and experienced the last couple of weeks. They waited a few more minutes and nothing happened. Then just as he was about to begin to try to explain and to tell them about the great wind that had blown him about for days now, he saw the associate pastor and one of the well-known local alumni from the college he was to attend enter the sanctuary. He knew immediately that they had not come there to seek the solace and quietude that sacred room could afford them. He turned to look at Pete and Paul and at that very moment he also knew that at least one of them had not believed a word he had told them, even from the beginning. Somehow while he was on the phone to John's mother, one of them had gone to another telephone and called the associate pastor.

He knew all this instantly with the flash of light-filled intuition, and even though he knew that he was very tired, it was then that he became almost overcome by fatigue and exhaustion. The four of them stood there with him just as Lea Oxbridge had stood and talked to him somewhere on the edge of the parking lot at the swim club a couple days after he saw her and the baby boy at Dr. Taylor's house, and the remembrance of her innocence and naïveté made him suddenly extremely despondent. He was more than just a bit fatigued, and he quickly became somewhat confused and bewildered by all of the visions and images and the events associated with them, which like a great roaring river had taken him and his little boat on a long and demanding journey. It was painfully clear that no one believed anything that he had said, and of course they would have not believed him even if he had told them about Lea Oxbridge and the baby boy, the golden woman of heaven, and the ancient Hebrews of Uruk, Ai, Haran, Shechem, and Mamre. It was the heat, they said. They made it a point to tell him that even they were a bit overcome by the recent heat wave, even though they had not been out working in all that heat these past several weeks like he had. It was very likely that he had suffered a heatstroke and that he had been overcome by a slight delirium that often accompanies such a malady. He stood there stupefied, exhausted, and overwrought. There was nothing more he could do and he had no choice but to acquiesce and let bygones be bygones. Somehow he knew, though, that time would take its course.

When he awoke the next morning, he at first had no idea where he was. He was lying in a squeaky-clean bed that had been placed next to a rather large window that was filled to the brim with countless light rays streaming onto the floor and his bed and bouncing off the surrounding walls of a moderately sized but sterile room. How he got there, he didn't know. The last thing he remembered was talking to his four compatriots in front of the pulpit at the Great Presbyterian Church. If he had not fainted, as later his friends told him that he didn't, he must have just entered a state of conscious unconsciousness. The associate pastor and the college alumnus had taken him to the local hospital where he had been treated and observed during the night. The door opened, and he saw a nurse enter with a breakfast tray. She seemed a bit surprised but more than happy to see that he was awake. They exchanged greetings, and she left him to enjoy the meal.

On the breakfast tray, besides the usual egg or two and maybe a small bowl of cereal were many slices of bread and an extraordinary amount of preserves and jam so that he was compelled to choose from among a number of plastic containers of strawberry, marmalade, and grape jam. He was hungry and quickly ate most of the food before he began to reminisce about the events of the day just past. He no longer felt confused, and his thoughts were clear. The most striking thing, though, about finding himself alone in this strange and unnatural setting was that he did not feel at all alone. Not only that, he did not feel ashamed or self-conscious about all that had transpired not only the day before but also over the course of the past couple of weeks. With the exception of the evening and night just past, he could remember all that had happened and all that he had told his friends. He knew that it was unusual, but the strangest and most fascinating thing about it all was that somehow there was a familiar aspect to it, as though despite the extraordinariness of those events they were truly natural occurrences that had blossomed into his life, just as though a crocus blossoms and bursts forth with the most wondrous colorful leaves and petals almost overnight. He was somewhat to his own surprise happy about what had taken place, and he felt content to be there where he was, and the real reason for that was that he still sensed that the presence was with him, not like it had been before but it was there in that room, hovering about him gently and extending a soothing feeling of solace to his soul and his body. The moment he turned to the bread and preserves he was immediately reminded of the last meal of the Lord on earth and the Eucharistic celebration of the church for countless centuries. It seemed to him that all this now had become his secret and that as he ate the remainder of the meal, he was to celebrate the passion and resurrection of the one true Hebrew Messiah, the God of gods. It was his secret not only because he had not been able to tell anyone other than Pete and Paul something about it, it was as though Jesus himself, despite all the not-so-orthodox visions and images, had spoken to him even through the vision of the golden woman of heaven. He looked at the plastic containers of preserves and chose all the ones with grape jam to symbolize the wine, said a prayer, and spread the grape jam over several slices of bread ceremoniously as he pondered the life and suffering of the Anointed One of Israel who thousands of years ago had become uniquely divine and human.

Toward the end of the morning the director of Christian education from the Great Presbyterian Church bounded through the door with a warm and cheerful smile decorating her somewhat round and cheeky face. She stayed almost a good half hour and they talked ever so briefly about what had happened but mostly about the summer excitement of work at the pool and swimming. She knew something about the college he was to attend and, making a good attempt to put all this into some kind of relieved perspective, she let the following comment drop ever so casually from her lips: "Sometimes students who go to that college do the strangest things." With that a generous smile beamed over her face, and he also laughed along with her as he remembered his secret. That afternoon his father came to see him, checked him out of his room, and drove him home where he was to spend his first night not alone but this time with his secret. So it was that he became the first heatstroke victim of the Cedar Swim Club.

He didn't realize it then, but it would be some thirteen years before he had even the vaguest idea what had happened to him those several weeks, almost a decade and a half that unfolded with uncounted adventures and unique episodes and encounters that came wandering along with him on that future path he was to travel. He searched for ways to talk to others about the visions, but almost invariably each little avenue that might have led to something was blocked by the sober and rational worldview of not just the grown-ups but his peers as well. Then, too, almost the very next day after his father brought him home, the presence that had opened up the enthralling other world for him vanished. For the first time since the vision of Lea Oxbridge and the baby boy, he was left high and dry in the real world with all the others who knew nothing about all this. It was something like a sailor over a hundred years ago who after being out to sea tossed about for months finally sets foot on the stationary, solid ground of the earth. It took him a few days to steady his somewhat wobbly legs, to allow the wind that had been swirling about his head to abate, and to plant his feet firmly on the paths each day sent his way. Meanwhile both consciously and unconsciously he rummaged through the brief past of his young life for clues that could shed some light on these matters. July quickly gave way to August, the king of the summer, and a few more weeks of torrid heat and sun came along with it. But somehow it didn't bother him as much, perhaps because by then toward the middle of that month the angle of the sun's light is markedly diminished and he was diligently preparing for the coming of the frosty days of autumn when he would have left home for the first time. He had to buy notebooks and new clothes and get ready for college.

Only a few days passed before he went back to work at the Cedar Swim Club, and it was good to go back there. Much to his surprise Pete and Paul were the same as usual, and the rest of the summer workdays there unfolded in an immensely routine fashion. It was good to follow the same old work routine with the lifeguards and the others and to see all his friends again. The only thing out of the ordinary was that the pastor called later and recommended that he go visit one of the local psychoanalysts. There was really no choice, and he went somewhat reluctantly. But Dr. Whiteford was a kind and remarkable man and a real native Englishman as well, whose two sons he knew as they were also members of the swim club. He wanted to ask him how it came about that he had left the other side of the Atlantic and the fabulous fairy-tale land of England, the home of hobbits and elves, and Dickens and Swift, to come to the rugged wilds where once the "savage" Cherokee roamed about. But they never got to that subject.

Somehow sitting there listening to the melodic lilt and song of an English accent he felt very much at home and was able to tell him ever so slightly something of the recent adventures that had meandered into his life. Without painting for him any of the controversial images and pictures that the visions had brought to him, he was able to talk in a remarkably vague but sometimes also specific fashion about the episodes that enabled Dr. Whiteford to relate some or all of this to his psychoanalytic experience and analysis. Almost all of their conversations revolved around the new feeling and new awareness that had come to him, and he remembered telling him something of how he had felt and how the earth and his surroundings looked from the rarified angle of the sensations that accompanied the Lea Oxbridge vision and the starry night walk, though he dared not tell him about the specific vision. He made sure he did not speak about that vision or the golden woman of heaven or Christ; he simply spoke of God, the God who made the earth and who could be felt through the earth. He told him specifically about that very first day after the starry night walk, and how marvelous it had been to sense the presence of God in all that surrounded him—the very earth itself, the grass, flowers, animals, birds—and how beautiful the people around him—boys, girls, men, and women—really were. He even went so far as to say that the pantheistic aspect of God's presence, the formal name and concept he did not know at that time, could even be felt in the electricity of their homes and the telephone and power lines that had long now been put up all over the town and formed one huge power maze. He did not know then that great amounts of electricity adversely affect humans and often block out the natural presence of God. Strangely enough he felt somehow that Dr. Whiteford had more than some understanding for what he told him, and he wanted to ask him about this. But there was never a way he could make him be specific, and there was never a real give-and-take between them. It was as though Dr. Whiteford knew what he told him, but he knew it a different way. It allowed him perhaps to relate it to one or more of several somewhat similar but various theories that of course he did not spell out and elaborate on. But beyond all that, he sensed that Dr. Whiteford had his own viewpoint, about which he refused to talk. So there they sat, squared away, each talking from a different corner. After a few sessions he was told that he no longer had to come if he did not want to, and he chose to let it all stand where it was.

VIII

Before the New Reality

THE NEXT SEVERAL WEEKS he was preoccupied with the concrete, material world and his readjustment to it. He didn't realize it so much during those first days when the presence left him, but months later he began to comprehend ever so slowly that it would never be the same world it had been for him for almost two decades. Yet even then he knew that that was the essential question: Had the world around him become overnight something it had not been at all before? Were the visions pure and natural episodes that arose in the course of time out of a human life on earth? Were they not simply the fruits of the human seed that had been planted with another human life on earth? Or were they only aberrations of some kind, the imaginations of a maladjustment that perhaps comes to the fore when a person is not able to throw off the outmoded, obsolete heritage of the past world and tries to mix it all up with the transformed, modern world.

He began to rummage through his past for thoughts, feelings, and events that might help him understand what had taken place. As he did so, he couldn't really see much of his past life that was at all out of the ordinary. He had been religious but not fanatically so. He was a member of the youth group, but it was split into two major factions, and he did not belong to the conservatives, nor did he claim to belong wholly and truly to the liberals, or "worldly religious," even though he socialized with them more sometimes. His life to that point had been much like the lives of his peers, and there was only one really quasi-supernatural occurrence he could remember. He was returning from a walk to town one afternoon with a friend when he felt a different sensation in his legs, and it occurred to him that he understood something about walking he had not experienced before. It was not that he could explain in any precise and scientific manner how the muscles and tendons and ligaments functioned; the thoughts he had were much more diffuse than that. They had just come to the five corners intersection where five streets meet, about halfway between town and his home. All at once he sensed that his legs were moving as though he himself was not causing them to move. It felt to him as though they were walking all by themselves, and with that came the thought that at long last he understood walking and was able to walk as he was meant to walk. How had that happened? There was no way to explain it; it was simply as though someone else were walking with him, moving his legs for him, propelling them along one after another with an extraordinary agility and lightness that made him feel as though he were floating along over the way. He said nothing about this to his friend, who noticed nothing at all.

Then there were those feelings and sensations he had experienced on countless walks through the woods and forests, and they usually came to him when he was alone or with just a couple of others, his sister or a friend. The knobs or small hills were only minutes away from his home by foot; once he was there, he eagerly bounded along those paths and small trails that wound about through and along the top to those enchanting, usually sun-drenched little mountains that rose toward the sky. Especially when the sun was high in the sky and its golden beams caressed the plants and trees of the knobs, it sent spirals of light scurrying in all directions, which welled up into magical light waves that seemed suspended in midair between the earth and the sky, between this world and the next. The most glorious of those walks were in autumn, when the paths were covered high and washed by a sea of yellow, gold, and light red leaves that poured over his feet wave after wave as he happily made his way along a familiar path. He could still feel the tingling of happiness that stirred beneath his breast when he heard the sound of the leaves washing against his feet—*swoosh, swoosh, swoosh*—and see the light reflecting off the boughs of the trees, and then usually the feeling came to him. He was there but he was not just there, and a feeling of awe swept over him as he seemed to rise and fly with the waves of light to the border of another world, another place that lay in and through and yet beyond the magical forest, the other realm, unseen, invisible, but tangible, ever so slightly perceptible, marvelously elusive. Something was there around those high mounds of earth among the trees and plants and animals that was not bound by them nor was it dependent upon them; yet it was part of them, and it came to them and walked about with them, lending its ineffable presence of joy to those who came to wander there.

Often on many Saturdays all the household except his sister got up before sunrise to get all things ready for a daylong fishing trip. His mother diligently fixed a lunch of sandwiches and fruit, his father hitched the boat and trailer to the car, and usually just at sunrise they had found their way to the lakeshore where the boat was launched onto dark, green waters that reflected the color of the tree-lined banks. At that hour the slim fingers of a light fog often meandered and skipped over the water before melting into the misty, early-morning sun as the call of a crow and its mate and friends echoed out of a cove and cascaded into the center of the lake and mixed with the wailings of a flock of geese or ducks winging their way above. There was a fresh crispness in the air of the early morning that appears only at that early hour, so tangy and exciting it sometimes felt as though he could reach out and put some of it into his hand and spread it over the musty and slight fishy smell of the boat and fishing gear. As they unloaded and launched the boat, the supreme stillness that sat reigning over that broad expanse of water that stretched for miles in every direction rose up around them and seemed to drown out the jabbing, cutting sound of the small motor that sent the boat zooming over a clear and glassy mirror of water. He would go to sit in the bow of the boat and bend over its side where he could see the reflection of the sky above rebounding off the bottomless depths of water below, pulling him up off the water into an endless sky, magically transporting the marvels of the earth into the heavens. For a few brief minutes he felt as though he, too, flew like the rays of the sun and soared suspended between this world and the other, losing himself in water and sky to encounter the edge of the universe which seemed never to have begun but was just beginning.

There was one other time he sensed that time had been suspended, when the future returned to the present. Just after he completed the eighth grade and before he was to enter high school, the city demolished the old junior high school, which for years had been the old high school, dating possibly from the first decade of the twentieth century or earlier, and built a new junior high school with also the ninth grade. It was a low-lying, shiny modern structure made of pale-red, almost pink brick, quite a contrast to the dark red brick of the old school, a very high-up kind of building. The ceilings in the old school were for him immensely higher than those of the rooms of the new school, and he was more accustomed to them as he had spent two years there gazing each day at walls that rose some fifteen feet or more above the floor. One morning not soon after he entered the ninth grade at the new school, he was for some reason asked to carry a note to the principal, who was out of his office visiting someone with an office on the third floor. Once he reached the third floor office and walked through the doorway, he had the distinct impression that he had entered a splendid throne room of a royal person in a vast country on the other side of the world. But because the ceiling was much lower than in the old school, it seemed to him that he had all at once grown at least half a foot taller, for it felt as though his head was dangerously close to the ceiling, but yet, because of the royal presence, impolitely and discourteously so. Then to his amazement, as he walked toward the other end of the room and stood before the principal, he felt like a tiny dwarf summoned to appear before a huge king in a medieval castle. Maybe it was that he associated the principal with the high walls and ceilings of the old school, and once he saw him and stood before him, his subconscious took over his conscious and the room suddenly underwent some kind of metamorphosis. At one and the same instant it felt to him as though his head was hovering rather impolitely too close to the new ceiling while his feet padded over a floor miles below the ceiling of the old school. It was then that he thought he heard a voice summoning him to appear before a ruler far superior to the principal who reigned over the people of a strange and distant land, but who nonetheless had jurisdiction over him and all those around him. He hastily delivered the note into the hands of the principal, turned about as soon as he could, and scurried out of the room. Was all this just his imagination? Perhaps it was, perhaps not. He did not really know.

Except for these and some other times when these kinds of feelings and sensations came his way, his life up until the time of the visions had been ordinary. He had good friends from the neighborhood something less than middle class; good friends at church and school, many a bit more than middle class; and some close good friends whom he went to see on the weekend and with whom he had birthday parties. He was a Scout and went with dozens of Scouts on weekend hikes and camping trips. He was even then a patriot and believed that his country was unique among all the countries of the earth. He had never ever believed that one could see a golden woman flaming through the night sky! No such thing had even vaguely occurred to him; it was not something he had even heard of or talked about with anyone. Sure there were witches and goblins and ghosts in Shakespeare and even Dickens and Poe. There were heroines like Jean d'Arc and Pocahontas and perhaps Queen Elizabeth, but no one ever spoke of a queen of heaven. There was no precedent for that. But for years he had wondered about the ancient and the modern worlds. From the time he realized that the world of the Bible and the world around him were not the same, he became preoccupied with what he understood was not only a dilemma for him but for those around him, even the church, even his country and beyond. It did not happen overnight; it was not like one day he had a tremendous, flashing thought that said, "This is a great dilemma!" No, it was more like over the years as he began to mull over all those impressions that came from the different environments of his day, of his week, of the years that piled on top of one another from the time when he was seven or eight years old onward, he began to realize that the Bible and the church that had sprung from it were not at all like the school and the business and the factory and the corporation, just as the tiny village of the heartland was not like the big city or megalopolis. Of course, Athens was not like the Jerusalem of the first century, or was it?

Much sooner than he expected, the last week of August arrived and with it the farewells before the first week of September, the first week of college, that long-awaited time when he hoped that at long last he could begin to find the answers to the thousands of questions he had. He would soon be able to sit at the feet of learned professors of the Ivy League kind who were reputed to have obtained the ultimate knowledge, the fruits of hundreds and hundreds of centuries of human learning and debate that arose with the "ascent" of humankind. He called Lea Oxbridge and went over to see her several times before the last week at home. He said good-bye to Pete, Paul, John, and all the others at the swim club, and he saw all of his best friends at least once before he took flight and sped over the tall mountain that separated him from that renowned domain of cherished learning. Somewhat to his amazement, the more time he spent readying himself for that big day, the more the remembrance of the visions receded into the past. Pete and Paul had never said a word about what had happened, and during the hours he spent talking to Lea he was surprised to find that he no longer expected her to know anything about what had happened. Pete particularly acted as if nothing at all had happened and was as carefree with him as always, even more so, as though he knew all there was to know about "a heatstroke," as though he was happy that he had never had something like one.

Actually he was a bit relieved that everybody was like they had always been and that time was taking its course, moving on slower than the wind, more like it is when a person sets out on a long autumn walk on Saturday or Sunday through a sea of multicolored yellow, gold, and red leaves of maples, oaks, hickories, mulberry trees, and others that lick at one's feet as the trees stretch out their boughs of comfort and the sun-drenched sky blue above beckons with a smile. Lea was going the opposite direction and they would be separated by hundreds of miles, but they vowed to write to one another and planned to meet at least at Christmas if not Thanksgiving. Even though he went over to her house and sat again on the expansive floor of her living room, he found her a bit more distanced than he remembered her being. It was perhaps natural considering the situation, the expectation of a long journey that lay there before them. He talked about what he thought it would be like and she did too, concluding that it would for the most part be like things had been during those past years. It would be just another phase of life, or would it? He didn't really know. He found himself still considering her as someone he could marry, but then he didn't know how exactly that option still remained. Did he love her? He didn't know, and he supposed that he didn't yet know what love really was. First of all he had to find out what life was all about, what the human world really was. He was sure that there were people he was soon to meet who had the real answers to all those questions he had accumulated over the brief span of less than a few decades. A few days later he gathered up most all his possessions, gave his mother and sister a kiss and a hug, said good-bye to his father, and sallied forth to find the answers to all those questions that only the "real" world could conjure up for him.

IX

Before He Had a Place to Go

AT LAST IT SEEMED he had a place to go, and though he had not really realized it, he had long been preoccupied with this quest, to find a place to go. From even those earliest days he could remember, he was a bit puzzled about where he should go, and actually all that revolved around how he perceived the world and what he thought was real. But he didn't conceive of it like that then. He didn't walk around talking about what he thought might be real or might not be real; he asked questions and pondered the world he saw around him. He wondered about the people who lived in tiny little houses not too far from his house and why they seemed to be so different from the people who lived behind the formidable boundaries of Deerborn Estates and other such enclaves. He wondered about the few people he knew of who had come from the countries on the other side of the great waters that lay east of the hills where there were no hills or mountains. He had only met a few of them, and he wondered so much why they didn't look like the rest of the people he knew and why the sound of their voices floated so strangely with different lilts and unheard-of reverberations to his ears. How was it, he wondered, that he conceived of the great wide world some fifteen years or more before he was asked to give a sermon of sorts, a religious talk, to the high school assembly during which he got up the courage to tell all his schoolmates that as far as he could determine, the human race did not know where it lived since it had no clue about where the sun was or where the earth might actually be as it went whirling around the sun day after day. "Just think about it," he told them. "You know your street address, you know where your neighborhood is as related to the rest of the town, you know where your town is, and so also where your state and where your country is on the global map. But then you've got to answer this question: Where is the earth, and where is the sun and the solar system and our galaxy, the Milky Way? Even if you can put the solar system in an obscure arm of the Milky Way and you plot it on the map of the hundreds of millions of galaxies that the astronomers have discovered, do you really know where you are? You have no idea whatsoever where you are!"

Way back then, when he thought he saw and felt something suddenly standing in front of him, he might have thought about these things. That "something" had been a presence of some kind, but he had no idea what it might be. Though he didn't forget it, it really didn't bother him that he didn't know what exactly it might be. Whatever it was, it was a part of the world; he knew that he, too, was a part of the world he saw every day as his life unfolded from one year to the next. He could remember the tricycle days, which must have begun about this time, not long after his sister came home for the first time. He could remember when his mother told him that she had to leave and go to the hospital to get his little sister. It seemed a bit odd to him that his sister had to come first to a hospital when his mother had tried to tell him that she was going to have a baby, the round hump that she carried with her belly. But he really didn't let that bother him, even though he had no idea how that round hump was to become his little sister. He could remember that he and his father were suddenly the only ones at home and that his mother had left them. It must have seemed a long time to him, but then he remembered the very day that a long, white car drove up in front of the house. Two men got out of the car, walked to the back of it, opened one very wide door, and gently lifted his mother who was lying on a long bed with wheels out of the long car, and carried her up the front steps into the house. He was overjoyed to see her and went bounding over to give her a hug when he saw his sister for the first time. It was then that she first started to cry, the cries that were to fill the house for months to come, and somehow he was able to give his mother something of a hug, but not like it was before.

But he had his tricycle, and he had had it even before his sister came home. On those cold or rainy days that he could not go outside, he even rode it in the house. He had a tricycle course laid out. He would crank the pedals round and round to take him to the kitchen, where he went round and round the sink, the cabinet, and the stairs to the basement, and he would keep this going for a while until he zoomed through the small dinette to the also small and by no means expansive living room, where way back then there was no sign of the hideaway bed. So there was clear sailing from the front windows to the back walls of the living room where a sofa of some kind stood, but not for long because the door to the small hallway, a door without a door, lay just to one side of the sofa. So he would make a circle since he could not get far along the small hallway that led to the bedrooms and whiz around the width of the living room, which was really at least as wide as it was long and head to the front windows that looked out onto a small yard with a mimosa tree that grew nearest the house between two tall wild cherry trees, one on each side of the narrow, verdant yard. There after many roundtrips, which made his youthful body only just a bit weary, he would stop and peer out of the window at the birds, the trees, an occasional car that motored west or east past their house, and the huge, redbrick building that lay immediately in front of their house, the local high school. It was not, however, the actual façade of the school he saw from his window, rather the end of the south wing, which displayed the windows of the cafeteria that was then located on the basement floor, next to which lay a good-sized parking lot to the east side of the football practice field and immediately north of his home street, Queen Street.

Such a large building so close to his house didn't faze him then. He had no real contact with it since neither he nor his parents knew anyone there. It only began to register in his psyche a few years later when he began to venture farther and farther from home on his tricycle to the sidewalks around the school and the paved entrance and driveway in the front, elevated at a good angle uphill that gave a thrilling tricycle ride. No, those were the days when he spent most of the day in and around the house and next door, where his two cousins lived. His father's sister and her husband had come to live in the small apartment next door, and with them came two daughters, one his age and the other just a year older than his new sister. So when he wasn't at home with his mother and sister, he was usually next door with the older cousin, Zarla, and her sister, Careena, if he had not gone some three blocks across the largest street of the neighborhood to play with some of the boys his age there whom he had gradually gotten to know.

Those were the days when their small house was something of a mansion from his vantage point. He was captivated by the mimosa tree that grew just some three to four feet from the house that he could see also from the living room window. It had smooth, soft bark and the strangest kind of boughs filled with the most unusual tiny green leaves that grew on little yellow limbs that all joined to a larger stem that grew from one of its drooping boughs. The trunk of this tree had grown at a curve for some reason, and looked like the letter C or the crescent moon and in the warm days of early spring it put out dozens and dozens of reddish pink, purple, and white blossoms that did not look at all like an ordinary flower but were simply colorful strings attached to a center from which they grew something like the sharp needles of a porcupine. Once bloomed out they gave the impression of some kind of rainbow flowing out in all directions, and they were a great target for the honeybees, bumblebees, and even butterflies that landed on them and bored their long noses into their nectar sacs.

Those were the days when his mother would read to him during the morning, and often Zarla and sometimes Careena would come over with his aunt, and she and his mother would take turns giving something of a dramatic performance of the children's story they had chosen for that day. Those were the days of his childhood, even before those of his early growing up when he reached high school. He had to prepare then for a place to go, for his family did not have the money for college. So he learned as best he could and was so glad that he had been awarded a scholarship to study at Solomonson College. He thought that he had found a place to go.

X

Solomonson College and the University of Marburg

HOW HE CAME TO make the adjustment to student life at Solomonson College he didn't actually know. It was the most different place he had ever been to at that early stage of his life. Though at least a third or more of his classmates had attended a regular high school as he had done, well over a third to half of the others were graduates of private, college preparatory schools where they had completed advanced courses. Many of them were thus exempt from some of their first-year courses.

Solomonson was founded as a "manual labor school"—that is, as both a farm and a school—by members and clergy of the Concord Presbytery of the Presbyterian Church USA who sought to undertake with "the blessing of God" the education of young men "preparatory of the Gospel Ministry." Since those days it had evolved into a renowned private liberal arts college whose graduates now studied law, business, and medicine or entered academia or embarked on other secular careers. Then at that time it still had a distinct southern atmosphere, and a long heritage and tradition with good connections to the middle class and the Presbyterian Church throughout the South. These ties were just beginning to erode but held sway for another decade or more as the administration decided to minimize its southern Christian mission and fully embrace the modern world of academia.

A friend of his some three years his senior who was also a Solomonson student gave him a ride to the college. Besides selecting courses, visiting professors, and preparing assignments he had to endure Rush Week. The college was situated on a red clay plain covered with pine tree forests some twenty-three miles from the nearest large city where its students of the nineteenth century had lived something of a secluded, "monastic" life.

Traditionally it had always been a college for men and had been founded during that time during which most private colleges were "segregated" and only admitted men or women.

Solomonson had a rather small cafeteria since most of its students lived in dormitories and took their meals in moderately sized fraternity houses that had been built on the north side of the campus. So for relatively good food and some social life one had to select and join a fraternity, or rather the fraternities selected the students. They sent their delegates to the dormitories to meet and socialize with the new students, who used these contacts to get interviews with fraternities with the aim of receiving a bid to join a certain fraternity. Many of the new students already knew older students from different fraternities and so were able to forgo many of the preliminary meetings. Since he had come from the hill country on the western side of the great mountain, he had no such contacts and knew only one of the older students. He met scores and scores of the older students, but after a while all their faces seemed to merge into one. He was used to his old circle of friends at home where all was familiar. Now he had to meet these students more or less on their own terms and impress them so that he would have a place to eat, watch TV, and dance with women from nearby women's colleges.

Solomonson had been admitting students from outside the South for well over a decade, and as a result there were fraternities that were mixed. A third or more of their members were from many different regions of the country, especially the Northeast. At the last minute someone whom he had only just gotten to know offered to use his influence to get him a bid from one of the predominately southern fraternities. He thought about it, but after a while he decided to go with one of the mixed ones. True he was from the Mid-South, but he had a good ear and after years of watching TV some of his southern accent had faded out a bit. After all, his roommate, a quiet, easygoing, friendly northerner from one of the most "southern" northern states, had joined the same fraternity.

The memories of the visions of the heavenly woman and the scenes of ancient Palestine lingered with him still, especially during the first month or so. There could be no doubt that that event had changed his life and his view of the modern world that had blossomed profusely around him. It had been almost three hundred years since the seeds of the European Enlightenment had been planted on Western soil, and he had no idea what the religious worldview of Europe around the year 1700 might have been.

He assumed that most people then would have felt more connected to the biblical world than his contemporaries, but he didn't know for sure.

At one point he considered talking to the college chaplain about this. But he soon dismissed this possibility, when he realized that his response would not be much different than that of his hometown pastor. As far as he knew, the heavenly woman was not mentioned in the Hebrew Scriptures. His Bible did include the books of Sirach and Proverbs but not the Book of Wisdom, and the archaeological evidence for a consort or wife of Yahweh, his Asherah, had not yet been discovered. It was not until 1975 that inscriptions that spoke of the Asherah of Yahweh were found in the Sinai at Kuntillet 'Ajrud. Traditionally Christians knew only the Mother Mary as a unique, somewhat divine woman, whether they considered her to be the Virgin Mother or not, and from his point of view the relationship between the heavenly woman and the Mother Mary was not explicit. He was rather certain that they were two distinct figures. So he signed up for four classes and ROTC, and set out on the academic journey he hoped would lead to the much sought-after answers.

Prior to that year Solomonson students had been required to take four semesters of Bible—two of which could be Bible-related—four semesters of English, and two history courses for their degrees. Now, however, a new combined course was being offered that satisfied all of the requirements. It was a history of Western civilization or what the professors and students called simply "the humanities." It allowed students to graduate without completing one Bible course. They could read Cicero, Virgil, Homer, Tacitus, and others without ever having to complete any confessional studies of the books of the Old Testament from Genesis, Exodus, or Leviticus on to Malachi or any of the reports of the lives of Jesus of Nazareth, Paul of Tarsus, or any other books and letters of the New Testament. The readings for the humanities course were voluminous, and so despite the fact that he had come to seek out biblical faith and knowledge, he decided that it would be best to follow the old track. This would give him more time for science and math, and so he added physics and calculus.

There were about three days when he felt extremely different from the other students. Those were the days that he remembered the visions and the heavenly woman the most. That was the time that the mundane routine of academic pursuit seemed almost devoid of any essential meaning. True, most of his fellow students and many of the faculty were Christians and believed in another world. But was death the only gateway to this other world? Did they actually sense this other world? Did such an awareness well up within them so that it mingled with the routine of daily living, teaching, and relating to those around them? It was during these days, much to his own amazement, that he thought of suicide. He didn't really consider it, and he made no plans for it. But no one he had ever talked to had seen a heavenly woman. It would provide an escape for all dilemmas related to her, or would it? But those thoughts soon drifted away as he slowly discovered a connectedness not only to his studies but to the students around him. He began to sense something of the old traditions of Solomonson College as if he could almost catch a glimpse of the thousands of students who had passed through those hallways as they began the journeys of their lives, those who had come with questions much like his own, those who had spent hours and years poring over ancient and modern texts attempting to relate it all to their own psyches and their own souls. He could walk over the campus and feel the past emanating from the lawns, the buildings, and the classrooms.

But this time was different, wasn't it? The new world of modernity was swirling around their heads. Most of the students he talked to shared the expectations of some kind of new world, a new age that some related to some extent not only with the discovery of new knowledge but to a new political and governmental life for the nation, embodied for the most part in the current president, whom many considered to be some kind of modern prophet.

So he went to class, he studied, he dived some for the diving team, he had blind dates, and he went to parties, dances, and concerts. He met other students from other fraternities. For almost three months he felt somewhat a part of this new age as though the ancient hills of the Cherokees no longer existed, as though the Hebrews had never seen visions sent by Yahweh and perhaps Asherah and then wandered from Ur, wherever it might have been, to Canaan. Then one cool, sunny, autumn day in November after the leaves had bedecked the campus with their golden, red, and yellow hues, he went to the room of a friend from Mississippi who had a stereo and put on the soundtrack from the movie *Breakfast at Tiffany's* and sang along with Audrey Hepburn. Suddenly he was in Rome, Paris, London, and New York and left out all trace of Jerusalem as he sang at the top of his voice: "Moon river, wider than a mile, I'm crossing you in style someday. Oh, dream maker, you heartbreaker, wherever you're going I'm going your way. Two drifters off to see the world, there's such a lot of world to see. We're after the same rainbow's end, waiting round the bend, my huckleberry friend, moon river and me." He had left the door open to the hallway. Suddenly out of nowhere in the middle of the song some six or seven students came running toward that room almost shouting, "The president has been shot."

The end of the semester came sooner than he expected. For the first time in his life he wasn't going to have all As on his semester report. He was a bit concerned about it, but he realized that the visions had brought him another perspective on life. He breathed a sigh of relief when he learned that he could keep the scholarship with C+s and Bs. He had not been able to connect with his Bible professor or even the chaplain, for that matter. He later changed his mind and went to talk to him; but like his pastor at home, he also lived in the modern Christian world, whatever that was. The conversation unfolded in such a way that it was impossible to mention the visions. He got to know his English professor somewhat but not well enough to talk about the visions. He and the Bible professor were from the old guard and had been at the college for over forty years. But the English professor liked him and always made an effort to talk to him whenever he saw him out of class. The Bible professor had a slight lisp and seemed terribly remote. He lectured on the Old and New Testaments, but they read only general essays on the Scriptures and did not begin with any kind of exegetical study. He did not bother to give an overview of the scholarly debate.

Since he had selected a physics and calculus course, he was told that he had to take German. He objected at first, but he had studied both Latin and French, and so he agreed to. It was his best class and he made As. He was fascinated by the language, and his German professor was a unique and delightful person who almost always wore a broad smile on his face. He took one psychology course, but it was terribly disappointing. There was no mention of Freud or Jung since it was an introductory course. The primary focus was on the conscious and subconscious conditioning of an animal or person to the stimuli one encountered daily. The only thing he remembered was Pavlov's experiment.

So it was that he came to put all of his hope on the atom. On the surface it seemed a bit absurd and not at all related to the heavenly woman or God, for that matter, but he had read descriptions of the atom that posed many questions. One of his science projects had dealt with the attempt to achieve refrigeration by slowing the flow of air in a confined space, the Hilsch vortex tube. It simulated somewhat the known structure of the atom at that time with electrons orbiting the nucleus with its protons and neutrons. Related to this was his high school talk on God and the unknown universe. Though we have many specific addresses on earth with streets, towns, cities, states, countries, and so on, we do not have any kind of address as far as the universe is concerned. But are we actually lost in the universe? He surmised that if the earth and the universe are actually real, if matter is essentially real and not some kind of illusion, and if the atom is the essential building block of the universe, it might well have a religious component to it that would demonstrate the presence of God. Since humans by nature do not have the ability for interstellar travel, they might able to detect the Divine Presence in the atom, which would then be related to the God of the universe who might just be at the end of the universe! The atom might well be the key for our understanding of the universe. The college offered an atomic physics course. But even though he had made an A in an introductory high school physics class, he did not score high enough on a proficiency quiz to be allowed to enter the class. He was required to take another introductory class.

With the coming of winter came the girl from another world. She had red hair and freckles, and he had always been fascinated by freckles. He had brown hair and somewhat dark skin that he had inherited from his mother, and always tanned easily. So when he stood next to her, it was as though he, too, had freckles that were like little islands he could swim out to or like the stars of the night sky. He was just a bit taller but could always look into her sparkling green eyes that always lit up her happy, captivating smile and engulfed him. Being with her was like flying on a spontaneous cloud that always took him to places where he had never been.

She was his blind date for Mid-Winters, the second big concert weekend on campus, when bands and singers came to the college, and the men of some dorms moved out and doubled up with students of another dorm for a couple of days so that the women would have a place to stay. But she was rich. She lived in Coral Mansions, a well-known suburb just outside the center of Florida's largest city. Her father worked for the city's largest newspaper, and most likely he and her mother had sent her to Salom College some ninety miles north of Solomonson to provide her with a quiet, protective educational environment. Salom College had been founded by Moravians and was known for its special Easter services. He had attended these once a few years before this and had walked through their large cemetery early Easter morning alongside members of the congregation, most all of whom played instruments and sang as they processed along. But they did not go to church when he went to see her, neither to the church at Salom or elsewhere. They went to the Tavern on the Green and sat there for hours sipping beer or cider and eating.

Her name was Isla but she liked to be called Izzi. "Is he who he is?" he used to say to himself, but he never told her this. She left her light-green woolen skirt in her room, and so he had to call her to make arrangements to return it to her. That might have been the occasion for his first trip to Salom College to see Izzi. She came once more to see him for the third concert weekend, Spring Frolics, and they both began to float through the air, bouncing here and there as they set out to see where this feeling of oneness, happiness, and effervescence would take them.

The college continued to minimize its Christian mission, and it was during his second year there that this transition became very apparent. For over a century students had been required to attend chapel and assembly during the week and church on Sunday morning. They were given specific seats in the auditorium, and it was mandatory to sign an attendance sheet at church. But his second year all of these attendance requirements were suddenly dropped. Students no longer had to attend chapel or church, and they were allowed to take the humanities course rather than four semesters of Bible along with history. The administration had made the decision to allow students to choose to engage a religious life or not. At first glance it all seemed logical enough; the future lives of the students would grant them the opportunity to accept or reject Christianity. Somewhat related to this came the ruling that students would be permitted to keep alcohol in their car trunks. Of course a large percentage of the students drank off campus, particularly during the concert weekends when they rented small huts or party houses in the pine forests that surrounded the college. But now they could almost drink on campus, and whether Christianity and alcohol were compatible or not was not really the question. The matter had been settled for them without any real discussion about why the college tradition had such a ruling to begin with.

Then during the spring of that year the college made a provocative decision that proved to be an affront to some of the students and likely to the Presbyterian Church as well. The philosophy department announced that they had invited an atheist philosopher for a series of debates on the existence of God. Some of the students who had chosen Solomonson because of its Christian heritage were appalled; others who had come because of its academic reputation were just a bit bemused. As it turned out, most of the students attended the debates, and he was among them. He saw no reason why Christians should not debate with atheists. Yet the debates ended more or less on the note that one cannot disprove or prove the existence of God, and such a conclusion itself is not without essential meaning. But the primary statement he remembered from it all was that there can really be no debate between two parties unless there is some kind of essential agreement. The question then arose as to why the debates had been held at all. So while the nation reeled from the growing civil rights movement led by Dr. M. L. King and his followers, the military was commanded to go to war on the other side of the globe for no apparent reason, and many young Americans called on flower power to protest the complacency of the American middle and upper middle-classes, the administration at Solomonson decided to cast off the old Christian tradition for another one.

This might have been an acceptable approach to the many matters at hand, except that no one stepped forward to explain what the new tradition was. It was not evident how one was to proceed if one wanted to keep some kind of Christian tradition. The only protest staged on campus during these years came when some five hundred students marched on the president's house and burned the fraternity liaison officer in effigy because, after several years of his study and assessment of the fraternity system, he had recommended that they be abolished and replaced with just eating clubs. This prompted one of the most outspoken professors of the English Department to address the combined assembly of the college on the state of the college and the nation, whereby he concluded that Solomonson College was the only major college in the country to demonstrate for the status quo.

Those days he made the futile attempt to question his old-guard Bible professor about the "old" and "new" Christianity. His answers seemed to some extent pertinent, but they gave him no real understanding of the basis for them. He was left with the vague notion that the God of the Hebrews and Jesus of Nazareth of Galilee were still the source of true religious understanding and spirituality, which, however, had evolved over the centuries, especially during the modern era to become a different, more humanistic religion. Above all there seemed to be no way left to apprehend the presence of God personally and individually as had been possible before. There was no mention whatsoever of a goddess or heavenly woman.

He still had hope for the atom. If it were the basis of all matter and life on earth, then it would follow that just perhaps the presence of God could be detected there. Just possibly, he thought, this could be the arena in which one could discover somehow the old spiritual presence of the Hebrew God and Jesus, and allow one to demonstrate to the Bible professor that such presence still existed. Such a presence would consequently have to be accepted as a natural component of earthly matter, essential for human life on earth!

But the obstacles to such an endeavor were tremendous. The study of the atom was still in its infancy stages despite the research on the atom and nuclear bombs. Quantum mechanics was just beginning, and most of the exotic, atomic components of the atom had not yet been discovered since only a few small colliders had been built. His physics professor could only present him with the basics, the nucleus with its neutrons and protons and the electrons that supposedly orbited around them. But their movements could not be directly observed and calculated; only the aftermath of their motions—that is, their responses to energy—could be detected. So it was not at all possible to determine what kind of presence or atomic field was characteristic of the atom.

Just as he came to develop a sense of foreboding for physics class, where most of the students and the professor were impersonal, emotionless, and too mechanical for him, so, too, the atom became a foreboding component of nature. It did not fly randomly like a bug, it did not hover or fly like a bird that soars, it did not bark like a dog or meow like a cat, and it did not moo like a cow or run like a horse. It did not blow like the wind or sail like a majestic cloud or rise and set like the sun or moon. It simply sat there, much like the physicists and mathematicians sat at their tables and machines attempting to determine the mechanical regulations and rules and the sterile dynamics that permeated its existence. Most of all there was nothing at all remotely human about it. It did not walk or talk or exhibit any kind of emotion. True, all humans were made from it, but paradoxically they had become something else and the source of that something else lay outside them. Whatever made humans what they truly are rose up from their inner being because it had come there from the other world, or at least so he began to surmise.

He was mystified. Where was he to turn now? All roads should lead to Rome (but those days Rome was not to be found as any kind of concept in Appalachia), but all the ones he set out to embark upon led only to dead ends. Then came the announcement that the college had decided to offer a year of study abroad. He could leave with one of his German professors and his family along with some fifteen other students and spend a year at a German university. He would have time to travel to see most of Europe, some of Asia Minor, and perhaps the Middle East. But what would Izzi say? Would she want to go with him and study at the university? He doubted it.

His mother was not at all enthusiastic about the proposal. Though it later turned out that she had German-speaking Swiss descendants, most likely Mennonites or Swiss who became Mennonites so that they could leave Switzerland, she had no ties any longer with Europe and saw no real reason why he would want to go there. His father, whose ancestors were most all from Scotland (but there were some Dutch and a German here and there), didn't really form an opinion pro or con. His mother finally acquiesced and gave her approval when he argued that his was a once-in-a-lifetime opportunity. He might never again have the chance to see some of the world beyond his native land.

As for Izzi, that was another matter that was never really resolved. First of all he felt that he was socially inferior to her, just as to some extent he felt that way about many of the students at Solomonson. Then, too, their relationship had suffered because of the ninety miles or more that separated them, and so when he came to assess the matter, he realized that they did not know each other all that well. When he told her about his decision, she was completely surprised, and he sensed that she felt it meant that he was rejecting her. But that was not the case, and it had more to do with his own journey at that time. His religious quest and the visions were topics that he had not ventured to discuss with her. He could just hear her say, "What? You saw a vision of a heavenly woman?" Surely he told her that he might decide to enter seminary. As far as he remembered, she never gave him any hint about what she wanted to do, except that it seemed that she had implied that she might work for the newspaper as her father did. Church life did not appear to him as something she would consider. So he had told her he might go to law school, enter politics, and run for president! He felt that if their relationship continued, he would have to compensate for his lower social standing by agreeing to a secular career that matched her current lifestyle. But either way he was not willing to give up the year of study abroad, and he viewed it as a way he could improve his social standing. He would have a year's experience abroad and could improve his German considerably. She was not convinced that he would keep up with her. They agreed to meet when the year was over but did not write very often. They somehow let father time and mother distance come between them and went their separate ways.

From the outset he was enthralled by life on the other side of the ocean. To both his amazement and somewhat to his bewilderment, he felt so completely at home most everywhere he went. Maybe that had something to do with the support group of his professor amd his family, and the other students he went with. Yet he often traveled with just one or two other students or by himself, and wherever he went, he met people and other students to whom he could easily relate. It seemed that he could feel the beautiful earth beneath his feet for the first time, as at long last he had come to the real, cosmopolitan world.

They sailed to Southampton and Le Harve on an old German boat used to supply the German submarine fleet that had been bought by an Italian line out of Genoa. It was a seven-day, fun-filled ocean voyage with some twelve hundred other American students all going to a European university for at least a semester. There were movies, lectures, and even a civil rights demonstration that erupted when some of the students from the South, even some of his classmates, were falsely accused of prejudice and discrimination. But that was to some extent resolved and they made friendships that lasted a year or longer, particularly with some of the students on their way to Strasbourg or Florence.

After a couple of months at a language school just south of Munich, they made their way to central Germany to the university town of Marburg, the capital of the state of Hesse, the home of the former Duke or Landgrave of Hesse, Philip I, and the site of Luther's debate with Zwingli held in the attempt to unite Protestant Germany and Switzerland. There was the St. Elizabeth Church named after this saint from Hungary, the student dormitory where the Brueder Grimm had lived, and the famous castle of the Duke perched above the town.

The University of Marburg was the home of the renowned New Testament scholar of the twentieth century, Rudolf Bulto. He didn't know this until he arrived. Yet though he had had a chance to meet him at a dinner that was canceled because Bulto was not feeling well, he most assuredly had become familiar with some of his scholarship when he left a year later. Little did he know that he had arrived on the doorstep of one of the fathers of the modern Christianity. It was here during the 1920s that Heidegger, Bulto, and Tillich taught and set the agenda for existentialist Christianity. But he didn't know that then, and even when he left, he was not quite sure what existentialism was. He signed up for two lecture courses on the letters of the Apostle Paul taught by one of Bulto's well-known protégés, Georg

Kuemmel. That was routine enough and was followed by two oral exams. But even then as before he could never understand why Paul wanted to abolish the Law, not reform it, nor why he led such a life of torment if he had been saved by grace through the vicarious suffering of Jesus on the cross.

It was later when finally he became a seminarian that he studied the development of Christian theology, the influence of Greek philosophy on the Christian world, and the great debates of Christianity with universal deism, Enlightenment philosophy and science, and modern philosophy. But he did learn something then about the philosophical debates of the eighteenth century and the importance of Immanuel Kant's work, *The Critique of Pure Reason*, which was a milestone in philosophical debate as it synthesized the works of the rationalists and the empiricists. With Kant's analysis it became evident that ancient reality and religion were fallacious, since he demonstrated that metaphysical philosophy and ancient religion were based on human fantasy. He concluded that *a priori* precepts simply do not exist, and that one is not able to approach God directly from the mundane world where human reason is encapsulated and divorced from any kind of divine realm. Such as assessment of reality led Bulto to discover existentialism as he used modern, philosophical concepts of reality to develop his theological system of demythologizing, which he applied directly to the New Testament. The three-decker universe of the prehistoric and ancient worlds was obsolete. There was no tangible hell or heaven, only the earth. God did not determine life on earth from a transcendent realm, but he empowered humans to become his agents on earth. Therefore, numinous experiences, divine theophanies, dreams, and visions were only figments of the human imagination. The physical earth and the universe around it were not any kind of illusion but actual concrete reality. The New Testament could not be traced back to the actual words of Jesus himself, but only to the early Christian communities themselves as they reacted to and tried to remember what Jesus said and did. Jesus did not perform many of the miracles and made no apocalyptic pronouncements.

So where did all this leave him with his dreams and visions? At first he didn't know. He had a better understanding about what some at Solomonson College were trying to do, and much the same way he could better grasp what modern theologians were striving for. The church had been backed into a corner, had become fenced in on all sides, and seemingly had no place to turn or no alternative but to somehow accept the new philosophy and the new science. It was something like the pope trying to tell Galileo that he had not proved that Copernicus was right and that the earth was no longer the center of the universe. But such is only vaguely related to the matter, because now everything depended upon God. Was there really a God, did he actually exist, and how was it that he could be apprehended by humans on earth? But why, he wondered, did the church and her theologians persist on using the ancient Greek and Hebrew Scriptures? If the basic reality that lay behind them was not valid, then why were they not merely discarded? Perhaps they should just assume that God was dead?

As for his visions, he knew one thing and that was that the heavenly woman was very much alive. He had seen her. She had appeared to him, and it was evident that she had come to him from another world. Along with her had come those visions of Palestine of Jesus's day and those of the early Hebrews wandering through the Near East on their way to Canaan. Though he had not been able to talk to anyone about them, he knew that they had been real. As he assessed the matter, he had to conclude that modern philosophy and science, no matter how erudite, empirical, systematic, and convincing they appeared to be, were wrong. His visions demonstrated that the earth and its physical reality were not essentially real; they were superseded by another, nonmaterial reality that lay beyond the physical universe.

Still the question remained. Why had he not seen a vision of Jesus himself? If he were the divine Hebrew God incarnate, then it followed that he was the Being who had made all things, the earth with its waters, the land, the mountains, all creatures human and animal, the stars, and all things that lie beyond. Who was the heavenly woman, and why had others besides him not seen her? It was all a bit confusing, but somehow he knew that it had meaning. Perhaps Jesus had sent the heavenly woman to complete the messianic mission that he had begun centuries before there was modern Christianity.

A year is not that much time, but it is much more than a few weeks. Though he spent most of it in Germany, he spent over two months traveling from Naples and southern Italy to Spain, France, East Germany, Belgium, Holland, and England. He began to become aware of the greater world outside the United States. He was awed by the beauty of the earth in most of these countries. There were lush, green, rolling hills and countryside with villages and town laid out such that they complemented the lay of the land, its valleys, meadows, and hills, as though somehow they had grown out of the earth itself. He was reminded of the Native Americans and their creation stories. They believed that they had been born in caves of Mother Earth before they emerged from underground to live on the earth above. There was some semblance of this in the early American colonial villages and towns that had not been deserted or destroyed. But most contemporary American towns and cities had been built with no respect for the earth, which for the most part had been bulldozed and covered with asphalt, concrete, and steel. Certainly, large European cities looked something like their American counterparts, but there was still a difference. There were more parks, meadows, and heaths, fewer asphalted streets, little villages within the cities, and more people who walked or rode streetcars or trams or the subway than those who drove cars. All this despite the ravages of two terrible wars that certainly had left their marks on the psyches of thousands of people but who now wanted peace and quiet and who still had a sense of earthly time, centuries of time that led them back into their human past.

He found compelling this sense of the past that emanated from the villages, towns, and cities. He had spent more than a decade and a half focused on the future, on some kind of presupposed metamorphosis and transformation of life on earth, a new life that was evolving from all of the new science, technology, and industry that had engulfed his native land. Whatever the new might be, people there wanted more of it at an ever increasing, faster pace, with more personal rewards and gratification. He now realized what was missing. Those American expectations for the future had been conceived with no reverence for the earth, which alone can sustain human life, and no concept and appreciation for the past of humanity. The past stalked him wherever he went and wouldn't leave him alone. Churches, town halls, museums, theaters, factories, houses, schools, universities, and other buildings, some more than five hundred to a thousand years old, sprang up here and there such that he began to fathom those times long before, some three thousand to twelve thousand years ago or earlier, those countless eons of the prehistoric past when life was far more rudimentary that he could imagine, or was it really?

When he returned to Solomonson for his last year, something of controversy was brewing that bubbled over into a good exchange among students and faculty on the aims of the new academe. Some students had been labeled by others as "gnomes," not that they were actually dwarves or the little people who lived under the earth to protect its precious metals or who were fairylike elves. At Solomonson the gnome controversy arose from the view of the majority that gnomes were students who not only spent an inordinate amount of time with their studies, they had withdrawn themselves from their moral responsibility to engage in the ordinary activities that were offered at the college, from sports to drama, that allowed them to embrace the activities and values of middle-class American society. One professor hinted at the concern of some of the faculty when he let it be known with a note of sarcasm that some held the view that the ideal Solomonson student should be so well-rounded that he would actually bounce.

He understood a number of matters in a different light since his return from Europe. One was that many of the students were there simply to earn a degree for their own future and their own prosperity, regardless of their moral obligation for the earth and society at large, especially the poor. Another was that some of the faculty had arrived at answers and solutions to the perennial questions about the nature of learning without a comprehensive consideration of the many possibilities. He came to view the gnomes as those who were dissatisfied with the status quo for many reasons, so he wrote an article for the college newspaper in their defense. He stated that the gnomes were those who sought to embrace the true nature of the debate of how academe and lifestyle were to be related, which the majority already considered closed and settled.

All of this was related to the other great dilemma of his life besides that of the heavenly woman: the guerrilla war on the other side of the globe. It had mushroomed into a full-scale war, and the law of conscription was still a law of the land. All American males eighteen years or older were subject to the draft, and it was likely that his life would be at stake. He could remember that morning ROTC class some two years ago when the military instructor gave a report on the first official battle between the American-supported South Vietnamese and the Viet Cong of the northern segment of the country. He had predicted that the situation could result in greater warfare, although without giving many specific reasons.

XI

Saigon

SOLOMONSON COLLEGE RECEIVED GOVERNMENT funds under the Land Grant Act of 1862 for its ROTC program, and for that reason all students were required to take ROTC for at least two years. The final two years for the commission were optional. He could forgo the commission and face the draft, which would most likely mean that he would be assigned to a combat unit as a private first class. He could enter seminary or medical school and receive a deferment. At least a fourth or more of his class would enter medical school, whereas previously a couple of decades before this the same number of students would enter seminary. That year the number of students who applied for seminary studies had dwindled to only three.

Medical school had to be ruled out since he had not completed the required science courses. Seminary would have been a possibility, but he could not justify that. After reading Bulto and his theology of demythologizing along with his initial interpretation of the vision of the heavenly woman, he had concluded that Jesus was not the divine Messiah, the Anointed One of Israel. He liked German literature and was doing well, but a teaching position would not provide for a deferment. There was one other possibility and that was that his military service could be postponed for a year if he were to be hired to teach. The war was not going well for the Americans. He predicted that either they might somehow win the war within a year's time or that after a year or so more they would face defeat and have to withdraw. He submitted several applications to various schools, and much to his surprise he was hired by a private school in a neighboring state whose German teacher had to take a year's leave of absence. He was elated but not for long. A year was not a very long time those days.

He taught two classes of German grammar along with a short story now and then and two classes of American literature. The school also wanted him to serve as a dormitory supervisor and so he was given a small apartment at the end of the hallway on the second floor. He helped with the diving and swimming teams and some with the soccer team. Two of his students for German were sharp; one had a complete photographic memory and the other almost the same. So they kept him on his toes, and he had to prepare diligently to keep ahead of them. They and a few other students attended the state conference for the German language, took the competitive exams, and were awarded the highest honors. It was all in all a very good year. He liked to teach, and he began to consider this an alternative to the pastorate or graduate school.

All the while he had his eyes on the clock. Time ran out much quicker than he anticipated, and Cinderella's glorious slippers, her heavenly gown, and her magnificent carriage vanished into thin air. The first week of June he packed his belongings, drove home for a few weeks, and then reported for the basic training he had postponed before he arrived at a military school for the U.S. Army Signal Corps. He spent just about a year at several military schools, or forts as they were called then, where he completed the courses that enabled him to become a communications center duty officer. From the Southeast United States he was sent to the Northeast and then on to the West Coast, where he had an assignment with a signal company. All went well and was rather routine until he received his orders to serve in Vietnam. The news was unsettling. Though he had considered it a possibility, he had been somewhat confident that he would be assigned to the American troops in Germany. He had his B.A. in German literature and almost a double major in history along with a year's study in Germany. He was then partially fluent in the language and had become accustomed to life there. He knew some of his classmates who did not have this background and yet had been assigned to "ole' Deutschland."

Several of his sergeants who had already served two or more tours of duty in Vietnam looked at his orders and told him not to worry, "Sir," they said, "this is the best assignment you could possibly get in Vietnam. You are either in Long Binh or Saigon at the headquarters. It's almost like stateside duty. You will be nowhere near the fighting. Take it and forget it." But he could not forget it. The war was not going well, and though it looked as though the writing was already on the wall, the president showed no signs of giving up. But it seemed rather evident that the war could not be won, and he foresaw nothing but a quagmire that would never end.

Though he still had his doubts about Jesus and could not be certain that he was the Jewish Messiah, somewhat to his own amazement he could hear Jesus's words reverberate about his head: "If someone strikes you on the cheek, then turn the other one to him." Certainly Jesus did not always acquiesce and refuse to defend himself. There were his words to the servant of the high priest who struck him during the mock trial: "If I have not borne false witness and have spoken the truth, then why do you strike me?" As for the war itself, it was clear that the nation for some unknown reason had chosen to involve itself in a civil war tradition that, though not ongoing, spanned some eight hundred years or more. The United States had stepped forward to strike the North on the cheek, even though most of the war was being fought in the South and its aim was to liberate the South Vietnamese. But by far the most baffling aspect of it all was that there was no compelling reason for this war.

Just a few weeks went by before he decided that he had to submit an application for conscientious objector status. It had become clear that he was not by definition a complete pacifist; if his life were at jeopardy, he would make the effort to defend himself. But it was his view that Jesus never fought physically with anyone, primarily because almost always he did not seek to solve disputes or arguments with belligerent acts of aggression. He made it his agenda to avoid physical conflict and confrontation, and thus was usually able to avoid violence. As he had surmised just a few days before, the war should be ended. So whether it was a just or an unjust war, to continue it was not a sober and objective decision. He felt that he had to make a statement against it, and the only means he had for that was the declaration for conscientious objector status.

Thousands of soldiers along with fewer officers had come to what one would assume to be much the same opinion, if not for perhaps different, specific reasons. All of their requests were flatly rejected, and there was no recourse for appeal. Within a matter of months he found himself sitting in a window seat on a commercial jetliner flying over the Bering Strait on his way to Saigon. Those words that he repeated over and over then never went away: "What have I done to deserve this?" The first thing he remembered from his stay in this Southeast Asian country was the wall of scorching, torrid heat that swelled up on all sides of him when he first stood on the soil of Vietnam and that escorted him wherever he went. Fortunately, he did not have to go far before he entered an air-conditioned building to ward off the waves of summer heat.

He was most grateful that he was sent to the original assignment that was printed on his orders, the U.S. Army's 160th Signal Group Headquarters at Long Binh and later to the 69th Signal Battalion at Military Advisory Command Vietnam (MACV) Headquarters in Saigon. For the next eleven months he traveled no farther that some twenty to thirty miles between Saigon and Long Binh, and though it was required that he carry a weapon when he went out to inspect the border patrol, he never fired a shot the entire tour of duty. He did leave the country twice for a week at a time for allowed rest trips to India and Japan, and he toyed with the idea of desertion, particularly to Scandinavia from India. But he elected to return each time. To be allowed to spend the week in India he had to complete a special application, which took several months. Lea Oxbridge had mentioned that she might enter the Peace Corps and go to serve somewhere in or around Calcutta. So for a reason for this special trip, he reported that he had a girlfriend who was in Calcutta, and that if he did not go to see her this year, it would be more than a year before he could see her once more. He had been told that India had not been designated as an official site for rest and recuperation, so he was gratified to be granted permission for the trip. He flew to Delhi on a military flight after he spent a few days in Bangkok, where he visited one of the city's renowned floating markets and saw a fleet of old, traditional Thai boats, which he found captivating.

The dusty, narrow streets of Old Delhi were quite a contrast to the wider, cleaner streets of New Delhi, particularly around the neighborhood of the YMCA where he stayed. It was actually a good-sized hotel, and there he met a Jewish friend from Brooklyn, a designer, aspiring abstract expressionist, and lieutenant in the Signal Corps whom he had also met at the military schools on the East Coast. He had brought an African American friend with him from their signal base in the center of Thailand's lush, jungle forest where they had fortunately been stationed for almost half a year. He had attended his Jewish friend's wedding in Brooklyn about a year before this. They were not an observant Jewish couple, and religion was not a topic they spent much time with. A civil magistrate had performed the marriage ceremony in their Brooklyn apartment. But the friend had done a good bit of reading of Hindu and Buddhist texts, and the primary reason for his trip to Delhi was to continue on the Khajuraho to view the erotic Hindu art and statues that had been crafted centuries earlier. They spent a few days in Delhi, then paid thirty dollars for a British taxi and its Indian driver who took them to Agra to see the famed Taj Mahal. Though he spent only some four days there, it seemed like four months. He found the countryside, the cities, and the people, rich and poor, captivating and was able to get a feel for the country and its people that both baffled and fascinated him. Before this he had not considered India a place that he would be able to relate to. He enjoyed the food immensely, much to his amazement, and continued to eat Indian curry for years afterward, even after he was no longer surrounded by Hindus, Buddhists, and Muslims.

A few months after his return from India he was assigned to a special communications center at the MACV in Saigon. This unit processed the daily war report that was sent to the Pentagon and the president. Furthermore, every day during the week it received and sent out the coordinates for the sites in the North that were to be bombarded by American aircraft. Ironically the signal personnel called them "arc lights," a term that they must have taken from the flame and light of the bombs that exploded but that must have meant anything but light to the North Vietnamese soldiers, many of whom did not live to see their light. As he worked there for six months or more, he must have been indirectly complicit in the deaths of thousands or more North Vietnamese.

Much to his amazement he was given a small apartment in a hotel in Saigon that had been rented by his signal battalion. A van picked him up just before the beginning of each twelve-hour shift and returned him to the hotel each evening or each morning depending on whether he worked the day shift or the night shift. He shared the apartment with a Yankee from Connecticut, a rather tall, slender, mild-mannered, unassuming man whom he did not get to know all that well. He was not introverted, but he was quiet and almost never bared his soul or expressed his opinion on matters. He was there to do the job for Uncle Sam and that was that. He was a college graduate, but one who might have been much more at home at Haight-Ashbury or in Greenwich Village. How it was that he had not found a way to avoid the military was something of a mystery to him, but he assumed that much like his Jewish friend he took the draft and his obligation for military service seriously.

One evening he returned to his apartment to find a book he had never heard of before lying on their reading table. It was a somewhat small book with an alluring, sensual picture of an angel-like woman adorning the cover. He picked it up immediately and found himself totally captivated by the style of the author and the content of this otherworldly novel, as he followed the unfolding of a story about a man named Sinclair whose life is eventually transformed by his encounter with a mysterious person named Demian and a woman who is supposedly his mother. That Demian is a character not fully human becomes evident as he begins to interact with Sinclair during the trials of his rather routine, mundane life. He presents a radical interpretation of the stories of the Bible and later introduces another god, Abraxus, who like the Zoroastrian godhead is made up of the essence of both evil and good. Sinclair finds all this more plausible than the Christian worldview of his upbringing, and as he becomes more acquainted with Demian, he is liberated from the people and events of his life that troubled him.

One day in a park Sinclair sees a woman who is so beautiful and alluring that he is immediately charmed by her. As it turns out, he never even speaks to her; but as he takes up art, paints a picture of her, and gives her the name Beatrice, she becomes for him a symbol of pure love. Later as Demian reenters his life and after he visits Demian's old house where he finds a picture of his mother, Frau Eva, he is overwhelmed to discover that she looks almost like Beatrice and a bit like Demian as well. Then Demian at last invites Sinclair to his new house. Once they enter the house, a beautiful, sensual, ethereal woman greets them, almost as if she has just appeared on earth from another world. She and Sinclair are instantly attracted to one another as if they had known each other somehow before, and they are full of joy and happiness as they talk incessantly about his life's journey, his quest for love, and his affinity for the other world.

As he read of this joyous meeting of Sinclair and Frau Eva, something of that presence that came to him days before he saw the heavenly woman descended around him. It was not as pronounced as it had been almost seven years ago now, but it was there. He could not deny or avoid it. He was somewhat startled by it, since though he had not forgotten it, he had not thought about it for over half a decade. He could almost see her once more, that golden, voluptuous woman surrounded by celestial light and whose face was adorned by a friendly, loving smile that sent his soul soaring into the heavens. For a few fleeting moments it seemed that she was there in the room with him, and he was so happy and enthralled to see her. He had assumed that he might never see her again, though he did not see her then as he did when he first saw her.

The author of the novel was Hermann Hesse, a neo-Romantic writer whose home had been southwest Germany. Though he had German Baltic, Swabian, and Swiss French ancestry, his family were members of a German pietistic group that had moved to a small town near Stuttgart and who had served as missionaries to India. His mother's father was an Indologist and his father, son of a doctor, worked for a theological and academic publishing house that was managed by his mother's father. They both wrote for a missionary newspaper and had written biblical works. They kept up contacts with Indian Christians who came to visit them periodically in Germany. So at a rather early age Hesse must have begun to read Hindu and Buddhist texts and to compare them to the sacred texts of the Christian Bible. Though he attended one of the best Latin schools for a few years to prepare for university, he refused to follow the path to academe. As a neo-Romantic he opposed the traditions of the European Enlightenment that had given rise to the modern world. Though he supposedly remained a Christian, he did not enter the priesthood and serve the Christian world directly. With his writing he sought to integrate Christian doctrine and belief with Eastern religions, for he felt that a deeper spirituality was the only way left for the Western world in the aftermath of two devastating wars. His novels had been discovered by the hippies and later the flower power people of the American anti-middle-class movement, most of whom believed that he had rejected Christianity and converted to either Hinduism or Buddhism. But it was not at all as simple as that.

He had to find out about this man Hesse and discover more about his literary roots. That was not easy in Saigon since there were not any English bookstores that he could find, but his lieutenant friend had a few more of the novels. He knew at once that he had to discover how such a writer could live and flourish in the modern world, for he had never read such a story that had been written in the twentieth century. He had been planning to do graduate study in German literature, and so he somehow obtained an application for a fellowship to study at a German university. To his great amazement and joy he was awarded a grant to study German literature at the University of Munich. He was released from active military duty some two weeks early, and flew home to spend two months with his mother. There he made plans to attend a summer French course in Dijon, France, and another two-month German course in Bavaria's resort and spa town, Bad Reichenhall. His plane could not leave for Europe soon enough; he had to find outs where Hesse's heavenly woman had come from.

XII

Munich

Munich had begun to shed its Nazi past some twenty-five years earlier. Along with Frankfurt and Hamburg it had benefited tremendously from the isolation of West Berlin and the Communist control of East Berlin. Not only had it become a major hub for German commerce, research, industry, and new technology, it had begun to flourish as a cultural center for music, art, the movie industry, dance, opera, and theater. Rainer Fassbender made a movie there on average every six months, and Gruenwald had become a center for German filmmaking. The university had grown tremendously and boasted a student population from all parts of Germany intermingled with students from all over the globe.

As for the political scene the mainstream socialist party led by Willi Brandt held sway there as also in the rest of Germany, despite the influence of the traditional, conservative Bavarian party, the Christian Socialist Union led by Franz Josef Strauss. There were even considerable numbers of more radical socialists and some communists, especially among the university students who often demonstrated on the streets of Schwabing and the city with the Iranian students who opposed the rule of the Shah. Most of the university's socialist students were followers of Karl Marx and used his *Das Kapital* as their primary source for political doctrine. They were not as prominent in Munich as they were in Berlin, where Rudi Dutschke led tens of thousands of socialist students who were so dedicated that they alternated their study at the university with factory and agricultural work on farms in Germany and other countries such as Albania.

Hesse's novels floated into his hands and he became thoroughly fascinated by what he read. Time stood still in his novels and though his language and style were basically modern and contemporary, they did not reflect the modern world. It was clear that the source of his literary world lay outside the mundane sphere of reality and experience. He wrote from the vantage point of otherworldly experience, but it was not always clear what the experience actually was. He did not address this directly with his characters and plots, but he gave his readers hints and clues to point them in another direction, to set them on a path that led to their inner souls and to lead them to an encounter with themselves and with God. If, for most Christians, Jesus was the Anointed One of Israel because of his vicarious suffering for humankind on the cross, for Hesse one could say that he was the supreme Hebrew prophet upon whom the Divine Presence had come to dwell. It was this merging of the human soul with the spirit of the Divine that was Hesse's great story, but he did not use the name Jesus nor did he refer directly to the biblical tradition. He wrote symbolically, metaphorically, and mythologically. One must remember that that he suffered through two terrible wars and that he once stated that when the state of human affairs becomes so unbearable, the best course of action is to begin at the beginning once more. So in the beginning from Hesse's perspective, there were, figuratively speaking, Krishna and Arjuna, and later Buddha and Ananda, and then came Abraham and Sarah, Isaac and Rebecca, Jacob and Rachel, and then Moses, Elijah, Samuel, and the rest.

The first year in Munich zoomed hurriedly by like a flash of lightning. His first visit to the German Department was a total disappointment. There was not one professor there who offered even a lecture course on Hesse, not to mention a pro-seminar or an advanced seminar. Those days Günter Grass, Thomas Mann, Peter Hanke, and many others dominated the German literary world. Hesse, who had fled his homeland for the exotic, balmy Mediterranean alps of Tessin (Ticino), Switzerland, had not sought to further the German literary traditions and had reached out to the Orient for the themes and settings of many of his novels. Though he had been awarded the Nobel Prize for literature, he had dealt with themes and characters somewhat foreign to the traditional and modern German palate. Even so, his short stories and novels written before the first terrible war were widely read in Germany, and until then he took somewhat of an active part in the German literary world. But he didn't approve of much of what German writers were writing then, and disregard for him grew when he decided not to return to Germany.

To receive the grant he had to register at the university and attend lectures and seminars. This he did with a couple of introductory courses, one class of British literature, and a beginning medieval high-German class. He was left on his own to write a paper on Hesse's work and send it to the fellowship committee. Then toward the end of the year, someone told him of a new professor who gave some three to four lectures on Hesse's work as part of a lecture series on German Romanticism. He found his way to the lecture room and was intrigued by what he heard. Werner Vordtriede had recently returned to Germany from Wisconsin, where he had taught at the university there for over thirty years. He had fled Nazi Germany first for Switzerland and then America, where he took a degree at one of the Ivy League universities. He had focused on comparative studies of French, English, and German Romantic literature and translated a considerable number of these works and other literature into German. He was widely known for his seminal study on the influence of the German writer Friedrich von Hardenberg, or Novalis, on the poetry and prose of the French symbolists. He had never heard of Novalis, but Vordtriede had mentioned him in his lectures on Hesse, and he was soon to discover his unique literary and Christian world. He decided not to return to the United States, but to register as a full-time student at the university. For the next three years his world revolved around Hermann Hesse, Werner Vordtriede, Novalis, and the other German Romantic writers, most all of whom were Christians, along with a countless number of students and people who walked into and out of his life from the lecture halls to the streets of Schwabing, Lehel, the English Garden, and Marienplatz.

He avoided student dormitories and usually found a room in a student apartment. At the end of his Munich stay he had lived in at least three different student *Wohngemeinschaften* (shared apartments), several small rooms, and one house. He first shared a small apartment with a Venezuelan student who wanted to be a pilot and his girlfriend, and lastly a room in an elegant *Jugenstil* apartment in the artists' and writers' quarter called Lehel on the banks of the river Isar on the east side of Munich. There he had been befriended by Olga Huber-Hohbruck and her circle of artist friends. She had painted the stage sets for the Bavarian State Opera for some forty years. It was here that he wrote a thesis on Ferdinand Freiligrath's poetry and his translations of English Romantic verse into German for his professor Werner Vordtriede. Even before he had met Olga, he had taken some art classes in Schwabing but had not continued with them on a regular basis. Over the years he had taught himself a good bit of art history as he visited countless art museums in Munich and throughout Europe. Olga was impressed by what he had written and became a good friend. He could have stayed here to write, draw, and paint. But he decided that he had two choices only after a year there at Olga's Liebigstrasse address, either to return to America to enter seminary or to go to Holland to study with a Dutch woman who had become a Hindu guru.

He had spent years debating the Christian aspects of the writings of the German Romantics with Vordtriede, other professors, and students. Always the focus was on the religious worldview of Hesse and Novalis, for it was Novalis and others of the German Romantics who had had such a great influence on Hesse. If Novalis himself had not had a vision of a heavenly woman or the Mother Mary, then his lover and fiancé, who was only twelve years of age when he met her, had become something of one when she died some three years later, just four years before his own death. He believed that he could still sense her presence and somehow talk to her along with his prayers to Jesus. He was devoutly Christian and sadly bemoaned the rise of Protestant Christianity, for he believed that the Roman Church was the truest embodiment of Christian belief and doctrine. He, as did most of the German Romantics, believed that his prose and verse were intended to reflect the love and spirit of Christ and Mary on earth. Words for him were symbols and images from the world of nature and heaven that had been created by God to mirror and show forth his love, light, and glory to God's people on earth. Above all the heavenly woman was a reality for him. He sensed that she was the queen of heaven, the heavenly Sophia who gave wisdom to those on earth who revered her. He might not have known then enough about her past to trace her from her beginnings as the consort of the Hebrew God, how she was related to the other gods of the Near East, and to learn how she had traveled via the Hebrew Scriptures and other writings of the Greco-Roman world into the songs of the Troubadours and the Minnesaengers of medieval Germany. But Novalis had come to know her.

Vordtriede and others he discussed this with knew this, but they refused to take it seriously or consider his viewpoint. He did not venture to tell them about his visions of the heavenly woman or the Hebrews for that matter, but he wrote seminar papers that sought to deal indirectly with this theme, for he was convinced that it was a major aspect of ancient Judaism, other religions of the Near East, and the Christian spiritual life. Along these lines he suggested as a thesis topic a comparison of the roles of a woman in the works of E. T. A. Hoffmann and Johann Wolfgang Goethe, whereby he proposed to demonstrate that the Romantic writers often presented women as an idealized symbol or image of the ethereal, heavenly realm, whereas Goethe and others tended to view her only as a human companion despite their love and affection for her. But Vordtriede would hear nothing of this. He was something of a writer and translator as well as a professor of literature, and he claimed that others had already exhausted this topic, though he did not give any specific references. From his omniscient vantage point he took the matter into his own hands and decided that he should write his thesis on Ferdinand Freiligrath's poetry and his translations of English Romantic verse. He was tremendously disappointed, but decided that he was fortunate to have this offer.

As the years rolled by, he met and attempted to discuss these matters with an array of students and others. There was the towering, tall American mathematician from the West Coast who with his long, curly, flowing hair reminded almost everyone of Albrecht Dürer's self-portrait, except that he never posed with his right hand raised to his breast with two fingers spread apart. He had befriended the daughter of the Muenster family who owned the tea parlor (*Teestube*) in the Tuerkenstrasse. The father of the family was something of a philosopher and literary critic as well, and he sought out his opinion on several occasions, sometimes over a peppermint tea, his favorite. There was the clarinetist from the wilds of Colorado who had devoted himself to classical music who taught him to eat mostly veggies. They spent days doing their horoscopes and throwing the I Ching. There was the vagabond Wolfgang whom the Germans called a "Gammler," who sat daily in the best pizza parlor also in the Tuerkenstrasse drawing with his crayons and magic markers. He always had a volume of Mozart's diary and some letters to his wife, Stazzie, and his sister, Nannerl, on the table beside him, but he never heard him read them aloud. One day he met one of Wolfgang's friends on a city bus and asked him why no one could help Wolfgang.

There was a handsome Turk who later became the chair of the Department of Hittitology, the study of the Hittites of the Bible who lived in present-day Turkey. They had met in the Weinbauer, an old pub and family-style restaurant in Schwabing that remained from the nineteenth century, and he often invited him over for tea or beer. An extraordinary German-Irish couple started a house theater, and with three lines he "starred" in one of their productions of an American play about people on welfare. There was Tiny, the Germanist from Bavaria, who helped with his thesis who must have become a very good German teacher. And there was Petra, a beautiful

German student he wanted to get to know, but she vanished out of his life. Two American girls—one Jewish from the West Coast and the other from a well-known family on the East Coast who had married a German man—were students of British literature he had met during classes. They often had tea or coffee together and sat for hours talking about any number of things. A local Bavarian girl became his second Lea Oxbridge, and they spent endless hours walking in the English Garten, talking over coffee and cake at the university, or strolling along the Ludwigstrasse toward Schwabing. Her sparking eyes lit up her face and she was a believer, one of the few Catholic students he got to know. But their relationship was platonic, and they could never really connect, as though there were some kind of wall between them neither of them could cross. She, as did many of the conservative Catholic students, had very little sympathy for the socialist students who opposed the lifestyle of the middle-class.

One night in late winter as he sat in the Weinbauer, he struck up a conversation with a student named Gizi from Cuzhaven near Hamburg. She had long, blond, straight hair and what he called a Modigliani nose. Those days he most always bought prints to hang in his room, paintings or drawings of well-known artists. One of them had been a portrait of an Italian woman with a long nose that dominated her face, and Modigliani had painted her in a simple blue and white blouse that highlighted her nose and hair. Fascinated not only by her German, Modigliani nose but also her marvelous eyes that flickered and fluttered as she talked, they spent hours together that evening and later day after day with one another. Though he had not at first thought of her as a lover, she insisted and he acquiesced even though she had not read Hesse or Novalis and knew nothing about the heavenly woman. Later he tried to talk to her about them, but she would not listen. Somehow she took all this to mean that he really didn't love her, which perhaps was to some extent true, because he felt even then that somehow all this was related to a true and meaningful relationship. One day he went to see her, only to learn from her landlady that she had packed up and left town.

He was more than a bit mystified by his own reaction. He sensed then that he was just getting to know her and that time would bring some understanding, but he wasn't sure. Now that she was gone, he felt a definite emptiness that before he had not thought was possible. He couldn't quite believe that he felt this way, but the feeling was there. That coupled with all the other rejections that had come his way as he had sought at least some kind of serious discussion of all the matters that pertained to Novalis, Hesse, the heavenly woman, and Jesus stirred his soul and brought him painful remorse. He could hear the chants of the socialists, the Marxist-Leninists, and some communists with their cry, "Hoch, die international Solidaritaet!" (Raise high the international solidarity!) as they drowned out the songs and liturgy of the Catholic Mass; the buzzing roar of the swirling, building cranes as they erected new stores, corporate headquarters, and mini-skyscrapers; and the zooming rush of cars that now filled the streets of Munich. All at once he felt engulfed by a prevailing darkness that had now blotted out the lively sunlight he thought he had seen when he first arrived there. He felt he had to leave also, though he had not had any idea about this before now. To his own amazement he packed a bag, walked to the train station, and bought a ticket to Venice. He wondered if he would be able to understand why Thomas Mann had come to associate life-giving, translucent, bright, and light-filled water with *Death in Venice*.

Not long after this he met her. Even before he had seen the heavenly woman and prayed only to Jesus, he had come to believe that marriage was made in heaven. He didn't know precisely how that was all to come about, but he felt that there had to be a spiritual aspect to it. He didn't meet her on the street. She had not been in any of his university classes. They did not meet in a pub, bar, or restaurant, not even on a trip to Italy or a walk in the park or on the heath. They had never seen each other before, quite a contrast to Hans Castorp's encounter with the woman he loved; he saw her almost every day but had never spoken to her. He went to London and simply rang her up, as she used to say. He called her from one of London's red telephone booths: "Oh, yes!" she said. "You are coming to stay with us, aren't you?" He was completely startled. Her voice sounded as though it rang through all the events that had befallen him since he saw the heavenly woman. Somehow he sensed that he was talking to a woman who would understand. "Well, I suppose so," he said, as he wondered why she had not just invited him to come by for a visit.

His sister had met one of her best friends in Switzerland on her return home from Greece. She had come to Munich to visit his first summer there, and she, a friend of hers, and he had ridden with a German student to Thessalonika and traveled for some six weeks. In Switzerland she had met a woman from Yorkshire named Laura who lived in London with Rachel and a documentary filmmaker. She had given his sister her address and told her to call whenever she came to London. It all sounded rather ordinary, but it was anything but that.

Somehow he found his way to St. Mary's Street on London's West Side, not far from Regents' Park, rang a doorbell, and knocked on a door on the second floor. Rachel opened the door, extended her hand to him, and they spent most of the rest of the afternoon sipping tea with milk in front of "the fire" in their living room.

Rachel's best friend was named Vela. She didn't live there but came by almost every day. The next afternoon on a walk through the park Rachel said, "Vela and I have been waiting on someone to come our way. We are so glad that you are here!" He didn't know quite what to say. He had not told her much about himself, just that he had come to Munich to study German literature and that he planned to teach after that. It seemed that she knew more than that about him, but he was to later understand that Jesus and the heavenly woman were not at all in the picture. Yet given the circumstance and how her words could have been understood, he was tempted to assume so, if not at least somehow subconsciously.

She had a cocker spaniel named Caleb who went with her almost everywhere she went except to work. He didn't know then that Caleb was the Hebrew word for dog, and that could have given him a hint. She and Vela had been friends for years. Both were nurses, had read Ivan Illich, and had begun to make tentative plans to move to India. "India?" he asked. "Why do you want to move to India?"

She was quietly beautiful. Her beauty was not glaring or stark. Her somewhat milky smooth face was dominated by glorious greenish-blue eyes that seemed to fly like swifts on the melody of her British accent that totally captivated him and helped drown out all memory of the German socialist chants and Freiligrath's bombarding poems for the Revolution of 1848. He had not spoken so much English for over half a decade. It felt as though he was able to express himself in his native tongue as he had never done before. Yet despite his attraction for her, he still felt somewhat removed from the scene, at least at first. He sensed that she was still very young, though she must have been at least twenty-six years old. Though he was eager to assume that she knew him or could get to know him, he remembered those first days when he sensed that she had assumed she knew him, but really did not. But she wanted to, if in no other way than on her own terms. They looked as though they would make a good couple. They were both about the same height and complemented each other with their body movements and demeanor. Both were youngish-looking; she was not to become typically womanly just as he would remain a young man, not typically manly. He should have kept his distance and let time play things out for him. But he didn't.

For the next couple of days he went sightseeing when she worked. Then one evening they went to the local pub, Ye Ole Rising Sun, for drinks and dinner. She chose a table in a corner a good distance from the bar, and it was then that he realized that she was in love with him. He should have made the attempt to tell his story, to let her know that he had been to the other world with the heavenly woman if only for a few fleeting moments. He still believed that Jesus was in the picture, but he didn't know quite where he was. He should have talked at least some about this, but he, too, began to think he was in love. He hoped that maybe she had had a vision also or that she would have one that would fully unite them as a young man and a young woman.

He remembered their first kiss but he could not remember where he first kissed her, while they were still in the Ye Ole Rising Sun or her flat. It was something like the starry night walk with the heavenly woman but still not the same. The next day he had become her lover, or should he have said that she had become his lover? That was the essential question that played itself out over the span of the next seven months or so. They should have said that they were each other's lovers. But what had begun as potentially a mutual relationship never really burst into full flower.

There were still some three weeks or more before he had to return to Munich for the summer semester. They took Caleb with them on long walks over Hampstead Heath, ate in Indian restaurants, and spent hours talking about many things, all with great happiness, exuberance, and simple joy. They bounced along from day to day as though they might be flying with some of the angels who had descended to the outer reaches of the earthly heavens themselves. But his time began to run out, and he would soon be on his way to continue his quest that had brought him to Munich. It was then that he told her that Munich was a long way from London, and he wasn't sure how they would be able to keep up with one another over such a long distance. He was somewhat amazed to hear her say, "Oh, Munich is not that far away!" Surely it was not as far as Tennessee, but then again it was not like just a few hours to Brighton Beach.

It was then that the differences began to surface. She gave him a special bracelet, a Jewish keepsake of some kind. "I am Jewish, you know." He couldn't believe his ears, and he did not know how to react. There was nothing whatsoever about her appearance that even vaguely resembled Jewish features. She went on to tell him that her mother was a Jewish American woman from Cincinnati, that her father was an Irishman, and that she had grown up in Surrey south of London. She spoke impeccable BBC English, and one would have never guessed that she was not English. "Why didn't you tell me?" he demanded. She remained calm and saw no reason why it would have made any difference whether she was Jewish or not. He had had only one Jewish friend in his life until then, and he did not really know him well. "Oh well, I don't practice Judaism, you know," she replied. "Vela and I began with Tai Chi a few years ago, and now we have started to learn the basics of Hinduism. If we go to India, we will be better able to relate to the people there."

Still, even though they spent the next several days talking about these matters, that incredible, unfathomable, joyful feeling of love remained there with them. He came home one day to find her asleep. It was not often that he had seen a woman asleep, and she looked so wonderfully quiet, serene, and composed, just as though she had not a care in the world and was eternally happy. How their love had come to them was beyond comprehension; it could not be explained. But it also could not be denied; neither of them was able to say to the other that perhaps they should attempt to put it all into a more sober perspective and try to analyze it. It was all quite beyond them, and both would have denied that there was any kind of fence between them. Even if there were such, their love would be able to overcome it.

She took him to visit her mother in Claygate. Her mother was asleep on a sofa in the living room and woke up only after they entered the house. But she did not bother to get up to greet them, possibly because she thought it was just Rachel who had come to have lunch. They spoke to each other from different rooms, and he unknowingly wandered into the living room and saw her mother's back as she was lying on the sofa but didn't speak to her until Rachel entered the room. During this strange moment he realized that her mother was Jewish and that she very possibly denied the divinity of Jesus and had never heard of a heavenly woman. It was a rather awkward situation that he had not foreseen, but Rachel came to call them for lunch. They sat at the kitchen table for a tasty meal and lively conversation that put them all in a better mood. She and Rachel had read one of Goethe's novels, and he learned that Rachel's oldest sister was editor at a London publishing house.

A few days later it was agreed that he would return to Munich to register for the summer semester and then come back to London when Rachel would have time for a trip to Cornwall. He had once been to Bristol on the coast, but he had never before been to that windswept peninsula on the southwest coast. But Rachel had been there often to wander among those lush hills washed by the never-ending, roaring waves and listen to the cries of thousands of seagulls.

As he returned to Munich, he realized that his entire world had changed. He tried to remember how things had been before Rachel had wandered into his life, but was only partially successful at that. About a year before the London trip he had moved into a large student apartment in the Amaliensenstrasse right around the corner from the university, which he shared with two couples, the sister of one of the wives, and a philosophy student from Madrid. They were all extremely friendly and outgoing, and it was a pleasure to live with them. Yet he could never really relate to them as he would have liked. The two sisters were studying to be interpreters and translators and let it be known that they were descendants of Johann Wolfgang Goethe. However that might have been, it didn't seem to have any relevance for his relationship with them. The single sister had been attracted to him, and when he told her about Rachel, she became even more insistent about her feelings for him. So when he was offered a room in a student house some ten to fifteen kilometers north of Munich with good train connections, he decided to move there. After all, Rachel had said that she had always wanted to live in the countryside, and that if she came to Munich, she would prefer to live there. The sister shed some tears the day he left, but he felt he had to go to be true to Rachel.

Classes at the university were for the most part routine, but he had started to write his thesis on Ferdinand Freiligrath. He had read enough to realize that he was not going to really relish this academic task. Though the socialists and the communists claimed that he was the first socialist or Marxist-Leninist poet since he wrote verse to foster and defend the German Revolution of 1848, Freiligrath wrote these poems without understanding the great differences between J. J. Rousseau, Jefferson, Robespierre, and the other democratic advocates on the one hand and Marx's *Das Kapital* on the other. But besides this there were only a few of his poems, such as the *Sandlieder*, which were genuinely good poetry, even though most of his translations of English Romantic verse were rather good. He thought of going to his "Magister Vater" Vordtriede to talk all this over and to ask if it would be at all possible to him to write on the role of women. But at last he felt that he had no real choice in this matter, and that it would be better to accept the topic than to write no thesis at all.

So after about a month's stay in Munich he found himself on the train headed to Ostende, Dover, and London. He and Rachel had talked some three to four times a week, and he felt then that more of himself was in London than Munich. He arrived on St. Mary's Street late one night, walked up to the second floor, and smothered Rachel with too many hugs and not enough kisses. He was so overjoyed to see her. She and Velva had been busy but not only with work; they had begun to make plans for their first trip to India. He didn't know how much Hinduism they were familiar with, but he hoped that some kind of a miracle would soon take place that would give him a bit of the limelight. He had, of course, talked about Jesus, the heavenly woman, and Hermann Hesse but only briefly now and then. There had been no serious discussion of these matters.

One evening on the way back to St. Mary's Street he lost the bracelet that Rachel had given him. He was happily skipping along a London street when it somehow came loose and fell into a basement window ledge just below the street level. The strange thing was that he couldn't see it. He had leaned over the ledge and had tried to retrieve it but found no trace of it whatsoever. He should have perhaps rung the doorbell and tried to find it from the other side, but that didn't occur to him. When he told Rachel, he could tell that she was more than a bit disturbed. It seemed to be a sign to her of some sort. But she didn't give a hint about it and presented him with a large, amber-colored plastic bead to take its place.

The next day they set out with Caleb to hitchhike to Cornwall. Those days it was a good way to travel; people were usually talkative and friendly and sometimes even bought you a meal. He had hitched occasionally in Germany and Italy, and she considered it an adventure that connected one to the countryside and the people. But things didn't go well, and they made little progress the first day. So she decided to turn south through Dorset toward Bournemouth to Poole Harbour where we could cross the bay to the Island of Purbeck and Corfe Castle. Her mother had a little beach house there, and she had been there often. She hinted that she liked the place but didn't give any real reason why. She liked the beach and the lay of the land around the castle with little hills and slopes that complemented the ruins of the walls, windows, and turrets of the centuries-old castle, which had been built by William the Conqueror not long after his invasion of England.

She had thought that her mother might be there but she wasn't. She wasn't planning to stay in the beach house anyway. They ate at a little beach restaurant and spent the afternoon there swimming and wandering along the beach. The wind was up that day, and so the surf of rather high waves lapping at the beach was exciting to watch. He made the effort to count the number of days he had spent on a beach because he was about nineteen years old when he first ever saw the ocean. He found it thoroughly idyllic to stroll along this ocean land, especially with her—and then suddenly the contrast to Saigon and those war days flashed before him, and he was sorrowful for those who had not returned to spend time on a beach. They talked a few minutes about this and then the Marxist socialist world he had left behind in Munich. Or had he actually left it? That was the real question, though they didn't really discuss it, just as they seemed to let Jesus and the heavenly woman come and go without any consequence. He capped it all off with a comment that had never come to him before. "Just call me a man of burden," he said.

They ate dinner at the restaurant and took their things and made their way from the beach to the slopes of the hills where the ruins of the Corfe Castle lay. She sought out a cozy corner along the remains of a wall where they could lay their sleeping bags and make their bed for the night. The wind had stopped. It was a quiet, balmy spring night, and only a gentle breeze blew as a huge, full, golden moon began to rise over the horizon of the island and the ocean. He was awed by the place. She had been there often, and for her it was all quite ordinary. He, though, sensed an aura about the castle and the countryside that emanated from them as he could suddenly envision the countless thousands of people who had come here. But more than this, he became aware of a presence that came to rest all around him, somewhat similar to the presence that had preceded his perception of the heavenly woman in Saigon and his vision of her in Tennessee.

He tried to say something about this to Rachel, but she was so focused on him and his physical body that it all seemed out of place and superfluous. It was then that the feeling of that presence and the beauty of her body seemed to merge with one another, and he was overcome by it all, as though it was not just Rachel there with him but the heavenly woman as well. So it was that he was not her lover that night, but she could not understand why and he could not explain it to her.

As the morn dawned bright with a rosy-red sun beckoning them to arise from their slumber, they were at first very happy and in good spirits.

Still, though, it seemed that they spoke subconsciously with one another about that night just past, and they intuitively decided to let it become a relic of the past, at least for the moment. A few days later when they returned to St. Mary's Street and were comfortably settled, they began to make plans for the summer. But for him it was a bump in the road that wouldn't go away. She had been there with him and had sensed nothing of the presence. That baffled him and began to haunt him. Even prior to that night he had been somewhat reluctant to give himself to her and she must have sensed it. But whether she thought he might be sexually dysfunctional or just wasn't physically attracted to him, she didn't say. He had desperately hoped that she might have some kind of vision or theophany. That would have put everything in a completely different perspective, and the barrier their love had not been able to overcome would have vanished out of sight. But that never happened. He had to return to Munich for the rest of the summer semester, so they decided that they would go south to Italy after that. He wanted to go to Corsica, but she preferred Elba. So Elba it was, that island where Napoleon was imprisoned before he was sent to die in exile, not Corsica where he had first seen the light of an earthly day.

They tried it all once more. She flew to Munich and spent a week or so in the student house in the countryside. His friends liked her, and they got along relatively well. But there was an Englishman among them whom she did not particularly care for. None of the rest of them spoke British English. The Bavarian countryside was a bit too stark and impersonal for her. The landscape was mostly flat there, and she missed the friendly, flowing, rolling hills of Devon and Dorset. So after a short stay they made their way to the autobahn and soon arrived in Livorno where they caught the ferry to Elba.

For a few days all went well. They were then to some extent still in love and it seemed that their love would carry them joyously from day to day. But the night at Corfe Castle would not go away, and he was still concerned about her resolve to accept Hinduism despite her Jewish heritage, not to mention the relevance of Christianity. When at last after a carefree and happy week they came to touch on the topic once more, she merely bowed out and gave him the impression that she hoped that it was all a passing fantasy that would soon fade away. So it was that they never really reached the point where they could seriously discuss the matter. He could not really explain what he had seen and what it meant to him, and she could not give him any real sense of what motivated her to travel along the paths of Krishna and

Arjuna, Buddha and Ananda. It seemed that they subconsciously decided to let time and distance somehow solve the dilemma for them. How they came to such a resolve was best explained by the circumstances. He had to finish the thesis, and she had to return to work. Neither of them wanted to admit it, but it seemed that the great exuberance of love that had wrapped its arms around them at first was only a figment of their imaginations.

They returned to Munich and she flew home to London. There they sat for months to come. He tried to find contentment and fascination for his literary study, but it took great effort. He made progress, but it was slow. He was astounded to discover that there were far more Romantic poets on the other side of the English Channel than he had ever heard of. Freiligrath had translated their verse successfully, but he never quite understood their souls and their longings for the soaring rays of the sun beyond the sun. Rachel remained dedicated to her work and Vela remained at her side, her constant companion. Sometime before September he moved from Biberbach back to Munich and took a room in an apartment with Olga Huberhohbruck and a couple who were artists. He was happy to be back in Munich, and Olga and her friends were good company.

The phone rang one day and he was overjoyed as always to hear Rachel's voice. A few minutes passed as they talked as usual and then she told him. She had met a man named Chris. Somehow somewhere she had met a man whom she considered half human and half divine, and she was convinced that he would fly with her through the rest of her life. Despite all their differences he had hoped that a miracle might happen, and afterward he realized that it had. Certainly it was not the miracle he had hoped for; it was rather a miracle for her. It had come to her world, not his. He was full of disbelief and agony, for she had become the center of his life as no other woman had ever been.

He bought a plane ticket, flew to London, and stalked along St. Mary's Street to her door. She couldn't believe that he had come, but she introduced him to Chris, a tall Englishman so handsome it looked as though he had been cut out of a fairy tale. He had a farm in Portugal, and Rachel let it be known that she had always wanted to go to Portugal. She then asked him where he was going to stay, and when he gave no immediate reply, she suggested that he go to Ireland, since she knew that he had never been there before. A day or two later he took the train to Dublin, and from there he made his way north to the coast not far from the river Boyne, not far from the place on the eastern coast where the Broch of Tara had been found, and not far from the battleground where his ancestors had fought Catholic King James II. After a night in a pub filled with Irish and half a dozen of their priests, he wandered to the beach and thought he understood why so many of the houses in Dublin had Greek columns and Greek facades. The lush, green Irish meadows filled with little white sheep had disappeared behind him, and now all he could see was an expansive, sandy beach, the waves lapping at the shore, and happy seagulls swirling overhead as their calls echoed all around him. His memory of those days spent on the beaches of Thessalonika and on the islands of Mykannos and Ios flashed before his eyes, and he felt the magical, ethereal blend of water, sand, and sky that he had only experienced in Greece. There Smyrna, Ephesus, and Hieropolis had become the homes of Jewish people from Jerusalem and Palestine who worshipped Jesus of Nazareth of Galilee, the Anointed One of Israel, those who had been oppressed, persecuted, and driven from their homes by their fellow Jewish brothers and sisters. They had never returned to their homeland, but they had found their way home.

XIII

Amsterdam

JUST OVER A YEAR later he arrived at the Brussels airport for a flight to New York, where he planned to spend a few days before he went home to Tennessee for Christmas. He had met a Jewish poet and his friend in Munich who had spent years reading Blake. There were not many people who still read Blake, let alone a Jewish man. He had offered them place to stay in Munich in exchange for a room for a couple of nights in New York. His train from Munich was late, but he had made it to the gate before the last of the passengers boarded the plane.

From Ireland he had returned to London to say his last farewells to Rachel. She went with him to catch the train to the airport, and for some reason about all he could remember was the pair of jeans she wore that day that dropped below her ankles and rubbed along the sidewalk behind her shoes as she casually, somewhat slowly, but with great confidence—it seemed to him—walked beside him to the station. They were talking about what he would do with German literature. She added that whatever it was, it most likely would have something to do with religion. Surely he knew that, and he could have at long last used this occasion to tell her about the starry night walk and the heavenly woman and the Hebrew patriarchs and matriarchs. He had alluded to it already several times before, albeit only vaguely, but he was not going to spell it out for her now. He still believed that one day she might see some kind of vision herself and that he also might see another vision that would help make the first one more comprehensible.

He still had his room in Munich on the Liebigstrasse in Lehel not far from the river Isar. Frau Olga proved to be a good and constant companion. She had been retired for a while, but at her age of eighty-four years she was still lively. Their relationship was at first just cordial, but became a very friendly one after only a few months passed. By the time that another month or two slipped away, and they had made it a habit to watch TV together now and then. One evening there was a documentary on Richard Wagner's life and work. For decades she had painted the backdrops for the stage sets for his operas, and she knew his operas almost by heart. He learned then beyond a shadow of a doubt that she greatly admired and revered him, so much so that she believed that with his music he had succeeded in elevating the Germanic sagas, especially the *Nibelungenlied* and its mythology, to a religion that was superior to all other religions, even Judaism and Christianity. No matter where he turned, he came face-to-face with opposition.

His study and research on Freiligrath was progressing, but it was still a painstaking task that moved slower than he liked. At least Freiligrath had remained a Christian and had grown up in churches where his father was a pastor. He spent day after day in the Bavarian state library as well as the library of the university's German Department, where he struggled to keep his thoughts from wandering from his poems to those images and remembrances of Rachel that haunted him day after day. He still could not believe that she had deserted him and that his attempts to convince her of the validity of Christianity had floundered so sadly. He had so very much hoped that he had found a real companion who, despite all the initial differences, was somehow on the same path that Jesus and the heavenly woman had set before him. It was clear that something was amiss, yet at first he couldn't quite put his finger on it. It all revolved around the heavenly woman, and how he was to relate her to Jesus. If Jesus had sent her to him to set his message on a new path of elucidation and understanding of his eternal gospel, then why had his relationship with Rachel not brought about some clear meaning for both him and her? How could she continue to reject Jesus, and how had it happened that she had not also sensed the numinous presence that had hovered around them that night they spent at Corfe Castle? It was then that he perceived that the heavenly woman was some kind of sign of a more complete relationship with Jesus. He had only very reluctantly put Jesus aside for her. Still he had tried to relegate Jesus to the far distant past and put the heavenly woman on a pedestal of the present. But it was clear now that that was not what had been intended. Whoever the heavenly woman was, he was awed to realize that Jesus was still the Anointed One of Israel, even during the twentieth century which like those previous centuries since he bodily left this earth sought to push him off his throne.

With the coming of spring, some of his German friends asked him to go with them on a trip to central and northern Italy. One of them had a large car, and there would be plenty of room. It had been just a few years since he had returned from Greece through Italy. As this was his third or fourth trip to Italy for that and other obvious reasons, it could not be compared to Goethe's *Italienische Reise*, but it was a flight from Freiligrath, socialism, and Rachel. At a café on the streets of Florence he met an animated, red-headed American girl from Phoenix who had moved there from Arkansas. She was so full of energy she reminded him of a young girl who required her mother's constant care. He spent a day or two sightseeing with her and some of her friends, but it was not enough to deflect his memory of Rachel. She haunted him no matter what he did and where he went. An American girl was now too American for him, though Rachel was not fully British.

They went to Assisi, Perugia, and Ravenna—Italian towns that he had never visited. This took them south of the magnificent Italian countryside of Tuscany to the region of Umbria, both of which boasted verdant rolling hills, vineyards, fields of grain, and meandering streams and rivers. North of there toward the Adriatic coast lay Ravenna, where he spent at least a day at its early-sixth-century church, the Basilica of Sant'Apollinare, Casse and marveled at its apse. It was a semirotunda so wondrously decorated with mosaics that depict the hand of God, the face of Christ, and others from the time of Moses to the disciples around the Crux Gammata, all of which allude to the resurrection and the Last Judgment with a heavenly vision of earthly flowers and trees that supposedly transcended purgatory and sent its viewers to the infinite realm of heaven itself. There the days of suffering had been suspended.

Most all of the passengers had boarded the airplane, and he was one of only a few who were left standing with their boarding passes in their hands. The attendant made a last call, and they made their way to the ramp that led to the door of the aircraft. It was an old 707, and there were only a couple of aisles. By the time he began to make his way through the plane to search for a seat, there was only one seat left toward the rear next to a woman who had unfolded a newspaper and placed it atop her head. He couldn't believe this sight and wondered why on earth she would want to cover her head then. He was somewhat reluctant to take the seat next to her, but there was no place else to sit.

How long she kept the newspaper on her head, he could not remember. But it was well past takeoff before it was removed to reveal a woman with short, grayish-brown hair of late middle age. She must have been in her late fifties. Her face was a bit pale and gaunt, but her cheeks were still tinted with a rosy hue. She had a short, pointed nose and lively, sparkling eyes. He could tell that she was of slender build, rather tall, and that she most likely moved agilely as she walked. He could sense even before they began a conversation that she had a definite mission of some kind, and that she was not the typical tourist on some holiday excursion.

A few minutes later he learned somewhat to his surprise that she was Dutch, from Amsterdam, something of a writer and translator, but most startling of all a Hindu guru who had just completed seven years of study with a follower of Sri Ramana Maharshi, a renowned Indian master guru. He had been to Amsterdam several times from Munich and knew that it was the alternative lifestyle center of Europe and that the broad spectrum of alternative lifestyles there was polarized by the flower-power disco called the Paradisio and all its marijuana- and hashish-smoking followers as opposed to the Cosmos, a quiet, elaborate center for Eastern religions that boasted a staff of Hindu, Buddhist, Taoist, and Zen Buddhist gurus and monks plus a vegetarian restaurant, sauna, meditation rooms, and lecture halls. He had visited the Cosmos restaurant and sauna several times, but he had never met someone who was an active member there. She lived mostly from her work as a translator, but found time to meditate some three hours a day, an hour in the early morning, an hour at noon, and an hour before her evening meal. He soon became cautiously fascinated by her, for it was evident that she had no sympathy whatsoever for a Christian worldview. She had read German and English literature but had not read Hesse. They did not get into a literary debate on Classicism and Romanticism and its critique of the Enlightenment world as he had hoped might develop. To his amazement they spent almost half of the flight talking about Africa, a continent she said that she revered because of its people and the reverence she felt they had for the earth, the natural world there where one could easily get a sense of the relationship that should exist between people, the earth, and their God. Strange it was that during the next three years they knew each other, they never again returned to this topic.

Despite such a conversation it wasn't until they got off the plane that he decided he couldn't let this woman walk out of his life. They were on the way to the taxi stands before he asked her to have lunch the next day. He had at first considered her too old and too eccentric. But then it occurred to him that it would be good to taste the waters of Hindu spirituality to see how they actually compared to those of Judaism and Christianity. And besides, he was somewhat attracted to her. They spent three days or more sightseeing in Manhattan from Chinatown, which was at the top of her priority list, to Little Italy, Greenwich Village, Central Park, and the East Side plus the museums. Her name was Eleanor.

One cold day in January he called her from Munich. He had come to an impasse with Freiligrath, German literature, and his life's work. He had finished the first draft of his thesis and had started to put it into a final form when he remembered the visions of the Hebrew patriarchs and matriarchs and the scenes of a village in Palestine during Jesus's day. These thoughts were accompanied by a spiritual presence, not as pronounced as that he had first experienced but a definite presence nonetheless. He could no longer put the heavenly woman in the center of the stage. Somehow he felt that he would be deserting Jesus if he accepted a degree in German literature, when from another point of view he should have studied theology and biblical literature. Previously he had not been able to view the heavenly woman from a sober perspective. She had come to him to call him to his life's journey. But what did all this have to do with the Dutch woman? He didn't know for sure, but he had a strong feeling that she had not become a Hindu guru merely for the sake of it, not just to debate history, theology, literature, and philosophy. She had devoted her life to what she had come to understand as the ultimate reality and its related spirituality. He had to find out what she meant by all of this, and so he packed and left for Amsterdam.

She had a small attic room in a large apartment house in a very respectable Amsterdam neighborhood quite a distance from the canals and the center of the city. For years she had had a rusty-red and white Spanish sheep hound named Shiva whose legs appeared to be blowing in the wind when he walked. The Vondelpark wasn't too far away, and they went there a few times for walks. She had accepted him as one of her apprentices though he had not made any formal affirmation for the Hindu belief. He did not renounce Christianity and let her know that he had come to compare his views with Hinduism. As the days passed he sought to allow his romantic feelings for her run their course.

He expected a give-and-take. He hoped that they would be able to compare and contrast Hinduism and Christianity, to set Krishna and Jesus, Arjuna and Paul side by side. But from the outset she set out to obliterate his old spirituality based on the orientation of the traditions of Judaism and Christianity. Only reluctantly would she briefly discuss them when he offered some parallels to basic Hindu precepts. To prepare him for the *Bhagavad-Gita* she gave him a volume of Gurdjieff, a mystic, philosopher, composer, businessman, and spiritual teacher who synthesized the Oriental religions and developed his own concept of true, spiritual consciousness that properly enlivened the human soul. After that she put Lord Krishna and his confidant Arjuna on center stage as the battle between good and evil, the forces of humanity vs. those of the heavenly realm unfolded. As time passed she gave him some of the Upanishads and finally some of the Hindu writings of her own guru and his master, Sri Ramana Marharshi. Along with this he began his first yoga exercises and then they began to meditate.

A month or so sailed past them. He did his yoga, read the texts, and meditated a couple of times a week. She did not emphasize the meditation at the beginning, and it was not clear why she didn't. Perhaps she merely assumed that he was not yet ready for it. But from the outset she sought to wipe away all of the images and associations of the Hebrews and their sagas, the stories of their God. She supplanted stories of Abraham and Sarah, Isaac and Rebecca, and Jacob and Leah and Rachel with Krishna, Arjuna, Shiva, Genesha, and the Hindu goddess Parvati. He objected but somewhat mildly and with deliberation and sober arguments as he tried to develop some kind of romantic relationship. He was aware of a definite spiritual awareness that she had nurtured over a decade or more, and he first thought that for a while he was responding to that with the spirituality that had been imparted to him from the visions of the heavenly woman and the Hebrews. He could feel an aura that surrounded her, and he hoped that he could relate to that.

Someone told him about Amsterdam's English Church. Though it was in the city center, he had never heard of it before. After a few Sunday visits he found out that it was actually a congregation of the Church of Scotland, the home church of his family and Scottish ancestors. He met the associate and senior pastors and began to attend regularly on Sundays. There he got to know more than a few faces who were students at the university.

It soon became clear that Eleanor's primary goal was to convert him. They continued their debate somewhat, but she resisted any lengthy discussion of Christianity. She wanted to add his name to the small list of converts she then served as guru. Not yet a year had passed since she had been consecrated, and so she was eager to share her devotion with him. But she became weary of his comments about Christianity and finally told him that until he could be more receptive to her instruction and guidance, she would only be able to see him once a week or less. He agreed to leave her place and found a room in a student dormitory across the canal from the Anne Frank House.

A few weeks later he met a Dutch woman at a jazz concert. He was not an ardent jazz enthusiast, but for years he went occasionally to Munich's jazz club in the heart of Schwabing. Usually there was a group there that played a relaxed, soothing sound, which he preferred, but now and then he could endure someone like Keith Jarrett. She was almost a picture-perfect Dutch girl with rosy cheeks, light brown hair, and enticing brownish-blue eyes. Her smile was warm and captivating. They were both absorbed by each other and the music as they floated along on those casual, melodic sounds for several hours.

The next day they met for lunch and were both swept away by a strong mutual attraction. He and Miriam laughed and talked glibly through the afternoon, had dinner, and then spent the night at her place. The next morning when some of the euphoria had dwindled away, he met the real Miriam, a nurse from a small town north of Amsterdam who, like Rachel, had begun Tai Chi and Hindu meditation. He found it a bit hard to believe since he thought that she was a young businesswoman or university student whose home was perhaps Amsterdam. She had taken his mind off Rachel and Eleanor, and he found that her company brought him comfort. But after that first day he had many doubts. Would he be able to convert her? It did not seem so very likely.

A few months passed quickly. He continued to visit the English Church on Sundays, went to Eleanor's a few times a week, and saw Miriam quite often. Her invited her to church services, but she would not go with him. From time to time he visited Amsterdam's chain of organic and natural food stores, Manna Foods. There he found part-time work as a food processor in one of their quaint stores and met Arien, a young Dutchman who was a member of the Anthroposophical Society of Amsterdam. They became fairly good friends and spent hours talking about the essence and meaning of life as they debated the validity of Christianity.

He at last decided that he could not return to Munich to take the degree in German literature. He had mixed feelings about Olga and would have considered staying there, had she not been so adamant about Wagner. He could still remember her words: "Die Kunst ist die wahre und eigentliche Religion" (Art is the true and essential religion). Miriam accompanied him to the Bavarian capital where with just a little remorse he packed his belongings and books and sent them home and bid Olga and some of his friends farewell. He called his professor and went to see him. He made the final attempt to talk about the heavenly woman and Jesus, but it was useless. Several years later Vordtriede wrote a few novels along with a work on religious philosophy, which he never read. He did discover, however, that like Rachel he was ethnically Jewish. On the return trip he and Miriam stopped in Marburg, this time to visit a professor of philosophy whom he had met in Montagnola, that little village in Tecino on the shores of Lake Lugano where Hesse lived after he fled Germany before World War I. He had found the little hunting castle where Hesse lived when he first moved there and knocked on the door. The professor opened the door, introduced himself, and took him to the cemetery where Hesse was buried. But for some strange reason he told him that he was not able to find Hesse's grave and went on to say, "Wie im Leben so auch im Tod hat er sich immer versteckt" (Just as in life so also in death he has always hidden himself away). The professor shook his hand and walked away. He then turned to continue on through the cemetery when suddenly he came upon Hesse's grave. There at the head of the gravestone grew a small cedar tree just like the ones his father and he always found for a Christmas tree. Tears filled his eyes as he stood there in disbelief.

For a while all went well, but it was not long before things turned sour. There was nothing that he could do to convert either Eleanor or Miriam. Then Miriam announced that she was going on a trip to India for a couple of months, and Eleanor remained strongly entrenched in Hinduism. She had at last refused to even discuss Christianity when he went to see her. At the English Church he spent more time with the senior pastor and at last asked about taking part in the worship services. His reply was that it would be best that he attend seminary first, for there would be no possibility that he could ever be ordained until he had a seminary degree. He had been writing to the red-headed American girl from Phoenix whose name was Darla. When he called and asked if he could come visit, she told him that it would be great to see him. So when midsummer came he boarded an airplane and a few days later landed in the semiarid, hot, and dusty landscape of southern Arizona.

He met someone at the airport who lived not far from Darla's house, but when he knocked on her door she was not there. It turned out that she and her boyfriend had gone to the Sadona Mountains to ride their bikes. He rented a small mobile home and worked for a lawn and gardening company mowing lawns for several months. He got to know Darla and her boyfriend and their circle of friends as the sun blazed its rays all around them and the summer heat became torrid. It almost never rained, and the only grass that grew had to be watered every day. He was not able to convince any of them that Jesus of Galilee was the Anointed One of Israel, and so he made no attempt whatsoever to tell them about the heavenly woman.

Just weeks before Christmas he boarded a bus for Tennessee and sailed over hundreds of miles of North American landscape on his way home. His mother was beside herself with joy to see him, and he was overjoyed to see her and the verdant, comforting, familiar hills of the Cherokee homeland that had not yet been covered with asphalt and concrete. There he rested until he could feel the earth beneath his feet once more. At least a week before Christmas he went to wander about the valleys, hills, and meadows not far from his house, and made his way through and past brambles, bri-ars, and sticker bushes until he found the perfect cedar tree. With the shiny, bright lights and ornaments from Thirty-Fourth Street in New York that his father had bought at a local department store some thirty years before, it was set aglow as his mother and sister and her family arrived for Christmas dinner. It seemed that he celebrated Christmas for three months that year before he decided to return to Amsterdam.

This time Eleanor was different. She looked the same and was as dom-ineering as she had always been, but something had changed. She had left the sedate Amsterdam neighborhood for the Red Light District, where she found a small, bare, second-floor apartment in an old house on the Gelder-sekade. Her Spanish sheep hound, Shiva, was still with her, and she had made a Hindu meditation shrine on the opposite side of the living room that overlooked the busy street below. Here she continued to meditate three hours a day when she was not at the typewriter translating or walking with Shiva through a park or the neighborhood streets.

He was surprised but so happy that she asked him to meditate with her. He thought that perhaps that was why she seemed different to him. She possibly thought that he had changed and that now he would be more receptive to the meditation. He took the lotus position across from her and sat there as though he had long been planted in that very position. She had always told him that one has to find a place, a comfortable but unique place, and that once there one can truly meditate so that it helps hold the universe up, by which he thought she meant that human perception of the spiritual presence helps keep the world upright.

Day after day he returned to the Geldersekade, and there they sat for an hour or more at a time with their souls reaching for and feeding on the divine spirit that hovered around them. It was absolutely phenomenal, for one could sense and actually feel the presence as if one could reach out and touch it. But one could not really see it; it could only be felt. She was very happy. Her face beamed with enthusiasm and joy as a warm, broad smile that seldom lit up her face spread from one ear to the other. Yet he was convinced that this time he was right. "Eleanor," he said, quietly hoping that somehow she could understand, "this is not the spirit of Brahman nor of Nirvana, and this is not the spirit of Lord Krishna, though it may be related to them. This is the spirit of Jesus of Nazareth of Galilee, the Anointed One of Israel, the Hebrew God who has made heaven and earth and all the cattle and the stars."

He had gone back to work at Manna Foods. At the beginning of August he took about three weeks off for a trip to Scotland. If the pastor of the Scottish Church wanted him to attend seminary, he thought he might just do so. It was a good and rather exciting journey. On the bus to Edinburgh he met a Frenchman from Paris on his way to visit his Scottish fiancé, and they invited him to stay with them. Their house overlooked the Queen's Balmoral Castle and the St. Giles Cathedral, and he spent several days walking along St. Giles Street and through much of the city. He went on north past Glasgow to Inveraray and its castle, his ancestral home, all the way to Oban on the coast, where he tried to catch the ferry to the Island of Iona on a Sunday. But there was no ferry to Iona on Sundays, and so when Monday came, he turned south once more.

The visit to the seminary was a sad disappointment. He felt that his life and his study there would be too confining. He thought that he would feel more at home if he entered an American seminary, but he was not sure. When he arrived in London on the return trip, the drought that had begun during that summer had taken its toll. Most all of the grass in the parks and throughout the city had turned brown while all Londoners baked under a relentless heat wave. He was glad to reach Amsterdam once more, but his exuberance would not last long. He would soon see that it was not the same city he had left just several weeks before.

XIV

Manna Foods

THOUGH HE HAD ONLY spent something less than a month traveling to England and Scotland, he learned that there were big changes at Manna Foods. The natural, organic, and macrobiotic food business had turned big profits for the food group for over a year now, and the manager had decided that it was time to expand in a rather grandiose way with the purchase of a central processing building located just on the outskirts of the city. It would thereby bring about an almost complete restructuring of the chain of stores they owned, providing for a consolidation of their various processing centers, which had previously been operating out of the tiny rooms located in the rear of a number of their stores. He had been back at work only a few days when they began the work of moving the inventory and food processing machines, though few, to the new central building that had once been a business of some sort in a small village just outside Amsterdam. For a couple of weeks or so, they loaded up a large truck several times a day and drove for more than an hour to the new site where they spent hours unloading and sorting the food so that it could be properly labeled and stored. The old familiar atmosphere of the small, quaint Dutch store where some three to four clerks and or food processors worked quietly like hobbits in the tiny back rooms listening to music, poring over macrobiotic facts, talking, and telling stories vanished overnight.

If nothing else with the arrangement at the central building, the natural and personal aesthetic of the entire food processing operation was replaced with an almost factorylike, streamlined, modern mode of production, a word that the workers had not used before. They had not so much been concerned with volume as with quality that came about with the care with which the food had been sorted, prepared, and put on the shelves of those tiny stores. Almost every day customers came to browse about the store and talk to them. Now they began to feel like factory workers working on some kind of crude conveyor belt, pumping and steaming along so that the volume of production could be raised to higher and higher levels for more profit.

One crisp, sunny autumn day toward the end of September, the manager and director of Manna Foods came to visit the food processors at the new building. That was one of those rare occasions when he chose to spend almost an entire day with the work crew and gathered them together to give them a series of hints, tips, and guidelines that would make the processing more efficient and productive. He was a handsome, charming young Dutch man no older than his late thirties with a narrow, bony face covered with rosy skin, pulled tightly over the jawbones and cheekbones of a noticeably symmetrical face. He smiled a good deal for a Dutchman and seemed to make an effort to be extremely friendly and outgoing. The aim of all this, though, was to demonstrate the intrinsic fruits of the proper diet and food that, with time and care of the body, could set one in a proper and peaceful, harmonious alignment with the revered realm of nature and the true spheres of being fully human, not just on the earthly level but the cosmic as well. That fateful day of their first encounter he had never forgotten, as it was then rather much to his surprise that the director looked at his face and told him that it was much too full and weighty. True it was not a Dutch face, not a stereotypical European face, though it might have been considered somewhat European. But if having a somewhat round face makes it "unnatural and corpulent," then he had such a face, as did millions of other people who walked over all of the earth's continents.

He knew that it was not his face that the director objected to, but its full countenance and the persona that it projected. It was different than his, and for some reason he didn't like it because with its waves and beams it said things he didn't like to hear, though of course it was his opinion that the director was not at all sure what he heard. To his suggestion that he should eat more of such and such foods to reduce its corpulence, he didn't make a rely as he knew that his face was thinner than it had been a year or so ago. How could he help it that his face was not narrow and bony, and why on earth would he want one anyway? Was that the sign of true macrobiotic, organic harmony, and if so, then why didn't the Orientals of Hindu and Buddhist persuasion he had seen at the Cosmos, Amsterdam's center of Eastern religions, have such faces? If he was able to admire the beauty of the natural, ethnic features of the director's face, he saw no reason why the response should not be a mutual one.

It was not, however, as simple as one face vs. another face. It was also a matter of religion, and all of the group knew that he was Christian. For months now he had made sometimes implicit, sometimes tacit comments about Christianity. He let it be known that he agreed that mind, soul, and body were related and that it was important how one cared for the body. There were, to be sure, parallels to the Jewish kosher tradition that were not unrelated to this debate, and then, too, there was the spiritual essence of Jesus's message, which he felt had long been overlooked and which related it to Hinduism, Buddhism, Islam, and even Taoism and the other religions of the world. He knew that they would agree that religious, spiritual awareness was essential to life as it was intended to be lived on earth, but he could not at all agree with them that such awareness was wholly dependent upon the organic process of the optimum nutrition of the body. For the Manna people, the source of wholesome, natural, and harmonious attitudes and right spiritual understanding was the proper food that the natural earth provided. Their founder and leader was a man named Georges Ohsawa, a modern seer and sage who had prophesied that if one could change and control the dietary habits of the human race, one could ultimately affect the quality of life on earth in a way that would allow peace and harmony to arise among all the earth's peoples.

About the middle of the afternoon the director called all the workers to tea, coffee, and sweets. They gathered up crates and boxes to sit on and formed a circle on the lawn that sparkled and glowed with the hues of reddish-yellow and gold radiating from the fallen autumn leaves of surrounding oaks and chestnut trees but which was randomly covered with a glaring amount of gravel and rock as well that had somehow seeped out of the driveway. Quite unexpectedly, he thought, the conversation turned quickly to religion, a rare event for Manna people, for he knew that most of them never spoke of religion. He remembered the time in one of the quaint, tiny stores when an Oriental girl who had been there talking for an hour or so suddenly asked what Dutch people thought of Christ. He knew, though, that she was not really asking what Dutch people thought of Christ but what Manna people thought. But still, as they talked on for several minutes, not one of the workers there ventured to make even the slightest reply. He tried to explain that in Holland just like other European countries there were many different views, opinions, and doctrines. He went on to say something about the progressive and liberal movements and came to a few remarks about the new spirituality. Not another person asked about his comments or sought to take issue with them, and it must have been obvious to her that Manna people could care less about Christ.

But there that afternoon, for some reason he could not quite fathom, they talked openly about their views and ran on and on from one religion to another when at last they came to Christianity. Then it was that the director took the stand and threw out his opinion that the true origin of Christianity was the phenomenal effect of desert life on the human metabolic rate, not the ancient tradition of Hebrew prophecy nor of Jesus's unique interpretation of that prophetic tradition. He argued that Jesus had not been the first desert prophet, and that if he had not gone into the desert to enter into an ascetic mode of living, he would have never developed the remarkable spiritual powers that enabled him to heal and perform other superhuman feats such as telepathic communication, levitation, and the raising of the dead to life.

Yet he doubted that all those remarkable feats and miracles attributed to Jesus had actually been done, because some were so extraordinary and spectacular, it was far more likely that they were nothing more than the fruits of a most fertile imagination, myth, or mere superstition conjured up by somewhat fanatic followers who used some of the Jewish oral traditions of the coming of the Messiah and the new Moses as guidelines for their so-called life of Jesus. Most everyone there agreed with the director, while a few remained silent. Then the sole Christian present let it be known that it was most certain that it was the Gospels themselves that gave a definite record of a continuity between the Torah and/or Jewish prophecy and the teachings of Jesus of Nazareth. He himself was crushed by the arrogance of the director and his remarks, but knew from the moment he heard them that his rebuttal would likely be only a futile gesture.

With glee, humor, and obvious pleasure the director continued his frontal assault and talked on and on about the desert and the ascetic life, expanding on his theory of how they are related to the desert fauna, the desert floor itself, light and darkness, and the climate of extremes. For him it was certain that Jesus's insight and powers had been gleaned from his assimilation to the desert environment. At this point he should have sat back, relaxed, and realized that the director was at least, it seemed, giving Jesus some benefit of the doubt. He was talking about Jesus's spiritual understanding and powers; he was, after all, admitting that Jesus was a person of extraordinary character and knowledge who had likely accomplished superhuman feats.

But he knew what the gist of it all was. Not just Jesus but other humans, too—even those who had no belief in the Hebrew and Jewish traditions or their relatedness to the other world religions—had or could have performed the same miracles. Jesus was not the divine, Hebrew God incarnate on earth; he was just another holy man. This point angered him most, and he spoke out, loudly denouncing the Manna people. He aimed his remarks at the director, telling him that he and his followers, the disciples of Ohsawa, were nothing more than a vast, bleak desert, a modern desert of the soul so immensely dry, foreboding, and empty that their desperate clamor for only physical food, harmony, and pleasure was a threat to their own true humanness and understanding of the miracle of life on earth. They had nothing but disregard for the spiritual essence of the human soul and its abode with Christ, the one true God from whom emanated the true spirit that was intended to enliven and captivate their souls, sending them soaring through the universe.

To the surprise of those seated around the circle as well as himself, he heard his voice reverberate about the small enclave. It was good to say what he had wanted to say for some months now and to let them know that he could never become a convert to Ohsawaism! Then he stopped speaking very abruptly, and it dawned on him what the aim and motives of the director had been. It was clear that he had no choice. A few minutes of silence hung like feathery, gossamer cobwebs fluttering about them, and he sat there pondering their nonchalance, bravado, and smug pride bound up by their supreme confidence that they knew what people for centuries had forgotten or not known. After a slight eternity slipped by, he heard his voice ring out again, letting them know that he could no longer continue to work for Manna Foods.

Were they surprised to hear this? He thought so. Even the director himself after another interlude of silence launched into a lengthy rebuttal to let all seated there know that what had just been said was of no real consequence at all. It seemed as though they had really wanted to convert him; for just as he finished speaking a worker he knew and liked stood up and boldly blurted out in a determined tone of voice that he would never be able to convince a single one of them that Jesus of Galilee was the one, true, divine God who had lived as this incarnate God on earth. He went on to say that no one could prove this and that Christianity was not a valid religion.

All this he found even more appalling and dismaying, and he was now even more firm in his resolve not to stay on there. They all got up to go back to work; but since one worker was returning to town earlier on a special errand, he decided to ride along with him without finishing the rest of the day's work. He had no idea at that moment that this was the beginning of the most marvelous and memorable event of his life.

He was, of course, more than a little perturbed and overwrought by the heated debate, but at first he did not think of leaving Amsterdam, though he did detect a faint longing to return to the United States. The longing for some sort of Paradise on earth had long been with him, and he most always projected it onto some distant place when the most undesirable adversity surprisingly lifted its marred and tattered face and set out to beset him in his immediate surroundings. The faces of a few friends zoomed by amid all those other images that now appeared on the stage of his psyche, and so he set out to see them that very afternoon. But none of them had any real idea what had just happened to him nor any concrete suggestion where he might direct his efforts to further the cause of his quest, and so he struck off on his own. He remembered that Hesse had worked for a bookstore in a small town for years, and a few minutes later he found himself rambling off to several bookstores he had frequented ever so briefly from time to time where he left his name and address.

Yet the heated words of the debate with the Manna People kept pounding in his head. He had no desire to return to his room or seek out the one quasi Manna person, Arien, with whom he could talk. Arien had become a real friend and allowed him to rent a room in his parents' old house. But he, too, besides being more than ten years younger, was an avowed follower of Eastern religions and anthroposophy who would discuss Christianity from time to time but never really seriously and who persisted with his verbal meditations centered on the utterance of the universal harmonic "Aum." With meditative, reflective thoughts and musings sifting through his head, his feet were left to wander the streets and quais of Amsterdam. Walking was one of his favorite pastimes, and picturesque Amsterdam was one of the most walking-friendly cities of Europe. All of its canals were laid out parallel to one another in a grandiose semicircle with the train station and the heart of the city surrounded by the canals at the center of the semicircle. Bridges were almost more numerous than the streets and alleyways that meandered sometime along beside the canals or cut their way over and around them and often led to parks such as the Vondelpark or other stretches of the city that, against the rule, had been left high and dry. Surely there were some wide and big streets covered with a barrage of cars and other traffic, but most were small, quaint, quiet, tree-lined thoroughfares bordered by walkways on either side. Tall townhouses bedecked with high gables, some with even late Renaissance and eighteenth-century façades, rose above the trees; it was easy to imagine that this place could be some sort of Paradise as he had hoped it might become months ago. Now, though, these longings had suddenly vanished, washed away by the disappointing events of that day and others before.

As he glided effortlessly over the golden autumn leaves piled along the sidewalks, he could scarcely remember whom he had met first, as all had blended into one great montage of people and places all so very different. He was Christian, but Eleanor was the subtle guru who had taken him to the Cosmos and opened up to him the elusive world of Hinduism that had become for him somewhat the spiritual heart of Christianity he felt he now knew. He had tried to talk about it to the pastor and others at the Church of Scotland where the eternal Word was preached each Sunday. How he had landed at Manna Foods he didn't at first remember, but then his search for work months before flashed onto the screen along with the great excitement that had been engendered by that name. He had remembered Jesus's words about the physical and spiritual manna and thought how most breathtaking it was that natural food people—genuine, alternative Dutch people from Amsterdam—would want to make the connection between the Orient and the ancient Hebrews. It all revolved around life and spiritual awareness, and here were real flesh-and-blood people who had made great sacrifices to turn their lives around because they sensed that the world needed them to make a difference. Even if they prayed in their own way, they were all working to help hold the sky up, something like the guru does.

XV

The Guru of Amsterdam

HE REMEMBERED ELEANOR'S WORDS that the guru's prayer gave foundation to the world so that the sun could shine on it. This great panoramic view of harmony, unity, and understanding sprang up all on its own, almost out of nowhere it seemed, and with it a genuine exuberance that gave him all those goose-bump feelings of expectation. But now it seemed that it was all not to be. Each faction sat stuck in the mud, mired up to their knees in their own confidence that their way and their way only was the one true way. The Manna people said that eating right makes one a true human; Eleanor sat defiantly meditating three hours a day and said she would never reincarnate again; the Christians had each other's songs that flew with the Word that was to come fully only at the last day. As he plodded over bridge after bridge and trudged on along canal after canal, Christ's words about the kingdom of God soared along to him. The kingdom does not come with watching and waiting, but arises within and there it blooms and blossoms. If only Eleanor could realize that the true source of the spiritual presence that fed her was Jesus himself.

She had moved from the solitude of a middle-class neighborhood where she had an attic apartment above the trees to the border of the Red Light District about three blocks from the central train station. She hadn't answered his question about this move, but he guessed that it was her way of putting on the line her claim to live in the other world, the last attempt to realize the life of the Bodhisattva, the enlightened one who plods along the dusty way of the human world to help others escape and achieve enlightenment rather than withdraw selfishly to hover quietly alone somewhere until death. Twice a day for a couple of weeks he had been coming to talk to her, climbing one flight of stairs that took him to her threadbare, almost empty apartment that overlooked the clattering traffic of the Geldersekade below. He still felt that she had actually done the opposite of what she hoped to do. Though she knew some of the Singapore Mafia who bought and sold drugs and others of the Red Light District, he could see no evidence of any real interaction with them. Maybe she had visitors when he wasn't there, and it could have been that she went to see them and worked with them and just never bothered to mention it. He somehow found out that she knew the pastor of the Scottish church and one of her secret agendas was to convert his congregation to Hinduism. But for some reason he never confronted her on this score.

At one time he had thought that he was in love with her. She was eccentric, just past middle age, and too energetic for him; yet the thought was that she understood the spiritual world and so it would be easier to combine his and her spiritual world rather than two physical bodies as he had tried already a number of times by then. That was one reason he had brought the little black dog, part Pomeranian, back with him from Chero-keeland. She had had her Spanish hound, Shiva, for years, and he knew that she loved and adored dogs. The shy and unassuming mutt, Whittie, he had picked up off a rural road just minutes after he had been run over by the car in front of them and had carried him around for weeks on a homemade, makeshift litter until his broken pelvic bone healed. He hoped that she would eventually develop an affection for this little dog and for him as well, but of course that never happened. She would hear nothing of his pleadings about anything romantic between them. Her sole aim was to convert him, send him along on the way of "enlightenment," and add his name to her list of those who had come her way. He had intended his dog's name as some kind of theological statement, a comment on the paradox of the human and divine. Later, though, he had to admit that this didn't quite work. The color, black, is not always bound and delineated by what is human, nor does the color, white, always denote what is divine—quite the contrary! But she would hear none of his Christian jargon, for from her viewpoint she was no longer "just" human; she was already at least half-way to Nirvana and had left all things human years ago. Yet to make it distinctly clear that she knew he was up to no good and had embarked on some clandestine mission of sorts to subvert all her great, sacrificial efforts of true enlightenment, she renamed his dog Scaramouch, the name of a clown, buffoon, or rascal, the first step of the enlightenment process she had envisioned for him, not his dog, which was to retrieve him from the false way of his past.

For a while he still persisted even in the face of not just her adversity but something bordering on hostility. He went to see her often, and he talked about the essence of the phenomenon of the Incarnation, the wonder of the Hebrew God come to earth, the tradition of the Hebrew prophets and how their spiritual callings were similar to the concept of Hindu enlightenment, the miracles, the suffering of Christ and on and on and on. The great Eleanor of Amsterdam, however, would not be moved. She sidestepped all his direct arguments with great finesse and glee, always screwing up her white, somewhat washed-out cheeks around her pointed nose as a defiant and proud grin or glance of scorn emanated from her face. She would be nothing but the universal bastion of the glorious, superhuman, true Hindu understanding. No matter what hour of the day he confronted her, she was always the same impenetrable, defiant, stubborn soul who espoused the one, irrefutable understanding and who was supremely confident that she had nothing more to learn from anyone, let alone a vagabond such as he.

Then one morning as he set out with Scaramouch on his way to Eleanor's abode, the little black dog put up more than his usual effort to resist going the way he had chosen. Slinking along like a snake or a possum, and tugging and pulling at his leash in his squeamishly quiet way, as if to say, "Just one more minute; let me get this scrap and it will be the last," he soon began pulling him to a stop every third or fourth step. At last it seemed that he had had enough from that dog and angrily lashed out at him with a loud verbal onslaught that left even himself a bit perplexed. At first he felt a bit ashamed that he had become so angry, and then had a thought that had never occurred to him before. Could it be that he had helped that dog for all the wrong reasons? Had he gone to rescue the dog and picked him up off the road and cared for him only to impress Eleanor? If that was true, it followed that if he gave up the dog and let him go his own way, then he might be invested with the insight and "power" to persuade Eleanor that Christianity was the one, valid, true religion that both contained and subsumed Hinduism. Dropping his leash with the flashing thought that whatever happened the dog would not go far, he stalked swiftly to Eleanor's apartment.

Whether she was glad to see him or not, he didn't know; but there was a look on her face he had not seen before, as though she knew that he had made a resolve of a different kind. Filled with anticipation and excitement he seated himself on his favorite spot on the small sofa just opposite her huge chair as he remembered once more her saying that a person of awareness must know where they should sit and where they should stand. He delivered what he considered to be a brilliant argument centered around the spiritual presence of a personal God who speaks to people on many levels, the ultimate being the moment of personal, direct revelation imparted on the awing waves of the spiritual aura both similar to yet different from the spiritual presence of Hindu meditation. He went on to explain the view that these two manifestations of the spirit must be essentially the same yet experientially different modes. It was for this reason that a Christian devoutly devoted to prayer often arrives at an awareness of the spiritual presence, and Hindus absorbed by their meditation often come to apprehend the presence of Christ. He paused and waited for a response. If Eleanor had not successfully ignored him before, this time she made a supreme effort not to be moved one iota. An icy silence reigned between them. He sat there holding his ground and she hers. Not to be the least engaged by his compelling presentation and not backing off of her resolve these past weeks of not even acknowledging the argument with even a related comment or question, she sat there solemnly with that familiar cold and foreboding look on her face. Another slice of cold silence slithered past them, and then she asked with as much reserve and detachment as she could muster up, "Where is Scaramouch?" He should have replied immediately that Scaramouch was no longer Scaramouch and that he had become a true and "free" dog to wander about the earth on his own, to seek the genuine quest of a true Christian. But he didn't say this. He simply refused to answer her query and got up to leave. As he made his way to the door he noticed again that there was a different look on her face. She had at last been a bit moved by his comments, but she refused to even begin to ponder the reason for her response, or at least he thought that he had at last moved her just a little way off her iceberg.

Swiftly he made his way to the clatter of the street below, thinking only of Scaramouch, whom he had abandoned about a ten-minute walk away, and he hurried off rather certain that he should be able to find him. He remembered the street and canal, but when he arrived there he found no trace of his small, black, hairy body. There had been plenty of scraps of food strewn along the walkways, enough he thought to keep him preoccupied for the half hour or less he was with Eleanor. He began to search in all directions from the spot where he left him, and soon it became a frantic hunt that sent him scurrying all around the area blocks away. But Scaramouch was not to be found. A pang of sorrow cut through his breast, and he realized that Eleanor, if she found out about this, would accuse him of wanton negligence, mistreatment of an animal. He could picture Scaramouch during those first moments of his abandonment, hurt and sorrowful that the master he loved so dearly had just walked off and left him on his own. Was that why he had not followed him, and was that why he had not lingered near the corner where he was left? Would he have not at least wondered if he would come back for him? Or maybe someone had just happened by, a dog lover, who simply could not resist taking Scaramouch to what must have been a better home.

Without his dog or Eleanor he began to wander through the city. An hour or so passed before he eventually wound up at the renowned Dam Square, graced on one side by the Queen's royal palace and a remarkable marble crucifix on the other. Jesus hung there majestically on a marble cross soaring high over the square directly opposite the palace, separated by a major street clogged with cars and people. He walked over to the crucifix set some twenty to thirty meters back from the street and stood there in awe and wonder, admiring the manner and style of the sculpture and reflecting on the historic and timeless moment it immortalized. Despite the modern contours it was a tremendously inspiring work, marked by definite, clear lines that lent it an impressive aura of modesty and the apparent appeal of earthly reality. Christ's suffering could be felt, and the longer he stood there, the more palpable it became. But to his amazement and his own sense of that dejected moment, there was a paradoxical glow and a hint of the unfathomable transcendence that negated all the suffering and rejection. The joy of Christ's lifting up hung there also, superimposed over all that human misery, seeping victoriously through time, space, and matter, transporting Jesus to that wondrous realm beyond the earth.

Just at that moment he thought he understood the reality and timelessness of it all, he saw still something he had never seen before, though of course he had seen it before. On either side of Jesus hung on their crosses the two thieves who had been crucified with him. The traditional crucifix focuses on Jesus alone, and Jesus was the only one he had really seen until then. Now out of nowhere it seemed that the two thieves had miraculously materialized as he stood there, and he saw them as he had never seen them before. A semblance of flesh and blood washed over the marble contours of their bodies and with that the astounding thought that these were the two disciples or followers who were closest to Jesus! He knew of course that according to the Gospel accounts only one thief had believed him and the other blatantly denied him and that only one disciple, the unknown beloved disciple whom many through the centuries believed was John, stood with Mary the mother of Jesus at the foot of the cross. But why would not a true disciple be there with him? Over an hour passed as he sat and then paced about the square below the crucifix, and with time came the thought that the two thieves were not just thieves but living symbols of the truest followers of Jesus. They, too, suffered, were mocked, and scoffed at; but they endured because of the presence of Christ whom they worshipped and whose spirit dwelt within them and went with them from life, through death and beyond.

He remembered the puzzled look on Eleanor's face, that slight look of doubt. Maybe it was the beginning of a confession that she didn't really know him inside and out and that Hinduism, though a true and genuine religion, was not the ultimate. With hope simmering beneath his skin and the images of the thieves spinning around his head, he walked quickly back to Eleanor's apartment, rang the bell, and was amazed that she opened the door and let him stay. All along the way he had been pondering her own quest, her real self, and how she might find some way to the earthly humanness and transcendence of the person of Jesus the Christ. But even then, even after a year of calling, writing, and visiting her, he didn't realize how far gone her body was, at least not how she felt that her body was almost already gone, over halfway to Nirvana. So he tried again. He told her that he thought that something new, wonderful, and marvelous was taking place, and that the essence of it all was to be understood from the heartfelt manner in which the most beloved disciples of Jesus honored and served him. They were able to identify with him, they were able to be one with him because they had become like him. This was all bound up in the past because it had all occurred in the past, hundreds of years ago. But the past had come crashing in on the present. The true present was past made present. He tried to tell her of all these feelings and sensations that welled up in his breast and pulled and tugged at his heart and his soul. With that remark he became silent, sitting there again before the great Queen sprawling on her ornate throne. She remained once more unmoved and then to his utter surprise she bellowed forth the chilling words: "Two men?" What she meant by that reply was not clear. Was she as a woman offended that two men had been hung with Jesus and by the accompanying implication of the symbolism that only men were true disciples? Was she accusing him of asserting that both thieves had believed and worshipped Jesus? Or was she telling him that she, a unique and superior woman and a follower of Sri Ramana Marharshi, knew the true Jesus as no other human had known him and that the real Jesus was a Hindu? Whatever the meaning of that statement was, he was repelled by her most offensive, arrogant words and her complete disregard for his experience and the uplifting waves of awe that had made their way to him. Filled with disgust he rose quickly to his feet and fled from her sight.

XVI

Flight through the Universe

A BIT DAZED HE stumbled and rambled through the city streets, along the canals, and through the alleyways. The images of the crucified Lord and thieves went with him and hovered about him. Almost unknowingly he found his way back to Dam Square and perched on the steps below the crucifix. There were other people sitting there, most of them students, and he struck up a conversation of sorts. For a couple of hours or so they talked on and on, enjoying one another's company as they basked in the midafternoon sun caressed by wave after wave of a balmy autumn breeze of early October. As the dimmer light of dusk was threatening to descend around them, an American happened by and joined them. To his utter astonishment this newcomer told them that he was living in Lugano. With that report came floods of images of the writer and recluse Hesse and the pilgrimage he had made to Baden-Wuerttemberg, Lake Constance, and Ticino some three years ago to escape the commercialism of the Olympics in Munich and to pay homage to the well-known German neo-Romantic writer. He was so amazed to hear the name of the town Lugano, it did not occur to him to ask the American how he got there and why, but directly launched into an intense discussion of the novels Hesse had written, many of which were set somewhere between the Orient and the Occident. Hinduism and Buddhism were their primary themes, but many of the characters were European, culturally Christian if not also believers of some sort; that was a matter he had never really resolved. Was Hesse a crypto-Christian? He had to ask this question, and it was quickly on his lips, quicker than he had expected.

The American was obviously pleased to learn that he had not only read Hesse but that he had become so infatuated with his religious worldview.

He quickly confessed that he himself was an ardent admirer of his writings and had also spent quite a bit of time clamoring along the path that Hesse had left through and for the modern world. As for the question of whether Hesse was a crypto-Christian, he went on to say that he guessed that he would have to plead his innocence on this matter as he was an avowed nonbeliever and had little sympathy for the heritage of Christianity. But he had spent some time rummaging through the novels and argued that he saw no evidence that Hesse was Christian. As he saw it, Hesse's *Narcissus and Goldmund*, *Siddhartha*, *and Journey to the East* aimed to whisk up the remnants of Christian Europe and mix them with the religious essence of the East, which, as he saw it, was the focus of his religious world. It was a popular way to view it all, particularly at that time when the flower-power people had unleashed their condemnation of the Christian American and European status quo.

Here, though, he had to take issue with the American as he himself had spent years delving into the literary roots he had found sprouting through the odd and seemingly alien pages Hesse left behind. That quest had landed him in the latter part of the eighteenth century when Novalis, Brentanno, Eichendorf, and a host of other European Romantics spoke up for true and essential Christianity and adamantly opposed the cascading, billowing rise of the Enlightenment and its inherent materialism. Yet on what page of what work had Hesse let it be known that he was Christian? There was none.

The evening was upon them, and hunger had sent its tentacles pacing round about their stomachs. As the American got up to leave, a girl sitting next to him who had overheard the conversation unleashed question after question. She had not read Hesse and let it be known from the outset that she was not Christian, but she was curious to know why he thought there might be a connection between the two. He asked her to dinner, where they spent hours rambling on about this mystery. He had already explained his view to the American, but he reached back into the past for a broader and more historical, literary basis for the argument. But it was no use. She couldn't imagine why a person like Hesse, who had spent a good bit of his life writing about Hinduism and Buddhism, would also harbor Christian sentiments. She rambled on and on exclaiming that she was not Christian, but if she were, she would have nothing to do with Oriental religions. Why was she bothering to talk to him? It was not at all clear. Quickly the night came stalking thickly around them and soon engulfed them, sending them on their separate ways into the bleakness that sat on each street corner.

The next afternoon found him again for a while at the Dam Square, but it seemed that the excitement of the day before had already been subdued. He sat on the steps and talked a bit with a few people, none of whose paths crossed his. Late afternoon sent him homeward from a brisk walk through the park, when not far from the house where he lived, he happened to meet a regular customer at Manna Foods where he had worked for months. It was someone he liked, and he had just turned the corner onto the street along which he walked when abruptly with no warning they looked up to see that they were walking toward one another. In his hand he held an extraordinarily large bird's feather which he turned over and around and around, as he had become clearly captivated by it. This all seemed just a bit strange, but as they greeted one another, he decided to say nothing about it. He didn't know him well but assumed that he was a student as they had talked often at the store. Theirs was a bit more than a casual acquaintance, so they picked up where they last left off, talking about food and the "new" Manna Foods.

At last he could resist it no longer and complimented him on that fantastic feather. It was immensely long, full, and covered with different and unending colors and color schemes that wound around one another and sent out enticing, lively, multicolored rays. It almost seemed that he literally jumped at the mention of the feather and excitedly launched into quite a long exposé, telling him all about the exotic bird it had come from and all the details about the feather and how he had come to have it. He listened intently and was fascinated by every detail. But he sensed that there was something about the feather this person did not know about, and this preoccupied his attention so much that some ten minutes after he was told all the particulars about the feather, he had forgotten almost every one of them.

Somewhat to his surprise his friend abruptly left off talking about the feather, and the conversation rambled on and on from topic to topic. Yet as they walked on slowly, try as he might, he could not keep his eyes from the feather. They kept bouncing back toward it, and soon he was staring at that colorful, fluffy stem of plumage his friend kept waving to and fro, back and forth as they walked. Somehow the excitement of the past few days and his lucid imagination became focused on the feather, and soon his persistent gaze at that kaleidoscope of color gave way to a waking, strong fantasy that took full reign of his thoughts. At that moment he could see an American Indian chief far in the distance, and he imagined that the very feather his friend was waving before his eyes was a special, magical feather taken from the headdress of this Indian chief, an inspired, well-known, and devout Indian who was known for his incredible religious powers and wisdom.

At that very instant the oppressive heaviness of the concerns and debates of those past days vanished wondrously into thin air. A light, buoyant exuberance descended from nowhere all around him, and with it came a spiritual presence that miraculously erased the mundane border between the apparently material world and the ethereal, timeless realm beyond. It was much stronger than and more pervasive than the presence that had come to him in Munich. It felt instantly as though he had been picked up from the street and was now gliding effortlessly over the sidewalk. He knew at once that it was the same presence that had come to him that eventful last summer he worked at the Cedar Swim Club. It felt somewhat as though he had walked under an invisible waterfall, where tons of spiritual water were pouring down upon him; yet paradoxically at that same instant those very waters were lifting him up, sending him soaring through the air above the earth where he now flew effortlessly between this world and the other. A wonderful, pulsing, joyous sensation welled up in his breast, and everything around him took on a new, vibrant appearance. There was no longer any trace of the lifelessness and somber atmosphere of the past several days. He could sense only real life and vital energy emerging from everything he looked at, not just from his friend and the people walking by them but also from the earth itself and its plants, flowers, animals, and trees.

He said something to his friend about how he felt and asked if he, too, felt any different, if he had sensed anything unusual about the feather. But he had no idea what he was talking about and told him again that the feather had come from an ordinary yet exotic bird. He then told him of his dinner plans, said that it was a bit late, and said good-bye. It was not far to the house by now, and he gently floated on down the street. Just before he arrived at the door, he heard dreary music seeping from the windows and walls of the house. One of the new comers to Arien's parents' house was a violinist, a student at the university, and she had just begun her evening practice. Much to his consternation she had chosen the wrong music; at least for him it was wrong. Most likely it was some court composition from the eighteenth century, as it was dry, too stylish—even drab—and it clashed tremendously with the songs he had just begun to hear winging their way on the waves of light that had come to surround him.

The moment he opened the door, the floors, walls, furniture, and windows of the house seemed to undergo some kind of instant metamorphosis, as though they were not only centuries old but now had become supremely lifeless as well. The decadence of eighteenth century France seemed to rise up and snarl at him and waltz with a grimacing glee from room to room. It all resonated repulsively with the despondent sounds emanating from her violin; and it was not only out of date and out of tune with the time, it was a brazen affront to the waves of joy swirling about him. Nothing around him reflected the glory that was just beginning to flash before his eyes; it was all far removed from the harmonious sounds he had just begun to hear. Everywhere he looked there was a frightening dearth and lack of vitality. The tones she sent through the house lacked true, lyrical substance, and the house was void of the sparkling essence of life that emanated from the rarified energy and vibrancy of the eternal melodies and celestial sounds he had just begun to hear moments before. Then came the thought that even if he sat there for hours using the most descriptive, persuasive, and miraculous language ever devised by humankind, he would never be able to convey to them the awing feelings and sensations that had come over him before and were seemingly beginning to come over him again. It was at that moment that he decided to leave, but he could not tell them this. It took little time for him to pack some of his clothes in his long knapsack. Then he said that he was going out to do his laundry and told them all good-bye.

He had enough money to pay for a flight to the United States at almost the highest commercial rate of that time. As he padded along the streets of the city, a myriad of thoughts swirled about his head, buoyed along by the presence that hovered around him. He wondered if Eleanor would be able to sense something different about him, as she claimed to be a psychic of sorts. She may or may not have read auras, but they had never talked about this. But then he realized that he had already been by her apartment earlier that afternoon, not really to talk but to let her know that he could wait patiently for her to consider a more realistic view of Christianity. It was clear to him that the church had accumulated so much prejudice and negative baggage throughout the centuries it was not easy sometimes for people with a sober and critical distance on these matters to allow such a religion as Christianity to come into a fair and objective focus. The window of her living room overlooked the street, and as he had not bothered to go up, he called from the street and after a few minutes the window opened. They had exchanged a few words; but when it became clear what he wanted, she turned her back on him and vanished from his sight.

Now he doubted that she would even bother to come to the window, but he really had no choice. He had spent some two years talking and debating with her about the essence of it all; if anyone could understand what he was talking about, it seemed then to him that it must be someone like her. Little did he know that he really didn't know the true Hindu Eleanor at all. He rang, and somewhat to his surprise she appeared at the window. But it was not a friendly appearance. It was evident from the first words that left her lips that this was to be her swan song, and she let forth with a loud barrage of complaints, the foremost being that his Christianity was causing her undue pain and anguish. His karma was too much for her to bear, and it disturbed the supreme quietude that her Hindu world had brought her. He tried to apologize and say something about that past afternoon, but it was no use. If she had extrasensory abilities, she had turned them off. He told her that he was going back to the United States, that he had decided to pay a long visit to his father. He thought that she was a bit surprised to hear this, but apparently it didn't faze her the least. The window slammed shut with a loud bang; his words of parting must have at last brought her supreme joy.

It was around 8 p.m. when he arrived that evening at the airport. The terminals were almost deserted, and there were only a handful of passengers to be seen here and there. The attendant at the first international airline he approached let it be instantly known that there were no departing flights until the next day. He refused to take this as the final word on the matter, however, and scurried from one counter to another, all of which reported that there were no night flights to the United States. Somehow that didn't register, and he didn't realize that the Amsterdam airport at that time was not that large an airport. He then began to plead with the attendants, telling them that his father was sick, not at all well, and that it was imperative for him to see him as soon as possible. Yet not a word he said to a host of attendants would change the flight schedule, and with great reluctance he sadly left the airport.

He decided to visit Anna. She had been a member of Amsterdam's English Church for decades and came from a family that had had ties with the Dutch Reformed Church for at least a century. He was not certain whether her father or grandfather had been a pastor, but he knew that she had been a faithful church member all her life. She had encouraged him to go to seminary, and there was a hint of something romantic between them, but he considered her too old and middle-class. The bus brought him to her doorstep, but when he rang, two Africans from Ghana rather than Anna stood there to greet him. Things went better, though, than at Eleanor's and the airport. He knew them both from the church he visited each Sunday. They had been attending there for over a year, just about from the time they had arrived from Ghana. Anna, it turned out, had left on holiday just a few days before and had invited the two Ghanaians to watch over her apartment while she was gone. They were overjoyed to see him, and since they were in the middle of dinner, asked him to join them. It was a fun-filled evening as they picked up where they had left off from Sunday, talking about their latest Dutch adventures, meeting other Africans and foreigners, and looking for work to help them pay for their study at the university. He told them nothing about what had happened to him that afternoon and said not a word about wanting to go to the United States. He was and he was not there with them, as that presence remained with him and lent the impression that those familiar faces and the familiar surroundings of that apartment now existed in a more rarified state of being. There beneath the mundane and the casual was the essentially real, and it emitted waves of feeling that cascaded quite naturally around him. They sensed nothing. The evening ended with music and television that they found all to their satisfaction and delight.

The next morning they persuaded him to go to town with them. It occurred to him that though the pastor at the church was not at all interested in his ecumenical agenda, the assistant pastor and youth leader might just lend him an ear. Besides, now he had two escorts, so to speak, and there was no hurry about the United States. As the three of them made their way to the bus stop, he met a man not much older than he was whom he had met before somewhere in the city. It just so happened that this man worked as a mechanic in the neighborhood garage. One of the Africans was also a mechanic and had actually been to this garage before to ask for work and was turned away. He introduced them, and the man asked the African to come by once more as it looked they there might be at minimum something part-time for him.

By the time they got to Amsterdam, though, he had changed his plans. Seeing the Africans off on their way to the university, he set out to the Red Light District, this time not to visit Eleanor. He had decided that if he could find a woman, any woman, whom he could relate to and who might be just a bit interested in Christianity of a kind that he could also relate to, he would consider a lasting relationship with her. On his way to Eleanor's months ago he had passed a woman of the night who did not look at all like the others. She sat there content behind her window wearing the clothes almost any middle-class Dutch woman would wear. A pair of reasonable, medium high heels were topped by a pleasant skirt that came just above her knee, a fluffy blouse buttoned tightly around buxom breasts, and a comely style for her brunette hair that did not come quite to her shoulders. A somewhat subdued smile lit up her face, and two rosy cheeks turned upward toward her sparkling eyes that danced and fluttered around her face. Her robust, innocent look startled him at first glance, and he had found that he could not walk past her that day. To even his own amazement he had stopped and knocked at her door.

But once he stood there before her, all of that supposed innocence and that seemingly ordinary air about her evaporated within a matter of minutes. She muttered only a few impersonal words before she made it clear that she would not even talk unless he paid. It looked as though he had no choice. Spurred on by his desire and lured by her comeliness and the rather incredible but for him intriguing thought that she might just be an "innocent" prostitute, he paid her fee and wound up in her tiny bedroom in the rear of the store with his dog Scaramouch, who scurried quickly under the bed when he dropped the leash. He sat down on the bed, filled with the expectation that he would now at least have a chance to talk to her, and quickly came up with any number of things to talk about. He wanted to know something about her life first, and then he planned to get around to religion somehow, but was not sure how. She took a seat next to him but refused to talk. He didn't know at all how he could approach her now and had to admit that he had been duped. He could have left immediately, but the lure was too strong, and he was unable to resist a passionate embrace.

He now remembered her and wondered if she was still there. Would she react the same way? Would she, a fascinating young woman, refuse to open up and remain a lifeless body of flesh? Why had she chosen not to divulge anything about herself when he had been there before? He was more than a bit surprised to find her there, sitting behind the same win-dow dressed like a young Dutch woman on her way to work or to Sunday church! No sooner than he opened the door, though, did he realize that she had no intention of dropping that professional façade that like a knight's armor protected and hid her real self and all her thoughts. The jargon was the same, and minutes passed before he realized that she recognized him. That moment came when for one brief minute she dropped the cold, commercial pitch and asked him where his dog was. He was dumbfounded! Had she liked his dog better, and was she really concerned about the dog? It appeared so, for at that moment she began to ramble on about the dog.

He was not at all sure how to react, and for a few brief moments he wondered whether or not he should really tell her what had happened. But she had said nothing about being glad to see him again, and so he quietly mumbled that he had lost him. He was amazed to hear her say that she was sorry about that and hoped that he would find him. He then went on to say that he was glad to see her again and wanted to know what she had done before she came there. At that remark she sealed her lips tighter than before and made her regular demand. He began to protest and told her that he had come to get to know her but that was the end of it. She would not budge, and when a smile leaped smirkingly onto her face, he turned for the door thoroughly baffled and exasperated by the way she had acted. Appearance is not reality, though sometimes it can be.

He stalked along at first and then gradually slowed to a leisurely pace, meandering through the rest of the Red Light District. Parts of it looked a bit like a circus. Some of the houses were painted yellow and purple, and multicolored lights hung around some of the doors. Music blared from many of the street corners, and vendors and delivery trucks made their way through the tiny streets to pubs and stores. Autumn leaves still hung on some of the trees, and as he trudged along, Jesus's words about prostitutes, the chief priests, Pharisees, and elders came to him: "You hypocrites," he called to them. "The tax collectors and harlots will go to heaven before you do!" A few minutes after that thought, suddenly in his mind's eye he saw a brilliant flash of light descend over his head as the trees, the canals, the stores, and the multicolored widows of the prostitutes became imbued with an unbelievable radiance and a vibrant energy that bounded in waves from house to house. He felt these waves surging gently around him, and so strong were their palpating nudges, he felt to his utter amazement that he might be able to fly. For some reason the idea came to him that if he threw away all of his money, something phenomenally glorious might take place. He felt as though he might be able to fly just like birds do by flapping his arms the way they move their wings. It was all some kind of theophany without a vision of Jesus or God! The presence of heaven seemed to be there wafting on the morning breezes that blew gently by him, and with all this came the image of the end of time as perhaps any minute his stay on earth might come to an end. Would the earth merely vanish from sight, or was there to be a judgment somewhere on it with Christ and the heavenly hosts? He didn't know, but the feeling was so definite, he pulled his wallet and passport from his coat pocket and flung them high above him, letting them hit the walkway behind him. Then wheeling about he quickly walked off another way, not bothering to see who would pick them up.

Walking exuberantly and euphorically along, he left the Red Light District and made his way to the center of the city. As he passed the American Express a young American happened along and stopped to tell him that he was searching for an inexpensive Volkswagen bus. He, too, seemed more excited and animated than usual for the average tourist on the street, and for some reason launched quickly into an elaborate description of this special Volkswagen bus that was to have the horns of a bull mounted on front above the windshield! The interior and exterior were to be completely redone with nothing but the finest furbishing, and the colors blue, gold, and red were to be used on the outside. For a minute he thought this person must be joking or that it might be a practical trick of some sort, and waited momentarily to see what would happen.

He was about to burst out in a hilarious laughter, when all at once he himself was overwhelmed with a most pleasant feeling of euphoria and supreme sense of well-being. Whatever he meant by what he said, it was also clear that his announcement could also be understood symbolically. He smiled and told him that he hoped he would soon find his special bus, but that he had just thrown away his last dime. Furthermore, he didn't know of anyone who might have such a bus for sale. Then he added that he had been born under the sign of Taurus the bull and that it could well be that their shared mutual elation and excitement came from the same underlying presence that had brought them together. He went on to say that it was all a spiritual matter and wondered if this made any sense to him. At that point the American smiled as though he might have some vague idea about what had been said, but then drifted off his own way.

He wandered on through the city somewhere between the train station and the Dam Square and was for some reason drawn to the rails of the streetcars that ran on either side of many of the streets, some of which ran parallel to one another. One by one he stepped over the crossties on which the rails were mounted as he imagined that he was floating along over a magical river that flowed ever so serenely and majestically to the gates of heaven. As he looked down on those wondrous waters, which he saw rising up and overflowing over the riverbed, he sniffed the air drifting upward and over the waters and smelled a most unusual, magnificent, otherworldly fragrance which he fathomed must have surely come from thousands of heavenly flowers that grew on the banks of this river of all rivers. He looked about to see if there were flower-covered banks of the river, but not a single, bright flower came into view. At that very moment he became aware of the presence of an incredible, heavenly odor rising from the surface of the skin of his shoulders, neck, and face that drifted slowly into his nostrils, spreading a most exquisite scent that he had never smelled. He imagined that it might be a small portion of some precious ointment that had somehow drifted down from heaven and now masqueraded as ethereal flowers growing up from the waters. With that came a loud clanging sound from behind him. Something was nudging at his legs and tugging at his thighs. When he turned around, he was startled to see a streetcar beginning to push him along the track!

For over an hour he drifted through the streets and from neighborhood to neighborhood moving joyfully about that quaint town, which for him was something of large village out of a fairy tale. His fascination never ceased for that city and for the way the canals blended in with the quais and streets that then gave rise to the tall, silhouetted townhouses that peaked into a host of façades and gables, most more than a couple of hundred years old. It seemed to him sometimes that many of the people were actual fairies themselves, as they scampered along the walkways, usually with a light, lilting pace that resonated with the song that arose from their gleeful voices. Dutch itself was a curious mix of German and English and often reminded him of what a child might do with the language, tossing the sounds and images into one big pile and then picking out the sounds that rang out with the happiest tone. It was then that he realized that he had not eaten all day and quickly found a pub for a sandwich and something to drink. The comfort of the large room was welcome, and he took a seat at the bar so as to avoid having to leave a large tip. Sitting and then standing, the strangest sensations came to him as he savored the food. For no apparent reason the thought and feeling came to him that he just might be able to stay awake for the rest of his life, even until eternity dawned and transcended the earth's horizon. Yet within a span of only a few minutes that startling image of everlasting vitality gave way to numbing sense of his bodily weight and eternal drowsiness, and it seemed that he would surely go to sleep before he left the pub and might sleep forever! He had to pinch himself to keep awake but soon revived and left to catch the bus to Anna's apartment.

There were only two other people on the large, wide bus, and only one remained when they reached the outskirts of town. One was an attractive woman who kept looking his way, sending along looks of curiosity that roused him from his slumber. Then, just before they reached the final stop, even she got off the bus. The minute the driver stopped and turned off the ignition, a deafening silence rang out and sailed through the night that greeted him when he stepped down from the empty bus into the cool, autumn air. Walking softly along the way to Anna's house he gazed up into the night sky, drinking in the bubbling light of myriads of stars that shone down all around him. For some reason it seemed to him that all of the stars were much closer to the earth than he had ever seen them before. Not far from Anna's apartment he stopped and let his head fall back into a position horizontal to the light-filled sky above. Suddenly out of the deep vastness that rose above him, he saw a huge, extremely wide star falling out of the sky. It might have been the light from an airplane approaching the airport, but for some reason that thought never occurred to him. The closer to the earth it came, the larger it grew; then to his amazement in a matter of seconds it took on the definite shape of a large cross glowing brilliantly over the earth. Reflecting on this for only a few moments he became convinced that it was a symbolic star sent to him from Christ from the other end of the universe. He sensed that the moment it approached his location on earth, a special, spiritual alignment would be established between himself and Christ that would provide a spiritual bond between the two of them.

He stood there several minutes more awed by that sacred star cross, paying it great homage and reverence. It soon descended to a point not far from the ground, still a good distance from him, and then hovered over the earth not far from the airport, emitting a bright, radiant glow. Whether it then vanished or not, he did not remember as it then occurred to him that he should go to the nearest church and offer up his thanks and praise for this sign sent from Christ. He made his way about the neighborhood and soon came to a very drab, modernistic church. He walked swiftly up a low flight of stairs and tugged gently on the sanctuary doors, which of course did not open.

As he stood there, it seemed as though he heard a voice calling to him, telling him to get off the streets as soon as he could. He wondered why, and then came the warning that he should get off the streets to provide protection for the heavenly presence that surrounded him. Castaneda's Don Juan flashed before his eyes, and he remembered the warning Don Juan had given to his American apprentice, who had come under the influence of a spiritual presence. He told him that during the final onset of the magical powers he had ritualistically evoked, he was to find a safe and secure shelter to protect himself from a host of possible counterpowers that might arise to confront him. He turned and hurriedly made his way to Anna's apartment and knocked loudly at the door. No one stirred from within, and once again silence rang out around him. The Africans weren't there. Startled he stood there momentarily trying to imagine where they might be. He had no key.

Fortunately the stairwell of the apartment house was spacious, and as he looked about, he decided to wait at the bottom of it. He found a pleasant spot near a radiator and a large window and sat down on a step, wondering how long he would have to wait and how he was to know what would be the appropriate time to leave. He felt rather sure that this was a safe place to stay. Only a few minutes passed before he heard what he thought must be the siren of a large fire engine approaching the house from still a consider-able distance. The shrill droning of the siren grew louder and louder as it neared Anna's street, and the motor of the truck roared and bellowed as it turned and then sped past Anna's house. He sat there shivering in the dark as the stairwell lights had long since gone out and pulled his coat over his head to protect himself. He wondered what had happened and feared that either Anna's house or another somewhere around the neighborhood had caught fire! But he had no choice but to wait there. He was all ears, listening to the truck, which much to his relief lumbered through the other side of the neighborhood and apparently left this time. He welcomed the ensuing silence with great relief.

For a good while though for what might have been an hour or longer, he kept his head covered with his coat to shield himself and sat quietly wondering what might happen next. When he sensed that all danger had passed, he uncovered his head and relaxed. He wondered if the Africans would be coming back to the apartment and listened for them, but the house door remained closed. To his left was a large window of the stairwell-which afforded a good view of a wide, expansive courtyard, and he looked out onto it eagerly, hoping to catch sight of the church he had found earlier. But another large apartment house rose up on the other side, blocking out any view of the street. It was then as he looked out onto a maze of lighted windows across the way, he saw a most unexpected vision of Jesus! This

time it was a waking vision, not one in his mind's eye as the others he had
seen before then, but a waking, sober vision of Jesus the Christ whom he
could see kneeling before a small altar through the window of an upper
apartment on the other side of the courtyard. Someone had opened the
curtain to that large, full-length window that revealed to him a tall man
with long, shoulder-length hair kneeling at an altar, his hands folded in
front of his uplifted face, the stereotypical WASP picture of Jesus.

But Christ was not alone. To his utter amazement he saw Eleanor and
Arien, the anthroposophical outsider and part-time worker from Manna
Foods, standing there next to the kneeling Jesus, one on his left and the
other on his right. For a moment he almost laughed. Who of all people
could be more different than this stereotypical Jesus? In character, appearance, and belief they were diametrical opposites to this traditional image of
Jesus. Their presence challenged in a bold and daring way everything the
WASP image of Jesus stood for. Years later he realized that there before him
stood the pictorial embodiments of those religious segments of society that
had opposed him while he was in Amsterdam and that were to oppose him
for years to come. The vision was a panoramic overview of his stay there,
and the three of them, Jesus, Eleanor, and Arien, symbolically represented
the Scottish Church, the Cosmos, and Manna Foods. Then, too, it was as
though the Hindu Eleanor and Arien of "Aum" had conjured up the WASP
image of Jesus all for their own purposes, for it allowed them to depict their
own prejudiced view of Christianity. This was the fuel they had used to
condemn his personal devotion to the essential, transcendental Christian
faith. It was all just a bit too uncanny for him, and he found that though
he had never seen a vision quite like this one, he had to turn away from it
from time to time. For a long while he sat there, and each time he turned to
look at the vision, all three of them were there. They remained kneeling and
standing, framed by the large picture window as though they were frozen in
time, space, and matter, and kept their initial positions, full of life.

The night had begun to wear on. He found that he could no longer
resist the urge and temptation to go for a walk. He slowly got to his feet,
cautiously opened the stairwell door, and made his way toward a small park
and playground that bordered the apartment house at the end of the street.
Halfway there he suddenly heard a deep, vibrant voice telling him to take
off his shoes; once he heard that, he could not get them off quickly enough.
It seemed as though his feet longed for nothing else but the feel of the bare
stone sidewalk, the soft green grass of the tiny park covered with a heavy

dew, and the sand of the children's playground. He had no sooner thrown them under a little bush on the edge of the park, when he heard a car slowly approaching him from behind. He pretended that he had not heard the car and dared not turn his head to look around. Gathering up all his courage he glided over the grass of the park and made his way toward a clump of trees just beyond the park.

Yet he had taken only a few steps from his shoes when he heard the car stop and a door open and close. A tall, heavy-set man stalked quickly toward him along the sidewalk and asked him where his shoes were. For some reason at that moment he had no intention of telling the man what he wanted to hear. He replied that he had no shoes and that he merely had a great longing to take a walk barefooted. This was not the answer the man had wanted to hear, and he demanded an identification or a passport immediately. When he could not show either of these, the man then asked for a work permit or any other kind of legal papers, and when finally nothing was forthcoming, he waved to another man who was the driver of the car.

The car edged forward a bit, and the man took him by the shoulder, pushed him along toward the backseat, opened the door, and demanded he take a seat. He had no choice and soon found himself on the way to the nearest police station. It was a small neighborhood substation of some kind, and he was led to a small room where they all took a seat around a large round table and immediately launched into a lengthy talk about God. He had already made the mistake of trying to talk about some of the events of the past few days during the ride to the station. For some reason he had thought that they might believe some of it or at least realize that people can have a religious experience. But they had laughed at almost every word he said, and there seated around the table they were prepared for an even bigger and more hilarious feast. As they sat at the table listening to him ramble on about what they could consider only pure fantasy, their smiles gave way to chuckles—and it wasn't long before they were rolling in waves of laughter that sent them reeling in their seats.

For the first few minutes of it all he found them utterly obnoxious and disrespectful of his plight, but then he was astounded to realize how considerate and personable they were. After all, they had not conducted themselves as ordinary policemen, had not been overly concerned to present themselves as professionals totally lacking for the "human" side of this situation, and had to some extent at least not gone to great lengths to make all this unbearable for him. At one point even he began to consider the

FLIGHT THROUGH THE UNIVERSE

possibility that they were taking some of his story seriously. One of them had actually added to the discussion by muttering that a thousand years was but as yesterday in the sight of the Lord at a time, when he paused and could not remember the biblical quote. For some strange reason he had not been able to remember that very familiar saying from Psalm 90:4; the manner in which the policeman said it impressed him so much, he thought he had heard something he had not heard before. But when he asked him to explain what was really meant by the quote, they both roared with laughter almost like the fire engine that had zoomed past Anna's earlier that evening. The other then wanted to know why, if he had had such a meaningful religious experience, he did not know the meaning of that saying. He should have asked why they were so sure that they understood it and yet had no sympathy for religious experience. But he didn't. He sat there a bit dumbfounded, not knowing what he should say next. It was apparent that he had said all too much already. At last he said that perhaps he should get out his Bible and refresh his memory.

When all the merriment ceased and the mirth he had brought to these two police officers subsided, they simply got up from their seats and motioned for him to follow them. At that point some effort should have been made on their part to follow the legal process. But they didn't even begin the legal procedure; his rights were not read to him, and they did not take the time to make a formal charge of any legal wrongdoing. They merely selected a cold, sterile cell for him and made sure the door was tightly locked. It was a most incongruous place to spend the wondrous, otherworldly night that was to follow. He was, though, to his surprise only a bit distraught about spending his first night behind the locked doors of a prison cell. He had felt for a few days now that he was on a journey for which there was rhyme and reason, and he had confidence that this was the right journey for him. He lay down on a very hard, tablelike bed and was about to drift off to sleep when he thought he sensed the presence of Anna from the English church enter the room. He sat up and in his mind's eye he saw the faint outline of her massive, corpulent frame standing in the room not far from him. She was more unbelievably, voluptuously beautiful than he had ever seen her or imagined that she could be. She smiled a soothing, gentle, compassionate smile, and then walked over to his bed and stood there beside him, caressing his shoulders. Her sensuality was overpowering, and he felt drawn to her as he had never felt before. Unable to ponder anything else or look away from her, he got up and followed her across the room as she moved toward the window. It was then that he was amazed to see what he thought could be nothing else but her shining, bright soul, that beckoned to him and called him to join her as she flew through the window. Instantly he felt himself being pulled along with her, and he soared through the window into a spacious, sublime realm that appeared to have no beginning and no end.

Once he was fully immersed in that new and other space, he was startled to see the Mona Lisa in the shape of a woolen, magical carpet flying toward him through the vastness of an immense darkness. She flew a straight path down to his feet, made some kind of landing, and waved to him to tell him to take a seat on the upper side of the carpet. When he was comfortably seated upon her, she took flight again. He saw the earth receding behind them in a brilliant flash of light, growing smaller and smaller as the Mona Lisa carpet winged her way with incredible, superhuman speed to the distant reaches of the realm of darkness and then turned toward a tiny point of light that shone with a piercing glow through the dark vastness. He looked around the carpet on which he sat and saw a kind of small radio-telephone he had never seen before, something like a walkie-talkie but much smaller. At that moment he heard a voice tell him to take up the radio-telephone and call all his friends, relatives, and other people he knew on earth to let them know that he was leaving the earth where they had been born behind, the only world that they knew, and that he would likely never be able to talk to them again, at least not for a long, long time. One by one he called them all, euphorically relating all the details of the flight and reassuring them that he was safe and sound. He went on to say that he regretted somewhat that he was leaving them, but that there was absolutely nothing that he could do to stop the carpet that by now was already millions, untold light years away from earth. Of all the people he called, not one believed the report that he was sitting on board the Mona Lisa carpet bound for a distant, celestial object, but at least he had talked to them. He asked them all to remember him, and he let them know that he was supremely happy, for at long last he had embarked on that fabulous space journey he had long dreamed about.

That distant tiny light loomed at first far, far away on a wide horizon that spread out before them. But in what seemed like only a few brief moments, it began to glow brighter and brighter in that vast sea of darkness. Then instantly without any warning they landed in a huge but rather dim antechamber of that light, which he now saw was a tremendous palace of light. To his astonishment he was told to debark from the carpet and make all the preparations he should to be admitted to the awing presence of the Lord. He didn't know exactly what was meant by this. There was nothing there but a large empty room with a cold, white marble floor. On that cold marble floor he knelt down and prayed earnestly and with great fervor that he would be found worthy to look in upon the throne room, which he somehow sensed was to be opened to him. Minutes that seemed like hours and then days crept slowly by—and then at that moment, when it seemed like he was to wait there kneeling for an eternity, the door of the throne room swung slowly open, unleashing instantly the spectacular and unfathomable brilliance of a most powerful, wondrous, heavenly light. He made one quick feeble attempt to look up at it—but no sooner had he done so when he was wholly overcome by that brightness, totally blinded by thousands upon thousands of brilliant rays pouring down into his eyes that struck painfully deep into their flesh. Quickly as he could, he reached up to cover his eyes with his hands and bowed his head ever so swiftly to the floor. Only when the pain slowly ebbed and faded away from his eyes was he able to open them again, and then only with his head bowed low on the floor of that antechamber. From that vantage point he was able to look slightly in front of himself and was awed by the sight of the feet of the Lord Most High, the Holy One of Israel. Though he could not look directly at His person, he saw in his mind's eye and knew that He was Jesus of Nazareth, the Anointed One of Israel. Once he saw those feet, he lowered his head again to the marble floor and stretched out his hands in front of him in praise of His presence.

It was then that he heard for the first time the awing voice of the Lord Most High, and it reverberated with a most uncanny, deep sound about the walls of the antechamber, "Put your head to the floor!" Quickly he put his head to the floor and hoped that he had done this the right way, as he had already put his head to the floor before he heard the command. But that was clearly not what was asked of him, and the voice replied with a second command to explain the first. "That is not close enough. Press your head hard against the floor." He was a bit disappointed to hear this but with great swiftness pressed his head closer to the marble floor, hoping that that would suffice for already he felt pain all along his forehead and the top of his head. But even that was not enough and to his great consternation and disappointment he heard the voice call out to him a third time, "Press your head with all your might against this floor on which I stand!" With every ounce of strength he had available, he pressed his forehead hard against that white, marble floor until sharp pain cut through and across his head. At that very moment the glorious, celestial sound of thousands and thousands and thousands of rejoicing, singing angels resounded throughout the throne room and beyond and through the heavens who came now to surround it, as all the angels joyously proclaimed his obedience and fidelity to the Lord of Lords, the Lord Most High, the Holy One of Israel, the Anointed One of Israel, the Master of all humankind.

Then the singing ceased and the hush of celestial silence reigned throughout the throne room and all the heavens beyond to acknowledge the Divine Presence as he heard the booming voice of the Lord again, which now seemed to come from a source miles and miles above his head. "For many days I have poured out my Word upon the people of the earth and to scores of your friends, and I have cried out to the thousands and millions. Some have heard it, many have not. At long last you have both heard the sound of My voice and have followed its command. Oh may it be that many others too will soon turn and perceive the Word from which all has sprung. I have called you forth and have foreordained you to the task I now set before you. Rise up, I say, and go and tell them that I, the Lord of all, have sent you!"

The very moment the echoes of the Lord's voice ceased to rebound and reverberate about the walls of the throne room, the rejoicing of the angels rang out again through the throne room and throughout all the heavens. Peals and peals of harmonious music, the purest sounds of celestial joy and happiness so very exquisite and uplifting, spread forth to all the infinite reaches of heaven, resounding and pealing through all the heavenly spheres as the vast sea of darkness now vanished within a matter of seconds and the entire heavenly realm was lit up with the most incredible, unfathomable, unearthly light that pushed back and engulfed all the darkness, leaving no trace of it to be found. Only the purest of light was to be seen that stretched in all directions to the unending reaches of the infinite, heavenly universe. He was overwhelmed with a marvelous feeling of well-being and joy, and felt as though he were a voluminous, large bubble of pure delight that could now soar forever on the waves of the ethereal songs the angels sent bounding throughout the heavens.

As he sat there on that marble floor listening to the celestial song and marveling at the magnificent, unending light, he was told that all the songs and heavenly sounds of the spheres of that celebration and festival were being piped down to the assembly of the students and faculty at his old alma mater, Solomonson College. Sitting there he could see the vast array of students seated in the auditorium where he had sat many times and the varied reactions on their robust, young, and eager faces as they drank in the words of the speaker chosen for that hour. Wave after wave of the exuberant peals and sounds of heaven arrived and rang out in all corners throughout that assembly hall, but not one soul, not one person, seated there heard them and became aware of what was happening. After some time a celestial announcement was made that proclaimed the heavenly event that had just taken place, but even then not one heard a single sound that had been uttered. At long last one of the professors heard some faint sounds of the singing angels rejoicing and then the mention of his name. "Oh, him!" he replied belatedly and coolly. "Why him? He never said anything worth remembering while he was here!"

The next day he was whisked off to one of the largest prisons in Amsterdam, a large rotundalike building in the middle of Haarlem, the massive dome of which reminded him of the Dome of the Invalides where Napoleon is buried. As he was processed through the prison, again no formal, criminal charges were placed against him. The only reason for his arrest was that he had no passport, residence permit, or work permit, but even with regard to this matter no legal proceedings took place. Once he passed through the admissions to the prison, he was taken downstairs to a distribution center where they demanded that he give up all his personal clothes and personal belongings, which they promptly replaced with prison clothes. Then he was taken to another room where he was told to disrobe and put on his prison clothes. While he was standing there dressing, another prisoner who had also just arrived asked why he was there. He had not expected such a question and wondered why the man had taken the time to ask him this. They talked on a bit while he pondered an answer. At first he thought of the vision he had had the night before and thought maybe he would try to say something about it. But then he paused and thought of the hundreds of prisoners in their cells that lined floor after floor of the expansive, round walls of the great prison dome, and considering his and their plight and remembering that the Lord had just that night spared his life, he answered with reserve and remorsefully, "I have been a very bad man!"

Once he was dressed, the guards came to escort him to his new cell; as they walked onto the floor that lay beneath the great dome, he happened to look up and see a small, round window in the very center at the very top of the dome. For some reason he did not see it as a mere window, but as a pathway of some kind to the sky and heaven above. The ceiling of the dome itself had been painted a light shade of green, but the glass of the window itself was crystal-clear. Pondering this contrast and considering the rising walls of the rotunda it became clear to him that this was the very center of the prison, as everything beneath the dome converged on that center top window. The sun's precious light streamed voluminously down through the crystal glass, lighting up his face and pouring a focused circle of light on the center portion of the floor. Try as he might, he could not take his eyes off that light, as myriads of golden beams of light flew and flashed through the small window. The longer he gazed up at this light, the more convinced he became that it was a symbolic link to the heavens above, which now were beckoning to him to acknowledge the Lord who reigned above the heavens. Then as it had been in the Red Light District, he had the strange sensation that somehow he might be able to soar through that magnificent window; he actually jumped up a foot or two from the prison floor expecting that he might be able to fly. The guards on either side of him who were taking him to his cell thought that he was trying to make a more conventional escape. One of them instantly seized one of his arms at the same time the other guard quickly grasped the other arm and with all his might and strength it seemed pushed it up almost to his shoulder blades toward the back of his neck. A most stunning, piercing pain shot through all parts of his body, and he let out a wretched, loud cry of anguish as they continued on and mounted the stairs that led to his cell.

Only a short time after the door to his cell had been tightly locked, he heard a quiet voice telling him to prepare and ready himself for Christ's visit. As he was listening to this voice, he saw another vision, a vision that he assumed was intended to warn him of the awesome presence of Christ, the Anointed One of Israel, the Holy One of Israel, who was coming to visit him. At that moment he happened to look out of the window of his cell, which faced the space below the rotunda of the prison, and saw again the sun's light cascading down through the center window, forming a circle on the floor far below. As he peered at this light resting there on the floor, he was suddenly astounded to see the head of Christ appear in the circle, a tiny head of Christ surrounded by that phenomenal light. For a while as he stood there breathlessly gazing at the wondrous head, he noticed no perceptible motion; it sat there motionless for some time. But then after a while it began to grow, to become larger, ever slowly at first but then increasing at a tremendously rapid rate until suddenly he was aware that the eyes of the

Lord were approaching the extreme height of his cell almost a hundred feet above the floor below. Then just opposite the window of his cell the eyes of Jesus stopped moving upward and peered inquisitively in through the window, staring directly at him at the same time his head continued to grow and expand, filling every tiny corner of that immense dome. As his head spread throughout the dome, his eyes grew larger and larger and continued to gaze solemnly through the window at him. He sensed that they were asking him if he had properly made all the required preparations for the coming visit of Christ. Then just at that juncture when it looked as though the head of Christ would burst through the walls of the rotunda, it began to turn, revolving slowly at first and then with a rising tempo swirling faster and faster in a complete circle around the walls of the dome so that he could look into every window of the prison and see each prisoner. Not much time elapsed when, without warning, his large, round eyes appeared once more right in front of the window of his cell. As he stood there gasping breathlessly for air at the door of his cell overwhelmed by the immensity of the eyes of Christ, the voice that he had heard in the beginning now continued on to talk to him, imparting a strange message, saying distinctly, "You must be sure to make preparations for the coming visit of Christ, for you must prepare as though you actually lived surrounded by and partaking of his very own mind."

If all that were not enough for him, another vision followed only a short while after that that brought him that now long-awaited visit. From that marvelous vantage point of his mind's eye he could see the human person of Jesus in his earthly form and shape. He looked much as the Western portrait pictures of him had portrayed him for centuries, and as he imagined he might have looked as he walked time after time from Galilee over the Judean hills on his way back and forth from Jerusalem. Yet though he was a man of impressive stature with shoulder-length hair and wore a long robe as people of the first century wore, he appeared realistically to him in the vision. The exaggeration of the typical WASP portrait was not to be detected at all; he was not immensely tall, and the long European, Western nose and face were not to be seen. For a moment it was as though he could see something of the actual historical Jesus as he might have appeared as he walked with his followers. But when he glanced at him minutes later, it was certain that he was not walking through Judea or Galilee and not a single person trailed behind him.

As he peered compellingly at the image before him, he could see that Jesus was hovering some three to four feet above the ground as his body floated through thin air above the streets that led from the prison in Haarlem toward the Dam Square just opposite the Queen's palace in the center of Amsterdam. Millions upon millions of cheering, screaming, shouting people stood on both sides of the streets and lined every inch of his way to the Dam, while hordes upon hordes of others from all over the city and every corner of the world ran wildly to join the others already standing along the streets. It was as though the entire population of the earth was now running to see Jesus the Messiah and what could be the cataclysmic end of history and time, the apocalypse or the long-awaited eschatological Day of the Lord that the prophet Amos first wrote about. Yet the baffling and perplexing paradox of this scene was that not a single person among the hordes and crowds thought that it was the end of time!

Every last one of them had come to see Jesus expecting only the utmost personal gratification. They had come for the sole purpose of satisfying their own individual human wants and desires, to fed their own greedy souls expecting nothing more than earthly riches, as though symbolically they wanted only gold, silver, bronze, and enormous wealth. All this they hoped and expected they could attain if they came and paid homage to the magical figure of Jesus who floated unmoved and somewhat lifelessly along the streets where they stood screaming at the top of their voices. Everyone pushed and shoved one another frantically to get close enough to him to touch him, thinking that if they did so, they would be instantly, magically, and spiritually blessed and would then at long last be able to attain enormous wealth which would give them unending leisure to continue this wild and delirious celebration that had begun before now but would be continued from now on with an astonishing crescendo. He could not see one person among them who wished for anything else but to be able to celebrate like this for as long as they wished, eating and drinking to their hearts' delight.

Seeing all this, Christ did not reach out to them. He did not even turn his head from side to side to look at them or speak to them. He did nothing to acknowledge the tumultuous presence of the people and their outlandish demeanor, and he did not allow himself to be physically touched by them. He looked solemnly ahead to the way that lay before him and floated unmoved past them, not waving to them even once. Once he reached the Dam Square, he drifted over to the statues of the crucifix of himself and the two thieves on either side and then turned solemnly around to face the royal palace that lay directly opposite the square. He stood there silently gazing at the Queen's magnificent palace for only a matter of a few short minutes when to the astonishment of all those watching him his body began to grow at a tremendous rate, becoming larger and larger second by second. The crowd ran toward him and took hold of his robe, frantically attempting to keep him earthbound.

But all their efforts were in vain. As he rose above the square, the robe was torn from his body. Then within seconds as he reached the height of the dome of the Queen's palace, he stretched forth his hand and gently caressed the top of it with the palm of his hand. Suddenly within seconds after the hand of Christ made contact with the stone of the palace, its walls, its roof, and the magnificent dome crumbled as if they had been hit by] a flash of lighting and came crashing down to the lawn and the street surrounding it. What was once a most luxurious and splendid palace was reduced to a mere pile of rubble within the twinkling of an eye. The rubble from the palace was so enormous it blocked all of the major streets leading to the Dam Square and the center of the city.

Seemingly taking little note of what had happened to the palace, Christ continued to grow and expand, reaching soon after that episode a tremendous size much larger than any man-made ship or airplane. But even then his body continued to grow and increased rapidly at a phenomenal pace. As his bodily mass expanded continuously, he floated and sailed high above the city and then above the country of the Netherlands and then above all of Europe where thousands of clouds and strong winds blew past and swirled around him, carrying him westward across the entire Atlantic Ocean until his feet extended to the West Coast and his head was placed just above the East Coast of the United States. Yet even then at that enormous size and great mass, his body did not stop growing and expanding. He grew and grew until he became an immense, universal man of infinite and unfathomable proportions whose feet were placed on the west pole of the entire universe and heaven while his head rested snugly and firmly on the east pole of that never ending realm. At that moment the entire universe and the heavenly realms were filled and fully permeated with the actual presence of his bodily mass so that the corporeal form of Jesus the Messiah was transformed into the universal Being of infinite transcendence, the true heavenly man, the heavenly substance of eternity. Just when he expected to see and hear the celestials sounds of angels winging their way through the heavens coming to pay homage to their Lord, he was baffled to see millions and millions and billions of people from the earth appear in huge droves and begin to swarm in every direction over every inch of his body, scrambling along from his head to his feet. But these people were not like the ones he had seen running and standing along the street in Amsterdam. As they moved to and fro over the body of Jesus, only some of them screamed and shouted wildly while others danced delightfully and sang joyous, ethereal, celestial songs. The most unbelievable sounds of tremendous volume resounded throughout the universe that were divided into two distinct kinds of song and melody. Some of the people, most of them in a drunken stupor, crawled and stumbled along over his body at the same time others walked gracefully with joyous strides, gliding along with great happiness, glee, and joy, their heads held high and covered with kind smiles. From some came sighs of groaning and lament as they slowly made their way over Christ's body that later arose on their lips as base and degrading shouts and screams, sometimes giving way to riotous revelry and drunken orgy. From the others came the tones of heavenly song that rose as harmonious melodies pealing and bubbling forth on ethereal waves, a most exquisite display and celebration of golden love. Harmonious, celestial songs rang joyously from their charming lips and light-filled faces of happiness, arising and wafting over from the impeccable glory that lifted them up and sent them flying from one golden light beam to another. Then the voice came to him again and said, "Look up and count out seven windows in your prison cell." He did as it commanded and looked up to count out seven windows." The voice spoke to him once more and said, "Now mark them out." He did as he had been told and marked them out and then stood there and marveled at all of the visions Jesus the Messiah, the Anointed One of Israel, had sent his way.

Appendix I

Dreams

D<small>URING THE AUTUMN OF</small> 1978, just a month or so after beginning a course on depth psychology taught by one of Ann Ulanov's assistants at Union Theological Seminary, I began a dream journal, which I continue to keep. The following dreams are ones I consider to be most significant.

THE GREAT TREE DREAM

August 8, 1997

Hi Ayala,

I hope you and all your family are fine and that you are enjoying a very pleasant end of the summer despite all the recent events. As I wrote before, I did not take the trip to Pennsylvania and neither did I go to Richmond. I have spent most of the summer working on my dream diary, gardening despite a drought which this year luckily only lasted four months, and working on projects around the house which needed attending to.

On Tuesday, July 29, just ten days ago, I had a very short dream which might, however, prove to be very significant. Usually it is those dreams which are more developed than this one which have meaning, but the real import of a dream actually depends on the symbols, not the length. And it is the symbol which serves as the center of this dream that I find most fascinating.

As the dream begins I am astonished to see a very tall, old tree appear before my eyes with the heads of four men or people protruding from or, perhaps one could say, growing out of the four sides of its upper trunk! The trunk of this tree is very wide and covered with a thick, rugged bark which shows signs of having endured the elements of several centuries or more. Above the trunk hundreds of limbs and boughs support an expansive canopy of green leaves which stretches skyward toward the depths of the ocean of the blue overhead. One might guess that this is an ancient oak tree, but the dream does not make this specific identification.

Each one of the four (4) heads looks out over the earth in one of the four directions of the globe, north, south, east and west. It might appear that they also represent the world's major ethnic groups which are sometimes referred to with regard to the color of the skin of the earth's peoples, yellow, red, white, and black. But only one head can be positively identified, and that is the head of an African whose twinkling eyes blend harmoniously with a face filled with a prevailing sense of exuberance and optimism.

For a moment it appears that this tree is filled throughout with a pervasive vitality and sprightliness, but then I suddenly discover that many of its roots have somehow come mysteriously to the surface of the earth! A closer look divulges the painful recognition that all of its roots including the tap root have died not recently but over the span of several centuries or more. It is now only a matter of time until the leaves turn brown and flutter and spiral to the ground. Actually at this very moment one could walk over to the tree trunk and push gently, and the tree would come crashing to the earth!

The interpretation of this dream depends on the determination of the entity which the tree symbolizes and the time span involved. On Thursday, August 7, I had a very brief dream which might suggest the amount of time alluded to.

I have a dream that I am surveying the night sky, and as I look toward the heavens, I see four tiny moons orbiting an immense moon which is perhaps some 12 times larger that each of the smaller lunar orbs. These four tiny moons can be seen to be grouped together and lined up only on one side of the huge moon.

So as I gaze at the very large moon, I see the four smaller moons parading one after the other against the face of the large moon.

What is the meaning of this dream and how should I proceed to interpret it? It seems to me that there are two possible approaches. Either this dream refers directly to the current state of affairs which are unfolding in Israel and Palestine, or it is a direct reference to the excavations which are currently being conducted by a group of Turkish archaeologists at the sites of the Church of Mary and the Church of John in Ephesos, Turkey. The tree could symbolize Israel, the Hebrew nation which was chosen by God from among the other nations of the earth, and which is located at the center of the earth. Thus the four heads look over the entire expanse of the earth. Or it could symbolize the current state of Christianity which has spread throughout the earth from its home which was Israel. The second dream specifies the amount of time which will transpire before the event of the dream comes to pass, four (4) months. So one can perhaps conclude that within four months either in Israel or Palestine a very significant event will occur which will determine the fate of those two nations, or a discovery will be made at Ephesos which will alter the course of Christianity.

Anyway, Ayala, I thought that this was a dream that I should send to you. How would you interpret the dream or do you think it has any real significance? I also wanted to ask if you got my last fax? Tell everyone "Hello" for me.

Shalom
Robert Rhea

It is rather obvious that the interpretation of the dream given above is for the most part false. It has been left as it was originally written, because that was the initial response of the dreamer to the dream. It could well have been that the dreamer did not remember the second dream accurately, and that instead of dreaming of the moon, he actually dreamed of the sun and found small suns. This would have provided a time span of four years and the date of 2001.

On the other hand if he rightly remembered that the second dream gave him a panoramic view of a huge moon with its four small moons, then there is a more accurate interpretation of this dream that is centered around the phenomenon of the four-sided mandala, which sometimes occurs in the Western tradition as well as Oriental thought and religion as perhaps the ultimate symbol of completion. From alchemy comes the perennial endeavor of attempting to complete the square, or transforming the square into the cosmic harmonious circle. Hindu and Buddhist traditions likewise work with the mandala as the expression of cosmic harmony. It could be that the dream intended to record this aspect of the expression of harmony to point to the interrelatedness of many of the world's religions, particularly the similarities of the spirituality of the Western and Eastern religious traditions. Thus the four moons would not refer to a time span at all but rather to the underlying, somewhat mystic religious reality that one encounters in both religious spheres and likely another element as well. The moon can symbolize both the unknown and the hidden or latent aspects of an event or matter. It could well be, therefore, that with the appearance of the moon here, the dream sought and still seeks to say that the content of the dream is not yet self-evident and refers to an ongoing unfolding of events.

As for the majestic tree and the heads of four humans that grow out of its stately trunk, there is little doubt that the original interpretation of this symbol is correct. The Judeo-Christian heritage is certainly alluded to here, but with a definite ecumenical thrust, for seemingly all of the peoples of the earth have been united by this immense, almost cosmic tree. Using the dream along with the characteristics of candidate for the presidency of the United States, Barack Obama, the dreamer predicted that Obama would be elected president well over a year before the election. So it is that the dream also focuses not only on Israel but the United States along with Western and Eastern Europe, and with that the interdependence of the first world and its primary source of civilization, the European Enlightenment of the eighteenth century. For the last three centuries or more, that movement has gradually gained unprecedented ascendency in the West and has engulfed the rest of the peoples and nations of the world as well. The acceptance or rejection of the new mode of secular living engendered by the Enlightenment is the great debate of the twentieth century and still demands the utmost concerns of the global village of the twenty-first century. It is not so much that one is called upon to either accept it outright, or reject it totally, but rather that one develop the capability to view it from a sober perspective and see its temptations to which most of us have succumbed. Only when we realize that moderation could have been the catchword that saved the day will we be able to accept our complicity and embrace a genuinely realistic approach to a more holistic life.

DREAM ABOUT POPE FRANCIS

November 21, 2014

Pope Francis has come to my hometown of Bristol to visit me. Someone calls me on the phone to tell me that he is on his way to my house! No sooner than I hang the phone up, when I hear a knock at the front door. I go quickly to the door and see the Pope standing there on the porch knocking on my door. I find this all hard to believe, but I am thankful and grateful that he has come. Full of excitement and a bit out of breath I open the door, bow before him, shake his hand, and invite him to come in and take a seat on our beautiful old sofa, a turquoise blue antique from the nineteenth century that my mother had refurbished. I move my favorite chair, also an antique covered with red velvet, in front of him and take a seat.

There we sit for more than an hour talking about an array of topics and events that range from political developments to the latest ecological, scientific, industrial, and commercial news to biblical, theological, archaeological, ecclesiastical, historical, and doctrinal matters. Suddenly I feel myself compelled to get up, take leave of His Holiness, and walk through the dinette to kitchen to the back door of the house that opens onto a small terrace. There I remain standing looking right and left through the backyard to the southwest and to the southeast through the large valley that lies behind our house. Then all at once, to my utter unbelief, complete amazement, and horror I see tremendously large, thick, dark, and foreboding storm clouds that reach from just above the ground to the sky blowing at lightning pace through the valley from the hills on the west side moving with phenomenal speed to the east on to a mountain range and beyond to the rest of the world!

I turn immediately and almost run back into the living room to the Pope and exclaim: "Your Holiness, you must go home immediately, this very minute!" "Home?" he asks. "Why must I go home?" I reply breathing heavily, "A most horrible, terrible, immense, and foreboding storm is coming from the West! It will last for a very long time. How long I don't know. But I am certain that if you succeed in going home now before this storm reaches the East, you will be able to live and remain in safety, unharmed by the storm and its devastation to most of the world."

I accompany him to the door and take leave from him. Then as he walks to a few aides and his car, I stand on the front porch and wave good-bye to him as his car climbs over the small hill in front of our house moving at an ever faster speed as it disappears from sight.

THE RATHAUS OF COLOGNE

I am taking an extensive bus tour through Germany. One day I look out to see that the bus has ascended an extremely tall mountain which is majestically poised just below a host of low-lying clouds. Through the clouds I catch glimpses of an opposing wide and expansive valley which appears to drop into a vast, unknown depth beneath the soaring mountain. As the bus begins to descend into the valley, peering out the window I am utterly amazed to see the highway dropping into the valley at an angle of descent of some 80 to 90 degrees! I begin to feel as though I have entered some hither-to-fore unknown fairy tale of the Brueder Grimm, for even a layman such as I knows that this highway has surpassed the maximum angle of descent possible by some 30 degrees or more! Moreover, I am a bit perplexed by the reaction of the rest of the passengers who appear to have noticed nothing unusual at all! Since the bus remains steadily on the highway and continues to progress at a reasonable rate of speed along the upper reaches of the valley, I decide against calling this unusual state of affairs to the attention of those seated around me. The bus descends for what seems like aeons of time along the rim and the mid-section of the valley, and at last reaches the valley floor at a point which gives the impression of being the center of the earth. When at last this omnibus of unusual fright rolls to a halt, I eagerly disembark from our crafty vessel and scan the valley floor. Much to my amazement I discover that we have arrived in the main city square of the city of Cologne. As I continue to look around at the urban sites which have miraculously come to view in this deserted valley, I am most awed to see towering before me the venerable, medieval, edifice which the church built centuries ago, the famed "Rathaus of Cologne." I discover that it is literally unfathomable how high this edifice actually is. As I stand gazing up into the sky, I can see that it reaches for miles and miles and miles, literally hundreds of thousands of miles into the sky into the vast reaches of space beyond the earth's atmosphere, far beyond the top of the mountain, literally out of the view of the human eye! I am more than a bit dumbfounded and not the least bit reassured by the fact that it looks vaguely like the cathedral of Cologne, yet there can be no mistake about the fact that it is the actual Rathaus of the city. The facade is comprised of some four to six impressive columns, each well rounded and of tremendous height of course, and though they resemble Greek columns of some kind, most particularly those of the Doric style, they are most certainly not Greek columns. I at last decide that they remind me of the columns erected inside the Cathedral of St. John the Divine on Amsterdam Avenue, though of course much higher. And since I was not able to develop a fondness for this mass of stone dedicated to St. John, or more properly speaking John the disciple, I am not at all reassured by this fantasmagoria which has suddenly materialized out of thin air. In fact I am rather repulsed by it, its immensity, its heaviness, its monstrous enormity, until I notice the clouds swirling around it, sometimes floating gracefully around the columns, sometimes flying past at a tremendous rate, all sailing off into the vast reaches of the heavenly sphere which lies well beyond the blue sea. But then I question if that is actually true or, rather, if that is symbolically true. It could well be that just as the real blue sea reaches on endlessly into the vastness of time and space, so too this Rathaus reaches from the lowest depths of the earth to the highest reaches of the heavenly realm, moving beyond time, space, and matter to that ephemeral, ethereal realm of vast and infinite light sailing over the blue sea, for there at long last one might encounter the true, golden light. I am overwhelmed by this event, this sight looming before me, and it seems that either my feet freeze to the ground or my arms become wings and I fly high over the earth never to return.

THE GREAT TREE OBAMA DREAM

March 15, 2012

Dear Mr. Obama,

The year was 1963, way back then when from many points of view it looked as though the USA was entering tumultuous times of social change which would never leave the country the way it was before. Not only was the civil rights movement for many people a threatening cloud which caused them much dread, there was also the music of rock and pop with its mostly negative critique of the sedate life-styles of the American middle class, the lure of a Bohemian life with its enticing promises many could not resist, the relocations of many Americans from a rural or small town settings to the stark landscapes of steel and concrete and asphalt of urban cities, the quest of many for a civilization no longer marred by the prejudices of the old past bound to the old religions and stifled social conformity, and the rumblings of war on the other side of the globe which many then said must be fought to prevent a socialist and communist domination of the world. Even the quietness of that old American small town on the Virginia-Tennessee border where I had lived for some 18 years during the late 40s and through the 50s had begun to reverberate with sound waves that no longer emanated from the verdant lawns, parks, and meadows and rolling but jutting hills that surrounded us on all sides, except to the east where the great Holston mountain thrust itself up heavenward to remind those whose perception had not been dulled by the onward move of modernity that even though heaven might not be found three miles above the earth or even beyond a distant galaxy, its existence could nevertheless be felt beyond the material confines of the mundane, even there in the transcendence of the earth which mirrors that wondrous light of the world beyond.

It must have been just a few days after Dr. King walked up to the podium of that stage erected before the Lincoln Memorial to talk for a brief seventeen minutes about his Dream that my uncle, a son of a cotton farmer of either Swiss or German descent and now in the peak of his career as a psychologist, anthropologist, and primatologist, came to visit us; this time not just at the airport, but he actually came to our house! It was not like those times before, when we drove a long way to the small airport lost in the green hills and sat behind the windows of the concourse to watch his turbo-prop plane drop out of the sky with great billowing, dusty, dirty clouds rising behind it. I remember that I was always horrified to see this spectacle and I remember when I first saw it happen. He came rambling toward us with a broad smile on the way from the plane and we all were thrilled to see him. But I felt I had no choice but to tell him that if more planes kept flying with all this debris coming out of them, the air would soon be filled with it, and since it was so dusty and *schmutzig*, I could not imagine that it would be good for the air and all of us who live from the air among many other things that come from the earth!

But that was the only time that I was allowed to say that, and this time as he came from the plane to the concourse he was chanting, "*Amo, amos, amat, amamus, amatis, amant*." No, perhaps I have forgotten when he said that because it seems that he conjugated the Latin verb for to love when I was fourteen years old and told him with great pride that I had started learning Latin. I blushed bright crimson because of his tremendous, scholarly presence and forgot what "amare" meant. A few years later listening to the Beatles I was to wonder if "all you need is love" is the same as the Latin for love, and if that was the same Love of the Hebrew God and the Love proclaimed by Jesus of Nazareth of Galilee and the great prophet Mohammad some six hundred years later as well as the Love proclaimed by Hindus, Buddhists, Taoists, and thousands of others of thousands of other religions. The ringing, joyous sounds of the Beatles left no doubt for me that they did know something about love. But was that love bound first and foremost by the enthralling sounds that floated from their guitars, their drums, and voices only, or did it emerge from the soul's reunion with Love eternal and transcendent? Years later, that year must have been late 1980, after two grueling years at one of the most liberal seminaries of our country where I sought to end the great Son of Man debate at 122nd Street among professors and students, none of whom took seriously a word I said or wrote, gunshots rang out on 72nd Street, where the quiet confines of the Dakota did not prove to be a protective barrier for the Japanese-looking Englishman from Liverpool. It seems to me that it was only then that I learned that years before that maybe Lennon had said something not quite right about Jesus. The sounds of their songs though still lifted and enlivened my soul and I can't hear them today without being at least somewhat happy, and even though as back then I was very sorrowful and troubled by the great austerity of "Christian academia."

So there we sat eating and talking out in our little front yard under the wild cherry tree, because our dinette was too small and too hot just as our house was too small for us and for my uncle who must have had to rent a motel or hotel room for the night. Back then the town still had a hotel! Or did he come and just spend the day and fly away again that night? I don't actually remember. That was my eighteenth year and my uncle had come to try to help us understand what had happened to me just a week or so before Dr. King declared to all the world, "I have a Dream." It was then that I had had an actual vision, not just a dream, and as I went walking in the middle of the night over the soft, warm asphalt of Queen Street barefooted like some Tennesseans and Cherokees sometimes used to walk, it seemed that I also flew very close to heaven but didn't see Jesus then. But I can't tell you what I saw, nor could I tell my uncle or my father or my mother or my sister what I saw. So I said to my uncle that if I go over to that college that is not quite like Princeton but something like it, it will all be so different than things are here. "And I have never been over there, so how will I know?" Then he said that even over there it would not be so different, because for the most part things are the same almost everywhere you go on this earth. And I said, " Is that really true? What about Dr. Martin Luther King talking there in front of the Lincoln Memorial to thousands of people who came to stay in tents for days all along the Mall, the great pool of water that sprawls between the Lincoln Memorial and the Capitol not far from the Washington Monument? Is he not different? Are they not doing something different? Just think, one day a man like Dr. Martin Luther King could become President!" To which my uncle much less enthusiastically said, "Well I suppose you are right." Then he turned to my father and said, "Let me take him with me to the university. We will try to study him." And my father said, "He is not going anywhere. He will stay right here."

So it was, Mr. Obama, but of course I did not stay there; yet on the other hand, perhaps from another perspective, one could say that I did. It all depends upon how one perceives and understands "right here." That in itself is perhaps the greatest dilemma of our time, this age, for even before the advent of the PC and the internet, we had already created a "virtual" world. One can perhaps conclude that even during the time of the ancients, from the beginnings of the rise of the great civilizations on earth, from Sumer to Akkad to Egypt to Greece and Rome, we humans have always built something of a virtual world of our own. Even the Hebrews and the Israelites did it, even during the times when they had no king, and even though they prided themselves on having brought about a theocracy, a human society ruled by the Hebrew God himself. To be sure even the primitives built shelters and villages and had to do so to live and procreate and actualize their views and understandings of life and reality. Yet even though there is such a fine line between what humans build to their own edification and what they build to honor and worship their Maker, there is a distinction between the two. If "right here" is understood to be the transcendent reality that humans can only experience but not guide or control for their own edification, then it is the truly "right here" that comes to us and fills us with the essence of all encompassing Love. This is the sole goal of our lives, to give ourselves over to that vision and those experiences that unite us with the other world of which this world is the mirror. Any attempt to distort this endeavor and make it "our own," to make from it only a material manifestation of our own creation to our own glory and hubris, negates the relationship between us humans and our Maker.

Mr. President, I write to you because I am deeply concerned about the definite decision of "our country" to attack the nation of Iran. One of the most puzzling aspects of this decision is that it is not at all clear who has made this decision. It seemed to many of us about a year ago that you had been able to make a decision about a definite policy concerning the establishment of a peace treaty between Israel and the Palestinians, and that soon there would be negotiations leading to the formation of a Palestinian state. I listened intently to what I might call your "1967 Borders Speech" at the State Department just less than a year ago now. As I recall just less than a year before that, before the onslaught of the Arab Spring, actual peace negotiations began between the Palestinians and the Israelis which, however, lasted for only two weeks! These talks were the fruits of your labor and those of the State Department, of which all of you should have been proud. But just as those talks were beginning, the moratorium on the building of settlements in the West Bank ran out, and the Prime Minister of Israel declared that that moratorium could not be continued for reasons which I didn't understand. As far as I remember, he stated simply that at the beginning of that decision to cease the building of new settlements, it had not been the intention of the Israeli government to even envision the continuation of that moratorium. Given such an approach to this matter, why then would he and others who made this decision have ever decided to allow a moratorium to begin with? The Prime Minister has stated that the Arab and Muslim peoples, with whom he seeks to make peace, do not want to make peace. Some ten to twenty-five years ago, many citizens of the USA believed this. But considering the pattern of attempted peace negotiations that have unfolded before our very own eyes over and over again for years and years, we have great reason to question the intentions of the current Prime Minister of Israel and those who preceded him and those of the Israeli government who have been delegated the authority to arrange peace negotiations.

Of course Iran is not the West Bank and Gaza. But many have suggested that if Israel could succeed in making peace with the Palestinians, then it would serve as a sign to Iran and other countries of the Middle East that Israel is not pursuing a foreign policy designed to provide for the so-called Greater Israel. I have read on this matter for over a decade now. I have read from a number of sources which are extremely critical of Israel and others not so critical, which have sought to point out that Israel still has a chance to prove itself a credible, viable nation seeking to live peacefully with its neighbors. From a religious point of view, I personally am skeptical of this venture because religion is so much a part of the Land of Israel that I consider it incongruous that the people of Israel should seek primarily to establish a secular state where once the attempt was made to establish the Israelite theocracy. Then also there is the matter of the tradition of the Messiah of Israel, and most contemporary Israelis, who for the most part are secular Jewish people, as well as religious Jewish people simply do not consider this a matter which is pertinent to the situation at hand.

Mr. President, I will not proceed to list the publications I have read here. Some are listed on the attachment below, entitled "The Earth, Jesus, and Light." What I do submit to you is a dream I had during the summer of 1997, the primary symbol of which is a huge, almost global sized tree with a huge canopy of leaves that reach to the heavens. From the trunk of this tree emerge the faces of four people who look out over the earth in the earth's four directions, such that the tree can been understood to symbolize all of the civilizations of the earth and their cultures. The face of the person facing south is that of an exuberant, joyful African man whose sparkling eyes glisten and glow with an uplifting enthusiasm and vibrant energy. It is this dream which enabled me to predict soon after you began your campaign for the office of the Presidency of the USA that you would win the election. That is what one might term the positive aspect of the dream.

But as I in my mind's eye stood there before the tree and looked down and around the tree as well as up, I was startled to see that all of the roots of the tree had died and had turned up through the dry soil that surrounded the tree. Even the mighty tap root, the very root that holds a tree upright, had died and withered. It was only a matter of time until the entire tree would come crashing to the ground. Actually I realized that if I went over and pushed with only my human strength, I very possibly could cause the tree to topple over on the barren soil that surrounded it. I sent the dream that very summer to an Israeli woman I had met while I was completing an M.A. for Hebrew Bible in the graduate school at the Jewish Theological Seminary of America, with whom I then still corresponded. She never replied with a comment about the dream and never mentioned it to me, even when she came from Israel to visit me in Vienna, Austria and to also pay homage to her deceased father who had studied music there during the 1930s. I at that time was a doctoral candidate in the Department of New Testament of the Lutheran Seminary of the University of Vienna, where I did research on the Johannine account of the Baptism of Jesus. I concluded that Jesus was not baptized by John the Baptist, but rather by the Holy Spirit of the Hebrew God during a theophany which Jesus and the Baptist experienced at the same time. An interpretation of the Great Tree dream and a summary of my research on the Baptism for a lay audience are to be found among the attachments at the bottom of this email correspondence.

Mr. President, I implore you to make every effort to solve the great dilemma of the Middle East only by means of seeking peace. For over a century none of the wars fought there have brought peace. If war were to pave the way for peace, then there would have been peace long before now. Even though it looks as if Iran is set upon the destruction of Israel that is by no means a reality unless the policies of the West compel the Iranians to follow such a course of action. The actual fact is that both sides, West and East, Christian and Jew versus Muslim and Arab, are to blame for the current impasse. Each side must seriously recognize the other and each side must offer their apologies to the other and ask their forgiveness.

May Christ help us.
Sincerely,
Robert B. Rhea

THE CROSS DREAM

March 28, 1993

I have been on a long journey traveling with Germans. At last we come to a certain highway where they decide that they will not be able to accompany me any farther. They explain that there is no alternative but for me to continue on by myself. Not far from the highway is a mountain crowned with a huge house which overlooks the surrounding countryside. I see them pointing to the house, and it seems that they tell me to make my way there. I decide that I might as well follow their advice and expect them to leave any minute. Yet as I trudge slowly up the hill, I catch glimpses of them in the distance, and see that they have stopped to observe my ascent up the mountain.

No sooner have I arrived at the house than I am startled to see an immense cross materialize out of thin air and fall over the roof. The cross came into view behind the house, rising swiftly up in the backyard to a height some three to four times the height of the house. Once it ceased its phenomenal growth, it fell like a flash of lightning over the top of the house, splitting the roof in two, striking the roof precisely at its midpoint. Thus the exact same area of roof was to be found on the right of the cross as on the left. I stood there in front of the house, somewhat bewildered, wondering what I should do next. I finally decided that I must take a look inside the house to see what the extent of the damage might be. Entering the house I went first to the living room, for it was that portion of the house which took the immediate impact of the cross. A wide crack extended from one side of the ceiling to the other, precisely in the middle; not one speck of plaster had fallen on the floor. Other than the crack the entire ceiling remained unscathed, except that two houses and two ceilings had been created out of one.

Appendix II

Letters

LETTER TO POPE BENEDICT XVI

February 22, 2013

Your Holiness,

During the summer of 1986 a month or so after I completed the Master of Divinity Degree at Union Theological Seminary, New York, N.Y., USA, where I wrote a thesis on the use of the Son of Man phrase and title in the Fourth Gospel for two renown Johannine scholars, James L. Martyn and Raymond E. Brown, a well-known Catholic New Testament scholar, I wrote a rather long letter to Pope John Paul II, asking him to consider recognizing the Fourth Gospel as the most authentic formulation of Christianity and perhaps the earliest and most historically accurate account of the life and teachings of our Lord, Jesus of Nazareth of Galilee. It was during the autumn of 1978 that I first wrote on this topic and then completed a seminar paper on this expansive topic which then contained essentially the same argument of the later thesis which Oscar Cullmann of Paris and Basel published as vol. 76 of his ATHANT series, Zürich, 1990. So for some eight years or so both in and out of seminary I had brought this matter to the attention of many people, not only my seminary professors but numerous pastors, lay leaders, and parishioners as well. To my great dismay all of them found my proposal somewhat intriguing but far-fetched, and thus they simply ignored and silently rejected this solution to the New Testament debate which, I later discovered, had been advanced by the late Cambridge professor of New Testament and Bishop of Woolwich, John A. T. Robinson, perhaps even a decade before his study, *The Priority of John*, was completed in 1983 and later published by J. F. Coakley during the year 1985. My seminary professors, so far as I know, knew of his study but did not choose to inform me of this remarkable, academic work, which in my opinion and that of several New Testament scholars solves the 2000-year-old debate on the nature of the Gospels of the New Testament canon. It was this state of affairs, the inability to communicate what had been imparted to me via dreams and visions as well as my academic study both in seminary and as a student of German literature at the University of Munich, that compelled me to write to Pope John Paul II to ask for his consideration of this matter.

One of the advisers of the Pope answered my letter and told me to report to the local Catholic priest and discuss this with him, which I did. I was told simply that the Church had decided this debate in favor of the Gospel of Mark and the letters of Paul and that the wisdom of the Church was to be regarded as the holy, inspired understanding of our Lord.

Since then I have continued the debate, once more both in church and synagogue settings as well as behind seminary walls. I entered the graduate school of the Jewish Theological Seminary of America, New York, N.Y., where I earned the degree of M.A. Hebrew Bible and sought to bring this matter to both Jewish students and professors alike. During the autumn of 2001 I matriculated as a candidate for the degree of New Testament studies at the Lutheran Seminary of the University of Vienna, Vienna, Austria where I completed the requirements to be admitted to the final oral exam. During this time I wrote six seminar reports for the advanced seminar, some four of them on the Johannine account of the Baptism of Jesus, whereby I concluded that Jesus was not baptized by John the Baptist but was proclaimed by John to be the true Jewish Messiah based on a mutual theophany he had experienced when he first encountered and met Jesus. During these years until Christmas of 2005, I attended the Vienna English-speaking Catholic Community and Christ Church, Vienna's Anglican Church. I sought to dialogue with the priests of these churches on this matter and often attended Mass and other services held by your friend and colleague, Cardinal Christopf Schoenborn. Some two weeks after I arrived in Vienna, I happened to meet just by chance

the retired Cardinal of Vienna, Cardinal Koenig, at a church near
the apartment house where I shared a student flat. He had come
to bless the new organ which had been brought from Innsbruck.
I then wrote to him concerning this matter and later continued
with a series of letters to Cardinal Schoenborn, the last of which I
completed on February 19 of this year. The German version of this
letter is attached below.

I have read several of your writings and your book, *Jesus of Nazareth*. I so very much welcomed your exegetical study of the Fourth
Gospel and the insight which you have given us with that study. I
sought to discuss this matter with my local Catholic priest at that
time, since I have attended Catholic Mass for over ten years. I attended his Bible Studies and sought to ask questions that would
enable a dialogue to unfold. He essentially refused to discuss this
with me until I accepted Catholic doctrine and joined the Church.
On April 17, 2010 while reading the lectionary the night before
the Sunday Mass, I discovered that based on the evidence of the
chapters 1, 2, and 21 of the Gospel of John it is very probable
that the Beloved Disciple was/is Nathaniel! I concluded this by
realizing that the unnamed disciple of chapter 1 and the others of
chapters 18 and 21 are not mysterious disciples whose names the
Evangelist have withheld from us for some secret reason or reasons, but simply that he has forgotten the names of the unnamed
disciples of chapters 1 and 21. The other disciple of chapter 18
must be the Beloved Disciple, and that he is Nathaniel is revealed
to us as a consequence of the vision Jesus sees of him under the fig
tree before Philip finds him and following the report of chapter
21 that he is from Cana of Galilee where he most likely goes with
Jesus following his first encounter with the Messiah to the wedding in Cana that Jesus, his mother, and others of his disciples had
been invited to.

Your Holiness, I ask you to seriously consider this matter before
your retirement. The Church stands where it stands today not
because you and other Catholics have intentionally sought to
stray from the faith, but for a lack of understanding regarding
the spirituality to which only the Fourth Gospel provides witness
and expression. You have devoted your entire life to the Church
and must be tremendously admired not only for your eloquence
and erudition, but for your vision of the tradition of the church
which you have sought to impart to your fellow Catholics and the
citizens of the world as well. I have followed some of your path

over these past years and I have prayed for you fervently. I implore you to recognize not only the New Testament scholarship which demonstrates that the Fourth Gospel is an eye-witness account par excellence that provides us with the basis for establishing the Catholic church somewhat like it was when the Mother Mary and the Beloved Disciple and the other disciples brought it most likely to Ephesos from Jerusalem and Galilee, but also the most recent archaeological evidence reported by Professor Francesco D'Andria of the University of Salento who makes the claim to have found the actual tomb of the disciple Philip who first found Nathaniel under the fig tree. As you well know, this means among other matters that the Eucharist which our Lord gave us was given with his sayings concerning the Lord's Communion at least a year before the Passion Week. Then and there after the feeding of the five thousand on the mountain, he stated that only those who eat of the flesh of the Son of Man and drink his blood have true life; but later he adds that it is only the Spirit which enlivens and gives life, the flesh is of no avail regarding spiritual nourishment. Here he is referring in my opinion to the nature of his Incarnation, for at least from the time of the Baptism onward throughout his ministry, John the Baptist, and Nathaniel knew that he was the Messiah because of the spiritual presence which emanated from him and which they thus gradually came to share with the other disciples.

May the Love of Christ our Lord and Mary the Queen of Heaven abide.

I have the honor to be Your Holiness' obedient servant,
Mag. Robert Rhea

LETTER TO POPE FRANCIS

September 14, 2016

Your Holiness,

That very special day of March 13, 2013 is still a vivid memory for me, that day on which you were selected by the College of Cardinals of the Roman Catholic Church as their Pope. As I recall, you made a special effort to speak about the role of the Bishop of Rome, and with those remarks you sought from the outset to place your selection as the ruling Pontiff over and against the background of the historical perspective of the Popes of the Roman Church.

Yet above all the name you chose in honor of St. Francis of Assisi, somewhat in contrast to your membership in the Society of Jesus founded by St. Ignatius of Loyola, was for me at least the most significant act of the early days of your papacy. As I understood it, you sought with this name to honor personal belief and individual spirituality along with private concern and action in both our individual lives and in the greater society of which we humans are all members. Thereby you seemed to assert the view that paradoxically we are all in a spiritual sense Bishops of Rome at the same time we are individuals who seek a special, private, spiritual devotion to Christ our Lord and the Queen of Heaven that enables us to act responsibly in our neighborhoods and the different human societies in which we find ourselves throughout this world.

The last entry in one of the biographical sketches of you which I read is the publication of your environmental encyclical entitled, "*Laudato Si,*" or "Praise be to you Lord." I went to a neighbor's house to watch you that day as you made your way in a small Fiat 500 to the Capitol Building to address the combined Congress of the Senate and House of Representatives of the USA on the crucial state of the earth's environment. That was on September 24, 2015, some twenty-seven years after James Hansen, formerly a leading NASA meteorologist, now professor of environmental science at Columbia University, New York, NY, testified before a congressional environmental committee on the critical state of the earth's oceans and seas, land, and the climate of the atmosphere.

Prior to the year 1988 thousands of environmental activists from the late 1960s on sought to raise the public awareness of this sad state of affairs. They were simply ignored and branded as radicals and extremists who could not give "concrete" facts about their claims. It is my view that Western Civilization with its extreme development of industrialization, technology, and globalization has already destroyed our dear mother earth, particularly when one compares the state of today's earth with that of the one that existed some 150 years ago.

Since I began this letter well over two months ago, I have spent time reading about the papal elections of the year 2005 when I was a doctoral student of New Testament in Vienna, Austria and those of the year 2013. From the different articles that I read, it appears that you and Pope Emeritus Benedict along with the Cardinals and the Curia have spent at the very least over a decade dialoging about the significance of the Second Vatican Council and what should be its import and its influence on Roman Catholic dogma and doctrine. Is it correct to say that there are two primary schools of thought on this matter, one of which developed with the Bologna and St. Gallen schools and the other which Pope Emeritus Benedict, the Archbishop Agostino Marchetto and you Pope Francis set forth as the proper response to Vatican II? As I understand the debate, the concerns of both schools have focused on the ancient Roman Catholic tradition which unfolded primarily over the first four centuries A.D. after the death and resurrection of our Lord and Messiah, Jesus of Galilee.

For over ten years I was enrolled as a student in the formal study of the Hebrew and Greek Scriptures at Christian, Jewish, and Lutheran seminaries in New York and Vienna, Austria. During the autumn of 1978 I wrote a seminary paper on the use of the Son of Man title in the Fourth Gospel for a Presbyterian scholar which was later expanded into a thesis for a renowned Roman Catholic New Testament scholar whose exegetical study of 1966 sought to convince scholars and laity as well that the Fourth Gospel is the most authentic record of the life and teaching of Jesus of Galilee. This was precisely the view that I reached with the image of the non-apocalyptic Son of Man as well as that of an Anglican scholar and Bishop of Woolwich whose study, *The Priority of John*, was published in 1985.

If one accepts this conclusion, then the most authentic tradition of the Roman Catholic Church is most explicitly and yet symbolically embodied and explained by the theology, chronology, and history of the Fourth Gospel. Thus one encounters the Church founded by Jesus of Galilee, but one which is best exemplified by the faith and devotion of the Beloved Disciple, whose report of the works, miracles, and teachings of our Savior most vividly recall exemplary episodes of his ministry to the Jewish people of Palestine of the first century. Based on the reports of chapters 1, 2, and 21 of this Gospel, I have ventured to suggest that this Beloved Disciple is none other than the disciple Nathaniel whose home was Cana of Galilee.

It is my view that such a conclusion serves to extricate you, Pope Emeritus Benedict, the Cardinals, the Curia, and the Bishops and all other Roman Catholics from the current debate on the most authentic tradition of the Roman Church, a debate which seemingly some time ago reached a stalemated impasse. With the Fourth Gospel's story we encounter the actual Jesus of Galilee who can speak to us today via dreams, visions, and a tangible spiritual presence just as he spoke to the early Hebrews and the Jewish Christians of the first century. Let us, therefore, be bold, courageous and yet filled with humble reverence to accept these ancient words of love, awe, and compassion which our Lord himself uttered to the Jewish people and to all of the people of this earthly realm.

May the love of our Christ our Lord and Mary the Queen of Heaven abide.

I have the honor to profess myself with the most profound respect. Your Holiness' most obedient servant.
Magister Robert Bruce Rhea

LETTER TO FATHER TIM

April 19, 2010

Dear Father Tim:

The Sunday Mass you celebrated this past Sunday at 8:30 AM, April 18, 2010 was a very unusual and extraordinary Mass, or at least I found it to have been that. I am writing to acknowledge my share of the blame for the exchange between us at the end of that Mass, and to present something of the background for that event before, during, and after that Mass.

First of all I was the first present at that Mass to reach the Baptismal font and exit the sanctuary after the final procession from the altar. Several times prior to that Sunday I had left the Mass immediately after the celebration of the Eucharist, but as far as I recall I have never been the first person to exit the sanctuary. I had planned during the Mass to leave once more after the celebration of the Eucharist, but the atmosphere generated by the readings, your sermon, the reading of the letter from Bishop Stika and the

Communion kept me lingering at my seat. I was about to leave at the beginning of the second collection, but at that moment I looked over to my left and saw Dr. Dave Arnold leave at that time, and I did not want to be the one to follow him. At that juncture I tentatively decided to leave after the singing of the first verse of the final hymn, "Jesus Christ Is Risen Today," but then I realized that I would be leaving just ahead of you and the final procession and I did not want to do that. So it was that I found myself walking swiftly toward the Baptismal fount just after you had left the sanctuary, because I was already late for a discussion group that I had planned to attend elsewhere.

Let me say here that I found your decision to read the letter from Bishop Stika at the beginning of that Mass to be a very bold and courageous decision. I have long admired your ministry as a priest. You possess a very genuine, unique, and heartfelt insight into the Christian heritage and tradition which you have nurtured with an intense devotion, hard work, and compassion. You have matched you love for the faith with a wide ranging curiosity and study of the various facets of the Christian, Roman Church from the theology of the early Church on through the history of the centuries which followed the days of the appearance of our Lord and God on earth. I have learned a good deal from you and thank you for your sermons which you have offered up to the congregation each Sunday. Because of this selfless giving of yourself, I know something of the sacrifice you have made for the Church, and your intense desire for the Roman Church to become for all Christians the Church it perhaps once was and can perhaps still become for all the peoples of the earth. Above all in keeping with your emphasis on the Eucharist, I know that you treasure it most of all and that it is your fervent hope that the people of the earth, especially those who are non-believers, can come to share this mystery which lies at the heart of all human existence. For all these reasons I can sense something of the turmoil which you have been enduring over the past couple of months. Particularly this past Sunday the suffering which you have experienced over the past four weeks was palpable, though you were able to put it in its place and not allow yourself to be swayed by it. So thank you so much for the reading of Bishop Stika's letter and for your prayer that the celebration of the Eucharist be offered up to the God of All Creation, the one true God to whom alone we can turn for His Love and His Help to endure these days and to face the duty which He has given us to preserve the one, true Church.

The Gospel reading for that Mass was taken from the last chapter of the Fourth Gospel, chapter 21. Since the autumn of 1976 I have never been able to read from the Fourth Gospel or to hear it read without a feeling of awe, wonder, and amazement. Prior to that time I was a student of medieval and modern German and English literature, and I used literature as a way of pursuing a religious and Christian quest. I became something of a literary critic schooled in the academic approach to the interpretation of literature ranging from the use of psychological views on to the hermeneutic approach before I became a biblical exegete, if I may be so bold to proclaim myself to be such, for I never really became a scholar, though I might call myself a "half-scholar." For all these reasons and for others not mentioned here, I have never been able to read the Fourth Gospel without feeling many, hundreds? of goose bumps surging around my spine and over my body. It is from my point of view the most remarkable, unique, and profound religious document ever written by a human living on this earth. Saturday night before that Sunday I found the lectionary and read from Jeremiah, chapter 32 about the siege of Jerusalem by Nebuchadrezzar, Jeremiah the prisoner at the hands of King Zedekiah, and Jeremiah's purchase of property in Anathoth for the day of the return of Israel from exile from Babylon. I then skipped the reading from Revelation, and read once more chapter 21 from the Fourth Gospel. At the beginning of the chapter five disciples are named and two are left as unknowns, something not uncommon for the fourth Evangelist, and then while they are fishing and after Jesus appears to them on the shore, the texts states that the disciple whom Jesus loved turns to Peter and tells him, "It is the Lord." We can only imagine what it must have been like to be there at that moment. One thing I realized for the first time that night reading that story once more, was that not only had we been there we would know who the Beloved Disciple was and is, but also that rather than there being only one real possibility from my previous point of view, namely that that disciple remains unknown to us, it became for me a distinct reality at that reading that he might have been Nathaniel! For with the exception of John the son of Zebedee who is only mentioned a couple of times in the New Testament alone and otherwise only in tandem with his brother James, the other likely candidates are not named: Andrew, Lazarus, and Philip. It is Jesus who goes to Bethsaida to find Philip who finds Nathaniel whom Jesus saw sitting under the fig tree before Nathaniel then pronounces Jesus to be the Son of God, the King of Israel. The next episode in Jesus's life and ministry which follows this encounter is the Wedding at Cana, the hometown of Nathaniel! From Nathaniel's words to Philip we know that he had likely become something of an expatriate of Galilee which could mean that he had gone to live in Jerusalem and had thus gotten to know the High Priest. The mention of the fig tree could denote Talmud study according to Charlesworth. Add to these observations the facts that that he is never mentioned in the Synoptic Gospels, though of course some have proclaimed him to be Bartholomew or Matthew; that a companion disciple to Peter who is his "competitor" in that he stands closer to Jesus than Peter is not developed in the Synoptics; and that the disciples James and John remain as flat characters in the Synoptic depictions of them, then one has a good argument that Nathaniel is the Beloved Disciple. Finally he is greeted by Jesus in a very special way, for seemingly Jesus has had a vision of him sitting under the fig tree and greets him as a true Israelite in whom there is no deceit, whereupon it is possible that Nathaniel experiences something of a theophany imparting to him privately the awareness that Jesus is the true Messiah of Israel for he calls him the Son of God and the King of Israel.

So for these many reasons the Mass you celebrated on April 18 was for me a very moving and inspiring worship service. It was certainly not easy for you to endure. It might have been better for us both had I congratulated you for courage and for your candid remarks regarding the recent events which have burdened the Church. But during your sermon, you dwelt on the person of the Beloved Disciple and those enigmatic remarks which that Gospel tells us Jesus spoke concerning him at the end of chapter 21. A couple of weeks ago Father Franz read to me most of an article that a German priest from his diocese had written about the Beloved Disciple, whereby he held the view that the Beloved Disciple was not intended to be a real person at all, but rather a hypothetical, ideal disciple, something like the view of those of the Jewish people who do not believe that the concept of the Messiah is centered around a real Jewish person. Of course you are correct that you did not say that the Beloved Disciple was an ideal person, but as far as I recall, you did say that perhaps we are to see ourselves as the Beloved Disciple, that the Church can be seen to be the Beloved Disciple. Here it seems that you were not referring to a specific comparison which though one could well justify making, but to the time span alluded to by Jesus's comment to Peter about the Beloved Disciple. That occurred to me only a few hours later as I pondered all that happened that Sunday morning, that you were referring to the report of Jesus's words to Peter, "What is that to you, what if it is my will that he remains until I come?" As far as I can tell from the text, Jesus's statement is thoroughly hypothetical and has nothing to do with the future. But you were concerned about the time span alluded to, and so as I remember you took this statement and projected the future Church upon it. Still though there would have been the possibility that, at least from that perspective, you viewed the Beloved Disciple to be a symbolic, ideal character. Not that he cannot not also be that, but if he is the disciple par excellence, then he was first and foremost a real flesh-and-blood person. So it was that I asked you if you understood the Beloved Disciple to be an ideal disciple. I decided to ask that for all those reasons given above and because I am rather certain that he was and is a real disciple, Jesus's true friend. So it is that the Fourth Gospel gives us a real, second version of Jesus's life, teaching, and passion week as opposed to the account the Gospel of Mark gives us. The Christian world of the Fourth Gospel is totally different, for the entire story it gives us is based on the moment of the Incarnation of which John the Baptist is the first witness as that awing theophany which he and Jesus experience together at the beginning imparts this momentous event first to him.

I completed an undergraduate degree and wrote a master's thesis at a German university before I could really understand what I "should" study. After my first year at seminary I was certain that the Fourth Gospel provides us with the answer to the timeless New Testament debate. It gives us a report from an eye-witness disciple. It should be accepted for what it is, the basis for the first true Christian church.

Most sincerely yours,
Robert Rhea

LETTER TO PRESIDENT CAROL QUILLEN

December 4, 2013

Dear President Quillen,

On the evening of June 9, 2012 as a soft, early summer breeze wafted through the din of exuberant chatter around the dinner table set for some of the members of the class of 1967, I turned from a conversation with one of my Davidson classmates and saw you standing just beyond the dinner tent, surrounded by a host of other alumni of our class. That morning I had arrived at 9 AM to hear your address the combined alumni audience, and had become so mystified by your lyrical, captivating arm dance that I could not focus my rambling thoughts and emotions enough to present you with a pertinent question. It was my first ever Davidson Reunion, the second time I had visited the campus since 1967, now the home of hundreds of female students, my first encounter with the "new Davidson," and of course the first time that I heard the first woman president of Davidson give her assessment of the current status of the college and the agenda envisioned for its future.

The question that I perhaps would have asked is directly related to my life's experience and work as a teacher of German and English, and my student days as a seminarian, whereby I devoted much of my time to the exegetical study of the Hebrew and Greek scriptures. My student days at Davidson were marked by that tremendous time of transition which engulfed the college as it emerged and evolved from the former primary role of educating and preparing future southern Presbyterian pastors for seminary study to embrace the greater world of secular academia and contemporary humanism as a basis for its liberal arts curriculum. The role of religion with regard to Christianity and its significance for the college remains a question which many alumni still discuss and which has recently found resonance in the recent assessment of Davidson's role as a college affiliated with the Reformed tradition.

Prior to that evening dinner I had made the attempt to contact a good number of professors of Davidson's Department of Religion via email regarding the ongoing New Testament debate, particularly the significance of the Fourth Gospel for Christian teaching and doctrine. Only one professor responded to let me know that it is his opinion that the Gnostic Gospel of Thomas is more authentically Christian than the Fourth Gospel. I had also looked through the array of professors of the Department of Psychology, hoping to find someone whose profile would indicate some expertise in dream interpretation and a familiarity with the psychology of Carl Jung. As far as I could tell, it was possible that some of the faculty taught an overview of Jung's psychological system, but there was no one who had spent a good deal of time with his theory of dream interpretation, though it could boast of many national award-winning psychologists and one who was awarded the Presidential Award for Excellence in Science, Mathematics and Engineering Mentoring presented by President Obama.

Nevertheless I decided that I would go over and introduce myself. We talked briefly about your arm dances and you demonstrated another version or versions for me which I found even more mystifying. I had decided that I would ask you about dream interpretation and began by telling you that I had spent a couple of days at a Jungian Dream Conference two years prior to that week of June at the Kanuga Center south of Asheville. It had been sponsored by the Haden Institute of Flat Rock, N.C., founded by Bob Haden, a former priest at St. John's Episcopal Church, Charlotte, now a licensed Jungian analyst. There I made a number of contacts and was to begin an email exchange of dreams, when I was informed that Jungians do not engage in dream interpretation which has a biblical basis.

About a month ago for the first time I made a rough count of my dream journal and found that I have collected over 2,500 hand-written pages of dreams. Over a decade ago I revised and edited my dreams for a two-year period and thus have some eighty pages of dreams for which there is a final copy. Because I have been recording dreams since September 1978, I estimate that my dream journal contains at present a minimum of some 1,300 pages. This does not compare to the tens of thousands that Jung worked with, but it does provide a sufficient basis on which to base and explicate a biblical view of dream interpretation. Just over a month ago I called Ann Ulanov, a well-known Jungian analyst at my alma mater, Union Theological Seminary, and asked if she might somehow find the time to discuss them with me. She refused, even though I completed two courses with her assistants. I also sent them to two professors at The Jewish Theological Seminary, Dr. Richard Kalmin and Dr. David Marcus, with whom I had previously made the attempt to discuss dream interpretation from a biblical perspective. They have not responded to my query.

That evening of June 9 I asked you if you might help me with this quest. You replied that you would consider this and that I should contact you. I have sent you email a couple of times. I would so very much appreciate the opportunity to discuss this matter with you.

Very sincerely yours,
Bob Rhea

Appendix III

My Christian Quest

HOW WIDESPREAD WAS THE Messianic movement begun by Jesus of Galilee, particularly during the time before Paul of Tarsus began his preaching? Could it have survived as a reform movement within Judaism without the influence of Paul? Did it rival the Qumran community during its formative years, if indeed there was a community at Qumran? Do the canonical Gospels give voice to and reflect a distinctly different form of Messianic Judaism than that preached by Paul? Was this early Christianity subsumed and eclipsed by the writings, preaching, and influence of Paul and/or the apostolic movement of the mid-second century? Has Paul's religious outlook been influenced by early Gnosticism, apocalyptic yearnings, and the Hellenistic mystery cults or Mithras? Is the Gospel of John the earliest and most authentic Messianic treatise focused on Jesus of Galilee, and is its biblical theology derived directly from the tradition of Hebrew prophecy, not early Jewish Gnosticism?

These are questions with which I have concerned myself both religiously and academically over the past thirty-five years. Yet the seeds for these questions reach well back into the past to my undergraduate days at Davidson College and earlier. It is rather clear now that unless more factual data can be retrieved from the first century, some of these questions may never be answered. Several of the others may not be answered definitely and factually, but only comparatively and/or introspectively.

As a youth I was rather perplexed by what I sensed to be the conflicting and disparate worldviews of the ancient world and the rational, post-Enlightenment modern era into which I had been born. Were modern science and philosophy the essential key to all knowledge and would they continue to transform life on earth to such an extent that one would no longer need to have personal access to the understanding of the ancient past? When the opportunity to study at the University of Marburg my junior year presented itself, at a time during which Rudolf Bultmann was still alive and his distinguished student, Werner Georg Kümmel, was lecturing there, I eagerly set out on an adventure which continued my quest for a discovery of the past and enabled me to compare my tentative answers to those these scholars had formulated. I was introduced first-hand to Bultmann's school of biblical thought, one which had focused diligently on the dichotomy of past and present. The puzzling questions which had been swirling through my head became focused in a manner which had not heretofore presented itself. Somehow to my own surprise I concluded that Bultmann was not only justified in his endeavor of severing the ancient past from the present with his program of demythologizing, he also had the right to take the process one step forward and announce the end of the Christian era altogether!

At that particular time during the middle of this century it seemed rather certain that Christianity and Judaism had not succeeded as viable religions, even though their "rotting and decaying" remnants had survived in the form of the institution of the mainstream church. If the rational and empirical assessment of modern science and philosophy was at long last a true description of reality, then Christianity had no choice but to concede the fact that Jesus of Galilee had not spoken the truth and that his pronouncements concerning life and eschatological judgment were not valid. The only true reality was that of the physical world and the inner self (the vast realm of the individual experience), not the mythological musings of ancient Christians and Jews whose antiquated babble had survived to become codified dogma.

Fascinated by the experiential world of literature and having discovered the phenomenon of the goddess in the writings of Hermann Hesse, I set out on a literary adventure and enrolled as a student of German and English literature at the University of Munich. As I traced the roots of Hesse, the famed neo-Romantic, I landed somewhat to my surprise in the late 18th century, among those whose criticism of the Enlightenment was pronounced and embraced not only the attempt to defend metaphysical philosophy but also the attempt to understand the thought of the East. Novalis, Fichte, Schelling, the Schlegels, and the school of the German Romantics opposed the rise and the "threat" of the dominance of rationalism. Hinduism and Buddhism became a fascination for some of them, particularly the Schlegels, and the parallels of these oriental religions to

Christianity must have certainly fascinated Hesse. But most compelling of all were the themes and images of the goddess which leaped off the pages of Carl Jung and Hesse and ran back into the captivating past to the works of E.T.A. Hoffmann, Novalis and his Sophie, Heinrich von Morungen, and on past the Minnesänger to Artemis of Ephesos, the cult of Baal of the Levant, and the Anatolian Mother Goddess. Was this too only a mythological religion, or did it have phenomenological roots and moorings which could also be anchored in the realm of the modern human psyche? Whatever the experience of God was for me at that time, it did not seem to be bound by dogmas, creeds, formulas, and religious practices which stifled the soul, and muted and subdued the expression of the body which naturally emanated from their innocent harmony.

Although I proposed a comparison of the roles of women in the literary works of Goethe and E.T.A. Hoffmann as a thesis topic, my "Magister Vater" had other ideas. Since he had then recently completed his translation of W. B. Yeats into German and viewed these and his previous translations as a continuation of the tradition of German translators of English literature, he selected for my study the works of Ferdinand Freiligrath, a 19th-century German poet and translator of English verse. I was not at all enthralled by his decision, but I made a valiant effort to carry out his request, as I sought to convince myself that I had no right to oppose his choice. It became a long and arduous task, which I thought would never end. Yet in the midst of this frustrating exercise as I poured over the conflicts of a man torn between the pull of "ennui," luring him off to the far reaches of the exotic South Pacific on the one hand, and an ardent fervor for the democratic idealism expounded by the English Romantics on the other, all of which landed him quite by accident in the bosom of Marxism, I unexpectedly encountered a new face of the Christian tradition, one which appeared to coexist with the vitality and exuberance of the human psyche at the same time it gave voice to the time-honored dogmas of the Hebrew prophetic tradition and its own unique, eschatological worldview.

As I viewed these matters from this perspective, I found that I could no longer justify the previous distinction I had made between religious and secular literature. It was no longer evident that the modern world was decidedly and characteristically different from either the ancient world or even the late prehistoric era for that matter. I was astounded to realize that the modern science and philosophy are for the most part nothing more or less than a new mythology. As I pondered this new view of the human predicament, it became clear that human answers and understanding are ultimately dependent upon mythology and symbolism for meaning. I realized that I could go so far as to state that without associative symbolism there is no "real" meaning, at least none that is essential and transcendental. Here the pervasive questions focus on the quest to determine which mythology or what type of mythology one considers valid and acceptable, and which systems of symbolism are ultimately meaningful.

Since that time I have pursued the study of Christianity and Judaism in academic settings in both Jewish and Christian seminaries, and I have attended a number of Jewish and Christian congregations for an extended period of time. I have considered ordination in the Presbyterian Church as well as conversion to Catholicism. But I have not been able to follow through on these endeavors because I cannot accept the ecclesiology and dogmas which form the basis of these churches, nor have I been able to relate in a thoroughgoing and essential way with a majority of the parishioners and congregants, who do not appear to be aware of the threat Western lifestyle presents to domestic ecological and social systems as well as the global environment and society.

I am very intrigued by the relationship between Judaism and Christianity, and the key this relationship may hold for the study of the canonical and Gnostic gospels and other Christian texts. In my previous studies I have focused upon the tradition of Hebrew prophecy, its nature and characteristics, and the impact it has seemingly had on the teachings of Jesus of Galilee. It is my opinion that the letters of Paul reflect an entirely different religious understanding. One of the questions which I would like to pursue during my studies is how such disparity could occur, since both men were religious Jews living in first century Palestine and the Mediterranean region during a time of heightened Messianic expectation. I would like to broaden my knowledge of the Near East during Antiquity and study the influences which molded Judaism and Christianity during the first century.

Most specifically I would like to continue my study of the Gospel of John and the religious worldview which it mirrors. It has long been held that this document was originally a Gnostic treatise which was later Christianized. Over the last four decades other scholars have sought to demonstrate how it might have been strongly influenced by the theology and religious postulates of the presumed Qumran community. Its relationship to the Synoptic Gospels is another matter which must be addressed here. To a great extent I concur with the findings of the former Bishop of Woolwich,

Dr. John A. T. Robinson, who had laid out his research in the work, *The Priority of John.* I am the author of two published works, one entitled *The Johannine Son of Man*, in which I have set forth a theory which parallels one of Robinson's suppositions which he formulated in his brief chapter on Johannine eschatology. Here he has surmised that the Johannine use of the Son of Man phrase and title may well predate its use as an apocalyptic title. I developed this view entirely on my own five years before I became acquainted with Robinson's study. I would like to continue to examine this finding along with my hypothesis that the phenomenon of Jewish apocalyptic is very late and not at all characteristic of the tradition of Jewish eschatology. The investigation of these matters would serve as my primary aim for continuing my study of religious and biblical literature.

www.ingramcontent.com/pod-product-compliance
Lightning Source LLC
Chambersburg PA
CBHW072355030726

47505CB00014B/1835